terrible things

"Suffused with atmosphere, populated by horrors half-seen and then, in startling moments of revelation, seen all too clearly, David Surface's stories stay firmly rooted in ghost story tradition. But where those oddly comforting classical terrors bubble up from grief or loss or regret or revenge, the menaces in 'Terrible Things' sprout from a disturbingly contemporary sense of bewilderment. These are the ghosts of lockdown drills and frayed marriages, identity confusion and forced retirement and that constant crackling hum of a world tilting out of true, and therefore new and now and terrifying all over again."

Glen Hirshberg
author of the *Motherless Children* trilogy

"Each of the stories contained within 'Terrible Things' is a small treasure to be marveled at. David Surface unpicks the scam of humanity to reveal the necrosis of our terrible secrets – the harms we visit upon one another, the lies we tell – but also that quiet hope that beneath it all there might still be something worth saving. Compassionate, astute and beautifully crafted, these are horror stories with soul."

Laura Mauro
author of *Sing Your Sadness Deep*

"David Surface is like no one else. His fiction has a precision of detail that is always unsettling, and often heart-breaking. One of our greatest contemporary writers."

Ralph Robert Moore
author of *Ghosters*, *As Dead as Me*, and *Father Figure*

David Surface knows home is an alien place and 'Terrible Things' is your expedition report – you'd do well to read it.

Adam Golaski
author of *Color Plates* and *Worse Than Myself*

"Location, location, location. Or, to borrow M.R. James' phrasing, places that are prolific in suggestion. One of the things I like about the stories collected in 'Terrible Things' – and I like many things about them – is the care David Surface has taken in what is sometimes called world-building. This is often taken to mean grand endeavours on a Game of Thrones scale, genealogies and maps and all the rest of it, but at its deftest and most effective, it is the delineation of place in a few well-chosen descriptive passages. Another of the things I like is that, having constructed these imaginary gardens, David proceeds to fill them with some all-too-real toads. Character and setting are two of the three pillars on which the weird story is established, so it's pleasing to discover that the third pillar – let's call it narrative enchantment – is also present, raising up some remarkable tales for your attention. If you feel at home in the October country of the imagination, you ought to enjoy these stories, in that complicated yet at the same time instinctive way we enjoy the best weird fiction. This is David's first collection, and I'm happy to recommend it, on the strict understanding that he comes up with another, as soon as he likes."

Steve Duffy
author of *The Moment of Panic*

"Knowing very little of the man aside from the warmth and intellect reflected in his fiction – and how his aesthetic has affected me – I've come to gain a sense that Mr. Surface, as a writer, operates like a combat medic. In the trauma unit of tale telling, David Surface is unable to provide too many precious answers; rather, he provides verbal sutures to the damaged and heart-sick, patching us up the best he can."

Clint Smith

author of *When It's Time for Dead Things to Die*

"David Surface's first short story collection is a reason to rejoice for all lovers of disturbing, off-beat, and ghostly fiction. Well-written and multi-layered, these stories are unpredictable in the best possible way: the author doesn't allow the clichés of the genre to dilute his own personal vision. Put simply, these stories are some of the very best weird fiction has to offer."

James Everington

author of *Trying To Be So Quiet and Other Hauntings*

Terrible Things

David Surface

BLACK
SHUCK
BOOKS

Black Shuck Books
www.BlackShuckBooks.co.uk

Version of the following stories have previously appeared in print:
"Terrible Things" in *Shadows & Tall Trees, issue 4* (Undertow Publications, 2012)
"Intruders" in *Supernatural Tales, issue 38* (2018)
"Writings Found in a Red Notebook" in *Shadows & Tall Trees, issue 6* (Undertow Publications, 2014)
"Faces of the Missing" in *Supernatural Tales, issue 26* (2014)
"Something You Leave Behind" in *Nightscript III* (Cthonic Matter, 2017)
"The Sea in Darkness Calls" in *Darkest Minds* (Dark Minds Press, 2015)
"The Last Testament of Jacob Tyler" in *The Tenth Black Book of Horror* (Mortbury Press, 2013)
"The Professor of History" in *Six Fingered Hand, issue 1* (2010)
"The Smell of Red Clay" in *Supernatural Tales, issue 19* (2011)
"The Sound That the World Makes" in *Nightscript I* (Cthonic Matter, 2015)
"Last Ride of the Night" in *Ghost Highways* (Midnight Street Press, 2015)

Cover design & internal layout © WHITEspace 2020
www.white-space.uk

First published in the UK by Black Shuck Books, 2020

978-1-913038-51-9

For Julia

acknowledgements

My thanks to Steve Shaw of Black Shuck Books for bringing these stories together in one place, and for all the fine books he helps bring into the world.

My thanks also to the editors who first gave these stories a good home: David Longhorn, who published my first "almost ghost story" and opened the door to a new world for me. Michael Kelly, who wisely pushed me to come up with the perfect ending for the title story (and also suggested the title for this collection). C.M. Muller, a man of great kindness and enthusiasm who labors like a Medieval craftsman to produce some of the most beautiful books around. The late great Charlie Black who gave me a place to let the monsters come out. To them, and to Ross Warren, Adam Bradley, and Trevor Denyer, I owe my thanks.

Many, many thanks to Lynda Rucker. Lynda was one of the first writers who introduced me to what the contemporary horror story is capable of, so it was a delight to discover what a wise, funny, and good-hearted person she is. I'm grateful for her kind introduction to this book, and for the years of long-distance support, wisdom, and friendship.

Literary friendships – which are often long-distance ones – are a lifeline for writers. I know they have been for me. So my thanks also to Ralph Robert Moore, a unique and mind-altering writer, and one of the most encouraging and generous souls I know.

Thanks also to the people who took the time to say kind things about my writing, not only in this book, but long before it existed: Glen Hirshberg, Laura Mauro, Steve Duffy, James Everington, Clint Smith, Adam Glolaski, and Ralph Robert Moore – all fine writers whose work I admire and have learned from. Thank you for your inspiration and your kindness.

My thanks to my mother, Linda Surface, an amazing woman who patiently tolerated my love of all things spooky, who held the camera for my first Super 8 homemade monster movies, and encouraged my love of music and writing through her own beautiful example. Thanks also to my sister Mary Hall and her husband Kevin for turning their beautiful home into a "writers retreat", and for their loving support and encouragement. And thanks to my children, Matthew and Cailey, who not only patiently survived the challenge of having a writer for a father, but who've both grown to be fine writers and book-lovers themselves, as well as amazing and beautiful human beings.

Most of all, heartfelt thanks and all my love to Julia Rust, my favorite author, editor, actor, and partner in all things, without whom these stories and my life would not be as good as they are.

David Surface
Cornwall-on-Hudson, NY
February 2020

introduction

I first "met" David Surface in May of 2009. He sent me a friend request on Facebook and wrote me a nice message, saying he liked my writing. We've had a periodic correspondence since that first exchange, and over the years I've watched as he's built a body of thoughtful, literate work, much of it (though not all) in the vein of what Charles L. Grant used to call "quiet horror".

These days, David is one of a handful of people I forget that I only "know" online – I think of him as a flesh and blood friend even though we have only ever communicated through the medium of words. I suppose this is not so strange for two writers. It gives me great pleasure to write this introduction to his first but what I think will not be his only collection.

In addition to similar literary sensibilities, David and I share one significant bit of back story as well – we are both, in words I've stolen from the writer F. Brett Cox, "Southern expats". Without wanting to generalize or romanticize too much, I do believe there is something about being raised in the South that lends itself to tales of the supernatural. As a region, it tends to look backwards more than it looks forward. Flannery O'Connor called it "Christ-haunted". Southern Gothic exists as its own little corner of the literary world for a reason. The prose of some of the South's greatest writers has an almost incantatory quality: Southern stories often feel unreal, like ghost stories without ghosts. The ghosts in David's story may be found in different landscapes than those of the Deep South, and may be more front-and-center than were those of our forebears, but these are not revenants, lurking in wait for hapless victims. They are usually born of the protagonists' psyches – their pain, their fear, their failure.

David works with veterans, who are often a marginalized group of people, and he writes about marginalized people in his work as well. His distinctly American style tackles distinctly American terrors – from school shootings to the collective guilt of our genocidal heritage to that sense of horrifying freefall you get when things start to go wrong in a society that offers few safety nets. Grounded in a gritty realism, many of their protagonists are lost before the first lines of the story in which they feature, like ghosts themselves, trapped in old patterns that are no longer relevant and unable to see a way out. It is often the supernatural itself that brings home to them the terrible clarity of just how lost they are.

If it's easy answers you're after, stories that tie things up neatly, David's aren't that – they leave you unmoored, emotionally and intellectually. You'll want to read his stories a second and then a third time – to try to identify the precise moment where the will-they-or-won't-they academics flirting-with-adultery setup of

"Terrible Things" takes a turn into something far darker, or precisely whether the monstrous in "Intruders" is born of institutional indifference, a teacher's misplaced care for his students or something much more sinister. That great American tradition, the road trip, gets its due in not one but two stories set in very different landscapes, from the arid miles of open landscape and sky in the West in "Writings Found in a Red Notebook" to the dark rural byways of the East in "Something You Leave Behind". And if you're in search of a more traditional type of storytelling, "The Last Testament of Jacob Tyler" is evidence he can spin a good historical yarn as well, a rollicking tall tale from hell in folk horror meets Old Testament-like mayhem and morality.

But I'll leave the rest for you to discover on your own – the anguished artists, sinister films, abandoncd carnivals and more that await you within. I'm excited that David Surface has a collection out at last, one that is long overdue, and pleased that Black Shuck Books is publishing it. I hope it brings him a wider audience.

For David, the supernatural tale is a thrill on its own merits, but it's also a way to explore broader issues of personal and institutional breakdown. I'm sorry that it looks as though he'll have no shortage of inspiration for more of those types of stories in the years ahead, but we're fortunate as readers to have him beside us in the dark.

Lynda Rucker
Margate, Kent, UK
February 2020

terrible things

It was one of those bars that could have been anywhere. The whole place had that carefully calculated look of old-time hominess that came right out of a can. Miles of wood-paneled booths gleaming under a thick layer of too-shiny shellac, decorative dartboards that had never felt a dart, framed photographs of grim-faced Indian chiefs and forgotten baseball teams. It was a look duplicated in strip malls and dying downtowns all across America. Sheila felt that if she pushed open those thick doors with their ridiculously large fake-brass handles, she might see the purple Nevada sky or the bristling black hills of Tennessee. But she knew where she was. She was in Dayton, Ohio, drinking a glass of red wine, waiting for a man named Douglas.

She'd met Douglas at a faculty party last month when she'd first arrived at the university. He'd said his name was Douglas – not Doug, but *Douglas* – which might have sounded like an affectation coming from someone else, but from him seemed perfectly natural.

Douglas was an associate professor in the Department of Anthropology. Sheila, who was, as she liked to say, *just another adjunct* in the English Department, had half-formed romantic notions of what anthropologists do. She'd asked him once if he spent his summers exploring ancient ruins in the jungle, and he'd smiled patiently. "You're thinking of an *archaeologist.*" Sheila didn't like to be made fun of for something she didn't know, but it had made him smile, so she let it go.

Ronnie, her husband, never smiled at the things she didn't know. Her general lack of interest in things beyond the world of books and ideas seemed to worry and annoy him. She knew there must have been a time when her lack of practical skills had been endearing or at least non-threatening to him. Otherwise, why would he have married her? The person she was when they'd met was the same person she was now. It was Ronnie who'd changed, she reasoned, who'd become less patient, less compassionate. Less loving. All she'd ever done was be herself.

The place was already full at five o'clock and the thick wooden doors kept swinging open with a soft sucking sound, letting in more and more people. She saw Douglas before he saw her. He was swept in, half-hidden, by a gang of laughing students, but she recognized his unkempt reddish hair and his worried, distracted look. When he spotted her, he smiled and started making his way toward her through the crowd. It seemed to take him an awfully long time to reach her.

"Is this seat taken?" he smiled.

"I knew you were going to say that," she smiled up at him. They were bantering, not flirting, not yet, although sometimes she had trouble telling the difference. That was what Ronnie had warned her of on more than one occasion. *You have to be careful how you talk to people*, he'd said. *Sometimes you send the wrong signals.*

"Damn, am I that predictable?" Douglas said, sliding into the seat across from her. She was preparing her response when the cell phone buzzed like a hornet against her thigh, making her jump. She glanced down at the white letters on the tiny black screen, *HOME*, and felt a flash of annoyance. She'd told Ronnie she was going out to meet friends from the school. He was probably calling to tell her to bring something home or to ask her to referee a fight between the kids, not because he really wanted to talk with her. He'd stopped *really* wanting to talk with her years ago.

"Everything okay?" Douglas asked.

"Sure," she said, pushing the 'silence' button and slipping the phone back into her pocket. "So, what are you drinking?"

Douglas ordered a beer from the young, harried-looking waitress, Sheila ordered another glass of wine, and the two of them began trading stories about work and kids. Neither of them mentioned their spouses. Sheila could hear the holes in their conversation every time one of them sidestepped the words *my husband* or *my wife*. Sheila knew from experience that this was what most men and women do at first. She also knew that the longer two people talk this way, the more likely it is to *mean* something. It felt that way now.

"So," she smiled, "explore any jungle ruins lately?"

Douglas grinned at her across the booth. "It takes a well-adjusted person to laugh at herself."

Is that how I seem to you? she almost said. *Well-adjusted?* "Seriously," she said, "I envy you. Studying all those different types of people, all those different customs. Must be wonderful."

His smile stayed in place but she thought she saw something shift in his eyes. "You think so?"

"Sure."

"Yeah, well," he hesitated, glancing down at his beer, "Some things people do…aren't so wonderful."

"Really?" she said brightly, not wanting him to slip away, "So, tell me…what's the most terrible thing you've ever seen?"

The harsh sound of glass shattering followed by a gale of drunken laughter came from somewhere behind them. Douglas said something she couldn't hear.

"What did you say?"

"I said you don't want to know."

"Oh, come *on!*" she laughed, "*You don't want to know?* What do you expect me to say after that? *Okay, never mind?* Nobody ever says that unless they really *want* to tell someone."

"You think so?" he said, a pained-looking smile on his lips.

"Yeah," she said, leaning closer, "I think so." And suddenly she saw how it would be, Douglas on his back looking up at her, his pale chest flushed red, the light in his eyes growing brighter and farther away.

Douglas ordered another beer and waited for it to arrive. When the waitress brought it, he took a deep sip and began.

"Ever wonder how I got here?"

"I assume you drove."

"Very funny," he said. "I mean the school. This town."

"I know what you meant," she bristled. Did he think she was stupid?

"Before I came here, I was an adjunct too. Six months in one place, six months in another. Couldn't pay my fucking bills. Before this job, I was at a college in Indiana, helping a friend finish his doctoral thesis. It was brilliant. One of the best I'd ever seen. I was helping him with the research, doing a little editing. Then he died."

"I'm sorry," Sheila said. Douglas gave her another pained smile, then continued.

"Car wreck. A drunk driver crossed over the median, hit him head-on. Anyway, the selection committee here wanted a writing sample. So, the day after the funeral, I went to his computer, took his name off the paper, put my name on it and sent it in." Sheila saw him watching her eyes carefully. "Are you shocked?"

"No," she said quickly. Maybe a little too quickly, she thought. "Why didn't you just send something *you* wrote?"

"Because. It was *better*." He glared at her, daring her to deny it. When he spoke again, his face and voice had softened a little, "I told myself I was giving his work a second chance, you know? 'Helping it see the light of day.' Besides, it wasn't like I didn't have anything to do with it. I worked on it too. What do they say…half of writing is editing? So, in a way, it *was* mine." He sniffed ruefully. "Crazy, right?"

"So…that's the most terrible thing you've ever seen?"

Douglas looked down and shook his head. After a moment's silence, he asked, "You know who Max Krieger is?"

"Director of Anthropology," Sheila said, proud of herself for remembering.

"That's right. He's like a giant in evolutionary anthropology. Practically invented it. I read all his books and papers in grad school. They were required reading. Kind of controversial, too."

"Yeah? Like how?" Her big sister had told her in high school that the way to hook a man is to be interested in whatever he's interested in, and the best way to do that is to pretend to be interested until you really are.

"Krieger said the reason some early humans died-out and others didn't was because the ones who survived had a longer child-rearing period," Douglas explained, settling into what Sheila imagined was his classroom voice. "The Neanderthals pushed their kids out into the world really early to sink or swim. But the other humans kept their kids around longer, gave their brains a chance to develop."

"That's controversial?"

"No," Douglas shook his head. "Everybody thinks that now. Krieger wanted to take it a step further. He said that because evolution is still happening, people today should do what those early humans did and keep their children from going out into the world as long as possible, give their brains a chance to develop even more. He said that's the way for the human race to remain viable, take the next step up the evolutionary ladder."

"Okay, that's a little weird…"

"Yeah, it is. Every brilliant mind is a little weird. That's why I wanted to work for him."

"So…you contacted him?"

"No," Douglas chuckled, shaking his head, "He contacted *me*. Two weeks after I sent that paper in, he called me and invited me to come for an interview."

"You must have been psyched."

"I was. He asked me to come to his house. You don't usually get invited to the department head's house until after you've been hired. So I thought that was a pretty good sign. I put on my best suit, my only suit, show up at the right time and ring the doorbell. Krieger opens the door himself. I'd never seen him before, just pictures on the back of his books. The first thing I notice are these scars on his face – not just on one cheek, but on both. Three scars in a row, three straight lines like someone dug into his face with a fork. I recognize what it is – ritual scarification. Here I am standing there, shaking this great man's hand, trying not to stare.

"He takes me into the den for a drink and says, 'You've come a long way. I hope it's worth it.' Now I'm wondering, what's *that* supposed to mean? Then he picks up a bell and rings it. A door opens and this beautiful black woman walks in, very tall, wearing traditional South African clothing. Then I see this thick coil of metal wire wrapped around and around her neck like those pictures of Mursi tribeswomen, so her neck is all stretched out like it's twelve inches long. She goes to pour the drinks, and Krieger says, 'You're surprised by my wife's neck.' I start to say no but he cuts me off.

'American women mutilate their bodies for beauty every day. It's called plastic surgery.'

"The three of us sit there talking. Krieger's talking, really, I'm just listening. I keep looking over at his wife. She's just sitting there, staring straight ahead, not saying a word. I think about asking her a question, you know, just to be polite. But I get the feeling that if I did ask her anything, not only would she not answer, it would also feel like some kind of…transgression.

"The whole time, I keep hearing this thumping sound on the ceiling, like something's moving around upstairs. After a while, his wife gets up and walks out of the room. Krieger tells me she's just gone to see about their child. I ask how old their kid is and he doesn't say anything. He just looks at me with this funny smile. Then he asks if I'm ready for my interview.

"My pulse starts racing. Krieger must have noticed because he smiles and says, 'Don't worry. This interview has only one question.' Then he asks me, 'What's the most important thing you've learned about anthropology?' My mind shuts down, completely. One question, and I have no idea what to say. Then, all of a sudden, it comes to me.

"'No judgments.'

"'Absolutely,' Krieger says with this really big smile. 'Anthropology is the practice of seeing human beings clearly. But first, you have to see *yourself* clearly. If you can't do that, you can't do anything.'

"We'd been drinking scotch. Now Krieger pulls out this clay

bottle wrapped in straw and pours some clear stuff into two shot glasses. It burns like kerosene but I don't want to offend him so I choke it down.

"Krieger asks about my work with the Borneo hill tribes. I realize he's talking about the paper I sent. I'm not worried, though. I know every word in it. He wants to know about the tattoos that the women wear on their faces. I tell him the practice is dying out. 'Originally, it was a way for the men to identify their wives if they're ever stolen or run away. Now that the tribes are becoming more modernized, more and more young women don't follow the tradition.'

"'That's a shame,' Krieger says. 'We all like to hold on to what belongs to us. That's not a bad thing. People should be responsible for their possessions, don't you think?'

"'Well,' I laugh, because I still think he's joking, 'people shouldn't *possess* other people. At least that's what I heard.'

"'That's a nice sentiment,' Krieger says. 'The trouble is it's not realistic. People *do* possess other people, always have and always will. That's not a bad thing, either. We like to say it is, but when you think about it, it's really not. When the slave-owner puts shackles on his slave's feet, or breaks his bones or cuts off his toes to keep him from running away, that may seem to us like an act of barbarism or cruelty. But that's because we're looking at it from our limited twenty-first century perspective. How far do you think that slave would get on his own? Out there in the world, away from his owner, away from the only home he's ever known? What's waiting for him out there? Starvation, injury, disease, death. When you look at it from *that* perspective, the perspective of the real world of that time, it's an act of love. These things that may seem cruel and repugnant to us at first, that's what makes them beautiful. The love.'

"I'm trying to think of something to say when Krieger's wife comes in and tells him he's got a phone call. He gets up and excuses himself, so I go down the hall looking for a bathroom. There are all these framed pictures on the wall of Krieger in the jungle, hanging out with various tribes. Some of them I recognize from his books, some I don't. There's one of him surrounded by a few younger people, his assistants or something. One of them looks familiar, a beautiful young black woman. I look closer and see it's Krieger's wife. I don't recognize her at first because she's smiling. And her neck. Her neck isn't stretched out by those metal bands. It's normal.

"I keep walking down this hallway, looking for a bathroom, but every door I come to is shut. For some reason I don't feel like opening them to see what's inside, so I go upstairs.

"It's even darker up there and I can't find a light switch, so I'm sort of feeling my way down this hallway. The whole time, I feel like there's someone watching me. Then I see something on the floor about six or seven feet in front of me. At first I think it's a pile of clothes, maybe one of the kid's toys. Then it moves. I think I yelled a little or jumped, because that's when it *hissed* at me. I'm thinking it's got to be a cat. Then it starts moving toward me, sort of dragging itself across the floor. I'm still thinking it's a cat, maybe it's hurt or something. Then it moves into the light. And it's not a cat. It's human. I see all these coils of metal wire wrapped around these tiny, twisted little arms and legs, all around its chest and neck. And this angry little face glaring up at me – not a child's face, all red and swollen with its eyes popping out. Then it opens its mouth and this horrible, choking sound comes out. Like *bleating*.

"All of a sudden, I hear Krieger's voice behind me. 'Don't move,' he says. 'Let him come to you.' So I stand there and watch this thing drag itself across the carpet toward me. It finally reaches my feet, stretches out one of those little hands, grabs hold of my pants leg and pulls on it. Then it makes that horrible bleating sound again. Krieger says, 'He wants you to pick him up.'

"I can't look down, but I can still feel it tugging on my leg. I want to scream or run. But then…I do it. I don't know how. I just reach down and do it. It's heavier than I thought, and I can feel it *moving* in my arms, against my chest. I still can't look, but the bleating noise stops. Krieger says, 'He likes you.'"

Douglas stopped. For a moment it looked like he was about to cry.

"I don't remember much after that. I got out of there, finally. I don't remember how. The next morning my phone rings and it's Krieger. That's when he tells me I got the job. That's it, nothing else. The only thing I can think to ask is *why*. He says, *because you gave the right answer*."

For a moment Sheila thought Douglas was finished. Then he said it.

"Now…I go over there once a week. I have to go again tomorrow."

Sheila heard a loud wailing and saw a red-faced child weeping at a booth across the room, the nervous-looking mother leaning close to hush it. Closer to them, in the very next booth, a big kid, maybe a football player, staring into space like he'd just lost the most important thing in the world.

Douglas's face looked pale and haggard like he hadn't slept for a year. Why had he told her this terrible story? What did he possibly hope to gain from it?

"Why did you *tell* me this?" she finally asked.

"Because," he said, looking up at her with weary, bloodshot eyes, "people do terrible things. And they don't think they're terrible."

The buzzer went off against her leg again. Sheila saw the word HOME on the tiny black screen, reached down and shut it off. The room suddenly seemed to tilt around her. Midnight already. The children would be in bed now. She could see them in their beds, the way their bodies seemed to stretch and grow long in sleep. Some day they would be gone. She suddenly felt all the minutes, all the hours, the days and years yet to come wrapped tight around her chest and throat, squeezing the breath out of her. Then the image of herself grown small, crawling on the floor in the dark like a broken, mutilated doll, wild-eyed and mute. The horror rose up in her throat so fast that it burst out like a laugh, shrill and harsh. She clapped her hand to her mouth to stop it from escaping again.

"Are you *laughing*?" Douglas asked. Afraid to take her hand away from her mouth, Sheila could only shake her head. The cell phone went off again, buzzing angrily against her thigh and she clawed at it, slapping it off.

"Jesus Christ," she whispered, *"Leave me alone…"*

"Sheila," she heard him say, "Give me your keys."

"What…?"

"You heard me." She could hear some of the familiar calm returning to his voice. "Give me your keys."

She looked across the booth at him. He'd just told a story that would make any woman run, and here he was asking her to give up her keys to him.

"I'm not afraid of you," she said, hating the drunken sound of her own voice.

"Sheila," he said. "Please. Give me your keys."

She tried to think of why she'd come here tonight, of what she'd wanted earlier. But there was only blackness inside her head. She knew she could not drive. She dug into her purse for her keys. Then she looked up and saw his hand reaching across the booth, the palm open, waiting. She thought about what that hand had touched, and those same hands touching her skin.

Suddenly she was on her feet and stumbling out of the booth toward the door. She ignored Douglas' voice calling after her, all the faces staring at her in disapproval and alarm. She reached the heavy wooden doors, shoved them open with both hands and the hot night air rushed into her face like the breath of some terrible beast. But she kept moving. *Home.* She was going home. If she could only remember where that was.

intruders

Greg found the email waiting in his inbox on Monday morning, the subject line shouting at him from the screen in capital letters: LOCKDOWN DRILL ALERT. Greg had seen pictures of lockdown drills – children curled in fetal positions under their desks, armored SWAT teams with automatic weapons charging down school hallways. In one photo, the face of one SWAT team member was flushed blood-red, his mouth frozen open in an animal-like howl. Greg could hear those angry shouts ricocheting off the metal lockers, stabbing deep into the ears of the terrified children huddled at the edges of the photograph.

"They're not going to do that here, are they?" Greg asked. "Armed police running through the halls?"

"Would you rather have armed police or armed snipers?" Margaret measured her words out slowly and impatiently, the same way she spoke to her ten-year-old students. Greg wanted to smack her across the face.

"I don't think there'll be a police presence," Carl said. Greg winced. He hated the way these ugly phrases were creeping into their school memos and conversations. *Police presence. Crisis preparedness. Lockdown procedures.* They were supposed to be teachers, not prison guards – although he suspected that some of his colleagues, like Margaret who'd volunteered to lead the lockdown drill committee, secretly enjoyed it.

"That's a terrible thing to say," Carl frowned when Greg told him what he'd thought about Margaret.

"I know," Greg said, "But *look* at her, the way she talks about it. It's almost like she can't wait for it to happen."

"She just wants the students to be safe."

"You don't think I want the same thing?"

Carl sighed. "Listen…you do fire drills, right? You don't have any problem with those, do you?"

"Jesus, Carl, it's not the same thing."

"That's right," Carl looked at him grimly, "It's not. But it *happens*, okay? Whether you or I like it or not, it happens."

Carl was right. It had happened at an elementary school in the next state. Not close, but close enough. Twenty-three kids, most of them first and second graders. It was all over the news for days, no way to get away from it. The message came down: *Talk with your students about it.* Greg had meant to comply. He'd read all the official talking points and protocols, he'd stood there in front of the classroom on the designated morning while his students came in and took their seats, leaning casually against his desk the way he always did, rehearsing the official words in his mind. But when he'd looked at their young expectant faces, something froze inside of him.

In the early days, he'd let the children get to him. Their noise and wild energy had felt like a threat, and he'd hit back, mostly with his voice, shouting ugly words to shut them up, and once, only once, with his hands, when a boy had been pushing a smaller boy around. Greg had grabbed the aggressor by the arm and roughly pulled him away. The parents had complained and the matter had come before the school board. It was Carl who'd intervened for him, speaking on his behalf. Carl was ten years his senior, and his word carried some weight.

And here he was, twenty years later, still in the same classroom, still seeing every face he'd ever taught. It wasn't that he could remember them whenever he wanted. It was more like they came to him when *they* wanted to. The thin, pale boy with the crew cut who dropped out of school and never returned, the big red-haired girl who wore only one dress – red calico with a white collar – who hit back and roared like a lion at the boys who teased her. The long-haired boy with the lisp who once wrote a poem that had made him cry. Their faces would appear to him, unbidden, sometimes in flashes behind his eyelids when he blinked, sometimes superimposed on the faces of the children in his classroom.

They're not your children. This was something Greg had heard many times, from Carl, and from his wife back in the days when she was still speaking with him. Greg had not seen his own kids in almost six months since she'd taken them with her to Oregon. The last time he'd seen them, he was shocked by how much they'd changed. His students, however, always remained the same. Their faces and names might change over the years, but their voices, the way they spoke and moved, the excitement and challenge he saw in their eyes, did not change. It was one thing he could depend on.

At the end of the day, Greg waited until the school was empty of students before he closed the classroom door, opened his laptop, and logged on to the school website. He entered his faculty password and began to read the official procedures for the lockdown drill.

Immediately direct all students, staff, and visitors into the nearest classroom or secured space.

Lock classroom doors.

Move people away from windows and doors.

Keep all students sitting on the floor and turn out the lights…

Greg snapped his laptop shut, closed his eyes and tried to breathe. He felt dizzy, and his pulse was pounding hard in his ears. *Shit…* What was he going to do if one of his students asked him what kind of drill this was? He knew his students. They were curious and they were smart. They would figure it out. What then? Would they be scared? He pictured their faces, pale and terrified, looking up at his, searching for calm and reassurance.

No school shootings had happened in their state. *Not yet,* Margaret liked to point out. Still, these things were like shock-waves, he thought, the vibration traveling outward in circles, eventually reaching everything and everyone. When he closed his eyes he could see circles radiating outward from a single point on a map, like an animation in an old educational film. Lately, he'd been seeing this map in his mind more and more, estimating the distance from the point where he was to the point where various threats were likely to originate. Tsunamis, tidal surges, and wind speeds. Terrorist attacks, germ warfare, nuclear explosions, radiation, and fallout. How far could you move away from one of those threats without putting yourself within range of another?

Locking the classroom door behind him, Greg walked down the empty hallway, listening to the echo of his own footsteps. He knew what he had to do tomorrow. He had to empty himself of fear. That was the face he would show his students. If he could do that for them, they'd get through this.

On the way to his car, he noticed a figure standing at the edge of the schoolyard just behind the chain link fence. It was a man, about thirty feet away, but Greg could make out the soiled, baggy coat and frayed pants, the beard and long tangled hair. *Homeless*, he thought. He'd never noticed any homeless hanging around the school before. The man was just standing there behind the criss-cross pattern of the chain link fence, his face indistinguishable, but Greg had the strong feeling that the man was staring at him. Immediately behind that feeling came another, even more strange – that this man had come here from a very long way away to see *him*, that *he* was why this man was here.

Greg looked away and walked quickly to his car, got in and, although he felt a twinge of shame, locked the car door. When he pulled out of the faculty parking lot and looked back toward the school yard, the man wasn't there.

The next morning, after he took attendance, Greg announced to his students that they were going to have a drill.

"A fire drill?" Raymond Benson asked.

"No…" he searched for a word. "It's an emergency drill."

"What kind of emergency?" This time is was Carlene Whitman. Carlene was smart, smarter than Raymond. Smarter than most of the other kids. He could feel her eyes piercing into his.

"Here's how it's going to work…" he said, addressing all of them. "When you hear the alarm, everybody come over here by this wall and sit on the floor. Here's the thing…you've got to be quiet. No talking, at all. Understand? That's very important. No talking until I say the drill is over. Okay?"

They were silent now. A heavy, uncomfortable kind of silence that made his heart sink a little. If they didn't know already, they would soon.

He tried to go about the rest of the morning normally, making an effort not to look up too many times at the clock on the wall. By 10:45 he felt like screaming. When the alarm finally did ring a few minutes late at 11:04, it almost seemed to be coming from a distant place, like he was sitting under thirty feet of water.

He moved into action quickly, motioning the students to come over to the wall. "Come on, come on," he said, startled by the sudden hoarseness of his voice. They came, much slower than he wanted. It seemed to him that they'd never moved so slowly.

They took their seats on the floor, giggling and whispering excitedly. He clapped his hands once, his signal for getting their attention, put one finger to his lips, and one by one they fell silent. He tried to lock the door without them noticing, but the lock made a loud *click* sound, louder than he'd ever heard it before. When he turned back around, a few of them were already wide-eyed, the confusion and uncertainty creeping in that he knew would soon turn into fear. He could not let that happen. Before any of them could ask whatever questions had started to form in their minds, he raised one finger to his lips again and made his own eyes go wide. It was one of his father's faces, the one he'd seen him use in church school, telling stories to the smallest children, trying to hold their attention and make them laugh. He could feel the muscles on his own face stretching, making that same face. He suddenly wished that his father could be here now.

He heard footsteps outside in the hallway, then the doorknob rattled and shook. He knew it was only the security team, Margaret and Coach Freedman, testing the lock. But what if it wasn't? How could he be sure? Wasn't that the point? That you had to take every precaution, because you could never really be sure of anything?

A loud knocking at the door nearly made his heart stop. He looked again at his students' faces. Some of them had turned pale, a few were trying to stifle nervous laughter. The knocking stopped for a moment. He listened for – prayed for – the sound of footsteps moving away from the door. Then a loud pounding began, rattling the door on its hinges. Fear surged upward in his chest, followed by rage. What the hell were they doing?

He looked down at his students again. Many of them were still giggling nervously, hands clamped over their mouths, but their eyes were wild. Two of them were clowning around, doing extravagant pantomimes of terror, clutching their heads and mouthing silent screams. Carlene was curled on the floor, her whole body twitching wildly, both hands clasped over her mouth. Her classmates were enjoying her performance, pointing at her and giggling uncontrollably. He was about to signal her to stop it. Then he saw the real tears streaming down her face.

The rattling and pounding at the door grew even louder. When he got out of here, he was going to find the person who was doing this and kill them. It was all Greg could do to keep from flinging the door open and murdering the person on the other side. Then the pounding stopped. He heard footsteps outside moving away and down the hallway to the next door, then the next, and the next.

"What the hell was that?"

He'd found Margaret in her classroom grading papers. She looked up at him, startled at first, then her face froze into that look of condescending superiority that he hated.

"What the hell was *what?*" she asked.

"All that goddamn pounding on my door! Jesus, you scared the hell out of my kids!"

"Classroom doors have to be tested," she said. "That's drill procedure."

"Traumatizing children – is *that* drill procedure? One of my kids was in hysterics."

"We checked your lock, Greg, that's all. I think you're overreacting."

It wasn't just your students who were terrified, was it? He could almost hear her say it, and by the time he'd left her classroom and walked back down the long hallway with those words repeating in his head, he was almost sure that she *had* said them.

For the next few days Greg kept a close eye on his students. Especially Carlene. She'd recovered well immediately after the drill, as if nothing had happened at all. True, she did seem quieter and more thoughtful than the rest of the class, but she had always been that way. Still, he watched her closely, and decided to have a talk with her whenever he got the opportunity. He rehearsed what he might say to her. *So, how are you doing? How are you feeling about that drill? Were you afraid? What can I do to stop you being afraid?* These were the thoughts that were spiraling deeper and deeper into his head when he looked up and saw Carlene standing in the doorway, looking at him.

"How are you?" she asked.

"I was just going to ask you the same thing."

"Great minds think alike, right?" It always startled and delighted him, this easy adult banter they had. He knew it was the typical speech of a precocious only child living alone with a divorced mother. *I'm old for my age,* she liked to say. He reminded himself that she was only eleven. He decided to go straight to it.

"What did you think of that drill yesterday?"

"It was stupid," she said, rolling her eyes. "I mean, if a real gunman got into the building with automatic weapons, he'd just shoot the lock right off the door."

She was right, of course. But he couldn't say that. He held his face as still as he could. "How did you know it was that type of drill?"

She blew air from between her lips, a rude dismissive noise. "It was kind of *obvious*. You don't hide on the floor if the school building's on fire, do you?"

"No. I guess you don't." He watched her picking up dry erase markers from his desk, inspecting them, then putting them down again. He thought about dropping the whole topic. Then he could see her again, huddled on the floor with tears streaming down her face. "Were you scared yesterday?"

Carlene frowned, playing with the pens in the coffee mug on his desk. Then she looked up and cocked her head, studying him. "How old are you?"

"Fifty-five."

"Gee…So you've already lived two thirds of your life. You don't mind if I tell you that, do you?"

"No," he forced a grim smile. "It's true. Why should I mind."

"My mother says I say inappropriate things," she frowned again. "It makes her angry. She gets really angry…"

She picked up another marker, a purple one, uncapped it and sniffed at the tip cautiously. Suddenly she stepped close to him and lifted her long auburn hair in both hands.

"See what the rain does to my hair?" He looked. Her hair was drying in long, wild corkscrew ringlets that spilled through her fingers. He found himself looking into her one blue eye and one green eye – they never failed to startle him. Her face was just inches away from his, and he could see a new red pimple growing on her nose and another on her chin.

Something else caught his eye as she lifted her hair in both hands; her sleeves slid down both arms, revealing dark, ugly bruises mottling the smooth pale skin.

"Do you think it's beautiful?" she asked, lifting her curls higher and shaking them at him. He smiled and said nothing. He'd learned long ago to never tell your female students they're beautiful, even when they practically beg you, even when you think it might help them somehow.

"Shouldn't you be getting to your next class?" He kept smiling at her so what he was saying wouldn't feel like a rejection. Her face darkened and he knew it hadn't worked.

"Sure, I get it," she pouted, *"Run along now, sweetie…"* Her face flushed with raw disappointment. He wanted to say something to fix it, but he couldn't imagine what that might be.

A group of girls passed by the open door, and the darkness passed. "Okay," she called back at him over her shoulder, running out the door to catch up with the other kids. "See you later…"

He stood there for a moment, thinking of what he'd just seen. Three years ago he'd taken a mandatory online course in identifying and reporting abuse. He remembered the drawing of a child's body on his computer screen, how he was told to click on the parts of the body where bruises might indicate possible abuse. Were the forearms one of them? He tried to remember, but all he could see was the cursor on his computer screen following the movements of his own hand, creeping and hovering over parts of the child's body. He'd made himself complete the course somehow, but never once in the years since then, or in the years before, had he ever made a report. There had been times, of course, when he'd wondered, but he couldn't bring himself to take the steps that would set something real into action, something irreversible. What if he was wrong? The stakes were just too high.

In the end, Greg thought, it all came down to this – that by focusing too much on evil and suffering, we bring more evil and suffering into this world. He'd told Carl this one night when they'd met for drinks. Carl, who'd been teaching ten years longer than him, scolded him for trying too hard to protect his students.

You don't want bad things to happen to them, Carl had said. *But bad things are going to happen to them. Bad things have happened to some of them already.*

At 12:30, Greg went out to the schoolyard to bring his class in from recess. He stepped out into the bright chaos of the schoolyard, squinting in the sudden daylight. As his eyes adjusted, he thought he saw something just behind the chain link fence. He blinked and looked again. It was a man with long, tangled hair and ragged clothes pressed right up against the schoolyard fence. Greg turned his head and saw another one standing near the schoolyard gate. Once he'd spent a week in a cabin in the California desert, and every evening a tarantula would come and stand right outside his cabin door. It wouldn't come closer or move away. It would just stand there waiting. Waiting for him to let it inside. That was the way Greg felt now, looking at the ragged man staring at him through the schoolyard gate.

The man was close enough that Greg could see his eyes were bloodshot, one eye almost completely red. The children ignored him and ran back and forth in front of him, but the man did not look at them. He was looking at Greg. As Greg watched, he saw the man's cracked lips twitch, then writhe and curl, baring broken brown teeth. It took Greg a moment to recognize that the man was smiling at him.

A rhythmic metallic sound – *ching, ching, ching* – made Greg look back to his right. The other man had raised his arms and started beating at the chain link fence, slowly and steadily, the same paralytic grin on his face.

Greg walked quickly back inside the school cafeteria and found Shavan, one of the public safety officers, flirting with a young cafeteria worker.

"There's some homeless guys out here, near the school yard," Greg began. "They're…Something's wrong with them. They're acting strange. They're too close. They're too close to the kids."

Shavan scowled, though Greg was sure it was because he'd interrupted him. He followed Greg outside, one hand on his radio. "Where?" he asked in his deep, serious voice.

Greg looked at the schoolyard gate. The red-eyed man was not there. He looked at the fence where the other man had been, but he was gone too.

The next morning when Greg opened his computer, he'd found another email flagged "URGENT."

"They're going to have another one of those fucking drills again," Greg said. "Some time next week. Did you hear that?"

Carl sighed. "Yeah. I heard."

"Well?"

Carl looked at him cautiously. "Well *what?*"

"You're going to do it?"

Carl's eyes grew wide "Am I going to do it? Of course I'm going to do it. What do you mean?"

"Well, I'm not. I'm not going to do it."

Carl's eyes narrowed suspiciously. "What do you mean you're not going to do it?"

"Just what I said. No way am I going to put my kids through that again."

Carl leaned closer, speaking in a low and even voice. "Greg…did you hear what you just said?"

"Yes. I said I'm not going to do the fucking drill."

"No. *My kids.* You called them your kids. You do that all the time."

"Do I?"

"Yes. You do. They're not your kids, Greg."

"I know…"

"No. I don't think you *do* know. Not really. If you *did* know that, you wouldn't get so upset."

"What – am I not supposed to care about my students?"

"No. Not the way *you* do, anyway."

"Not the way I do? Which way is that?"

Carl took a sip of coffee and cleared his throat before he continued. "Okay. That drill. You don't want to do it because your afraid of how it'll make your students feel? Or because you're afraid of how it'll make *you* feel?"

Greg shut his eyes for a moment to slow down the whirlwind of thought inside his head. "I don't know…"

"Exactly," Carl said. "Guess what? *None* of us know that. That's why we have rules. Guidelines. Procedures. Because we need them. Especially when things get confusing."

"So. You think I'm confused."

Carl smiled, reached across the table and gave Greg's arm a firm squeeze. "Greg, you're the most confused person I know…except for me."

Greg stayed late in his classroom again, grading papers and drinking coffee. When he looked up, he was surprised to see that it was already eight-thirty and dark outside. He put the rest of his papers into his briefcase to grade at home, turned out the lights. Just before closing the classroom door, without knowing why, he turned around.

The homeless man was standing right outside the window,

looking in. His arms were raised above his head and his fingers were hooked in the holes of the metal security grill. Greg thought of how long the man must have been standing there watching him, and his whole body went cold.

The security light in the schoolyard outside silhouetted the man from behind, lighting up the wild tangle of hair and the claw-like fingers that were moving and flexing in the window grate. Greg felt grateful he couldn't see the man's face. When he looked closer, his body went cold again. The man was not alone. There were more disheveled figures standing in the schoolyard; Greg counted at least seven or eight, silent motionless shadows. To get to his car he would have to walk right through all of them.

Taking out his cell phone, Greg punched-in 911, his fingers trembling. The voice that answered right away was female, official-sounding, and expressionless. "911. What is your emergency?"

"Yes… I'm at P.S. 45, on Harris Street. I'm a teacher. There's… there are intruders here, on the school grounds."

"Is anyone injured?"

"Injured? No. No one's… There are intruders here. They're… they're trying to break into the school."

"Are you inside the school, sir?"

"Yes. Yes, I'm inside. Can you…Please, can you send someone?"

"Stay inside the building. We'll dispatch a patrol car to your location."

"Good. Good. Thank you."

"Do you want to stay on the line?"

He thought about that, and a wave of shame burned through him. He wasn't a child. "No. No, thank you."

"A patrol car will be there in five minutes. Call back if you need further assistance."

"Thanks…goodbye…" Greg punched disconnect and too a deep breath, trying to calm his pounding heart. He turned and saw that the man was no longer there. Moving cautiously, he stepped closer to the window and peered outside. The schoolyard was empty.

Greg felt a wave of relief, followed by embarrassment. The police were on their way. What would he tell them? That he had seen what he'd seen, that's what he'd tell them. He'd seen what he'd seen and did what he had to do, what anyone else would have done.

His thought were interrupted by a loud knock on the classroom door. He stared at the door, shocked, unable to think. Were the police here already? How did they get inside the building? He was about to open the door when another thought came to him – how could the police know which classroom he was in? He had not told the woman on the phone that.

The knocking started again, slow, loud, and insistent. The doorknob rattled. Then the pounding began. The door shook from violent blows as if it was about to split open. Greg didn't want to see whatever was on the other side, but found himself inching closer to the small window in the door. He looked through it.

An angry red eye filled with blood looked back. A dozen other eyes, a dozen faces, disfigured by a rage and suffering so strong that it sent him sprawling to the floor where he curled up, hugging his knees and hiding his face while the door thundered and shook. When he heard the door burst open, he screamed. Opening his eyes, he looked up and saw two police officers with flashlights and troubled faces looking down at him.

A one-month sabbatical. That was what the school suggested for him. He knew it was not really a suggestion. It was to begin immediately after the conclusion of the Fall term, as soon as he handed in his grades. The question of who was to pay for the destruction of school property was yet to be decided. The police officers at the scene reported that they had broken into the school when they'd heard a man screaming and had followed the sound of those screams to his classroom door. Greg couldn't remember screaming until the classroom door had caved in. He told the police everything. He told the principal and the teachers' union rep too. He'd endured their questioning, suspicion, and pitying looks, and agreed to their terms. As hard as all of that was, being alone with his thoughts afterward was a hundred times worse. Was he losing his mind? That possibility wasn't as terrifying as it might have been; at least there would be an explanation, and he would be taken care of. There was something almost peaceful about the thought. But if what he'd seen was real…

Carl was already drinking when Greg arrived at the corner bar. Straight scotch from the smell of it. He gave Greg a look of pity mixed with wariness. "What can I get you?"

Greg shook his head. He wanted to keep his mind clear. He

wanted to, but it was no use. It felt like his mind would never be clear again. Still, he had to try. He had to ask Carl some questions. But before he could, Carl spoke out in a loud, slurred voice.

"So, you're not gonna help me celebrate?"

"Celebrate what?"

"My retirement," Carl smiled, but it looked like a grimace.

Greg was shocked. "You're retiring? When?"

"Next week."

"Why?"

"My doctor. Says teaching is bad for my health." Carl laughed, bitterly. "God, look at your face. You didn't think I'd ever retire, did you?" Carl shook his head slowly, his smile fading. "Well… neither did I."

Greg looked at Carl's face in the dim bar-light. He looked thinner and more frail than he'd ever seen him. "Jesus, Carl," Greg said, "What am I going to do without you?"

Carl chuckled and waved his hand in the air like he was swatting away a fly. "Ah, you'll do fine. You always do."

"What can I do?" Greg said quietly. "What can I do for you?"

Carl sighed. "Take care of my kids, will you? Just look in on them. Make sure they're okay."

Greg felt a smile forming on his lips. *Your* kids?"

Carl smiled ruefully. "Yeah, well…"

Greg didn't know whether to laugh or cry. The thought suddenly came to him that he might never see Carl again, that this might be his last chance. He had to ask now.

"Carl…have you ever…have you seen those people….the ones near the school?"

Carl's eyes went wide for a moment, then he lowered his face into his hands. "Oh thank God…" he said in a hoarse, weary-sounding voice. "Thank God. I thought…I thought I was the only one." After a while, he lowered his hands and leaned back against the wall, his eyes still shut. "I was hoping someone else would see them…I always knew it would be you."

A couple walked by, laughing loudly. Greg waited till they'd passed before he spoke again. "Who are they?"

Carl opened his eyes and looked at him. His eyes were wet. "Don't you know?"

"No."

"*Yes,*" Carl said, fixing Greg with a hard look. "Yes, you do."

On Friday, Greg planned to spend recess alone in the classroom, packing up the few things he needed. As he sorted through his books and papers, he found himself picking things up and putting them back again, wondering what he really needed to take back with him, wondering if he'd ever really be back at all, if, like Carl, the unknown time ahead of him was going to be longer than he'd thought.

He wanted to see his students one more time before he left. Closing the classroom door, he walked down the hall toward the schoolyard exit where he could hear them shouting and laughing.

When he reached the open doorway to the schoolyard, he froze in horror. There among the laughing, playing children were the ragged people, with their filthy clothes and long matted hair, more of them than before, more than he could even count. The children kept laughing and running right past and around them, not noticing. Once again, the silent figures weren't looking at the children. They were all looking at him.

One of them, an old woman, was standing closer to him than the rest. Her tattered dress was soiled with dirt and rust-colored stains that looked like dried blood. Her body was bent over nearly double at the waist, and her long matted hair covered her face. As he watched in horror, she reached up with her gnarled, filthy hands, lifted her hair and let it fall in dirty gray ringlets through her twisted fingers. Her arms, thin and brittle-looking, were mottled with bruises. Then she smiled with blackened, toothless gums, gazing at him with one blue eye and one green eye.

He knew her. He knew them all.

Greg's hands were shaking so badly, he had to punch-in Carl's phone number twice before he got it right. Carl answered on the fifth ring. "Hello…"

"Carl…" Greg began, then found he couldn't speak.

"You saw them again," Carl said. It wasn't a question.

"Yes."

"And you know." Again, Carl said it like he was stating a fact. "You know who they are now, don't you."

"Yes," Greg said, trying to keep his voice steady. "What…"

"No," Carl cut him off. "Not on the phone. Can you get over here? Right now?"

"Yeah…"

"Don't wait," Carl said. "Come right now."

When Carl answered his apartment door, he looked older, gaunt and haggard. He stood in the doorway but didn't invite Greg inside. Again, Greg could smell whiskey and the stale scent of something unwashed and uncared for.

"How…" Greg began, then stopped; it was a question he didn't even know how to ask. He tried again. "What do they want?"

"The same thing they've always wanted," Carl said. "They want your help. They want you to help them."

"Why *me?*"

"Because it's your job." Carl said, then looked down and shook his head. "It's not mine. Not anymore."

Greg watched Carl pull his keys from his pocket and twist one off the ring. "Here," he said, handing the key to Greg. "It's yours now."

Greg looked at the key in the palm of his hand, then back up into Carl's weary face. "What do I do?"

"Just go in late, after dark," Carl said. "The school won't know you're there. But *they* will."

Greg drove to the school at eleven-thirty but he sat in his car for almost thirty minutes, waiting for his heartbeat to slow down. Then he got out, locked his car, and walked quickly across the empty school yard to the front entrance. The key turned with a loud click, he pushed the heavy door open and slipped inside. As he walked down the empty hallway in the dark, he thought of the last words Carl had said to him.

Don't lie to them. They'll know.

When he entered his classroom, he almost turned the lights on, but stopped, remembering. He wasn't supposed to be here. Even if that hadn't been true, he wasn't sure that he wanted the lights on for what was going to happen.

He left the classroom door open. Then he walked to the front of the room, noticing the time on the clock. Eleven fifty-five. He didn't sit, but stood in front of his desk, resting his hands on its surface just behind him, the way he did every day. He could hear the low electric hum of the clock. The longer he waited, the more he thought he could hear it growing louder.

The first one came inside almost before he knew it, moving along the walls and corners of the room like a shadow thrown by the headlights of a passing car. When it stopped at one of the desks, he saw it more clearly. A thin, ragged man with tangled hair and a pock-marked face. Slowly, the figure lowered itself into the small desk and sat looking at him.

They were all coming now. One by one, through the door they moved like shadows, vaguely, slowly, but with a terrible eagerness that he could feel. They wouldn't hurt him, he told himself, just as he would never hurt them. But how could he know that? How could he know the hundreds of ways he'd already hurt them, the countless things he'd done and said over the years, the countless other things he'd failed to do and say? The realization came to him, swiftly, terribly. All these years, he'd been trying to keep out the things that might hurt them, when the thing that had hurt them had been right here in this room all along.

One by one, they took their seats until there were no seats left. Still more came and stood along the walls, filling the room until there was no more space. They kept coming and stood in the places where others were standing, filling them, looking out through their eyes, the eyes he saw every day, the same eyes he'd seen for years. Despite their wasted and crippled bodies, their scarred and ravaged faces, he knew them. He knew them all. He could feel them waiting, waiting for him to begin and teach them what he had never taught them before. Waiting for him to explain the things that had happened to them, and the things that were going to happen. Waiting for him to tell them what to do, and what it all meant. His throat swelled. How could he tell them? What could he say?

The clock on the wall hummed. He looked into their ravaged faces, cleared his throat, took a deep breath. Then he began.

writings found in a red notebook

August 12

Entered Nebraska today, crossing the Badlands on our way to Wyoming and the Medicine Bow.

Feeling of great distance everywhere. The space from one point to another feels like the space between stars – you can measure it on maps and charts, even see it on the horizon, but it still takes light years to cross.

Annie read what I just wrote. She said I make this place sound like Mars or some kind of alternate dimension, when it's all just sand and rock. So is Mars, I told her.

Annie says my imagination was the first thing that attracted her to me, my stories, songs, and poems that I showed her on the first night we met back in college. She said no one had ever done that on a first date – I told her that should have been her first warning.

I want to show Annie that I can be practical too. I can set up, operate, and strip down the propane stove. The tent is still hard and takes too much time. If it's late and we're tired (like tonight), we sleep in the car. We could sleep out under the sky if we wanted, but somehow it doesn't feel safe.

Annie's mother used to travel with a gun. I saw it once in the glove compartment of her old red pickup when we were on another camping trip years ago. I was looking for a roadmap when my fingers touched something cold and hard. She told me *any woman who travels alone without a gun is a fool.* I remember saying *But you're not alone; you've got me,* partly as a joke. When I saw the look on her face, I was sorry I said it.

When we were packing for this trip, Annie asked if I thought we should bring any protection. I started to make a joke about her choice of words, some lame crack about condoms, but stopped, knowing it probably wouldn't be funny under the circumstances.

Packed two sleeping bags for this trip and we're still using both of them. I don't know why. I thought maybe it would be different for us out here. I think being alone together like this, *really* alone together, makes us more self-conscious and uncomfortable. Maybe it's too soon. Maybe we just need a little more time.

August 13

Decided to try one of those roads that looks like a dotted line on the map. It was Annie's idea. (*The shortest distance between two points.*) Left the main road around dusk to cut across open land. Tires rumbling over nothing but dirt and rocks. Not really a road anymore – more like the memory of a road.

A half-tank of gas left – should be enough to reach Lusk in four hours.

Later

Thought we were going to die tonight.

We'd been driving in the dark for a while when I saw headlights behind us. No other cars for miles and it spooked me. When I saw how fast they were closing-in on us, I got ready to pull over to let them pass. But the headlights pulled up behind us, right on our tail, filling the mirror and blinding me.

Annie started yelling *what's this guy's problem*, but I knew. He wanted to kill us. We'd crossed over into a place where we had no business being; now he was going to run us off the road and kill us.

I took one hand off the wheel and felt for my knife in my jacket pocket, wrapped my fingers around it and tried to imagine what I'd do, whether a three-inch blade could stop a man. Our wheels were banging over rocks and rough terrain at seventy miles per hour with this guy right on our bumper, Annie yelling at me to pull over and let him pass, but I kept my foot down on the gas pedal – I knew if I stopped or slowed down, we'd be dead.

When I heard the truck's engine roaring louder behind us, saw the lights leaving the rear-view mirror and swelling past us on the left, I gripped the knife in my pocket and turned to face him.

There, just a few inches outside my window, I saw two stick-thin, talon-like hands clinging to the steering wheel, two dead eyes like black stones, a withered, hollow-cheeked face and a toothless gaping mouth that looked like the desert wind was howling through it. I watched this shrunken, ancient vision rattle past us, red taillights fading out like two sparks far ahead.

Took my foot off the gas pedal, we rolled to a stop and sat there, not saying anything. Then a star fell right in front of us. I saw it cross from left to right across the sky right in front of our windshield. It felt like it meant something. Even though I couldn't say what it was, I knew it meant *something*.

Decided to sleep in the car again. Locked all the doors before going to sleep, my knife still here in my pocket where I can reach it.

August 14

Can't find the road. Woke up this morning and realized we're on open range. A few faint lines or indentations visible on the landscape – can't tell if they're old cattle trails or something else, like those canal-markings on the surface of Mars.

Tried looking at the map to find the nearest road, the closest town. All I could see was the jumble of names, the spider-scrawl of highways and roads that go everywhere and nowhere at once; like paint spilled on a flat surface, my mind wanted to run in all directions at once, and I could feel it freezing to keep from coming apart.

Annie asked, *What are we going to do?* I should know the answer to this question, but I don't. Whatever gene other men possess that allows them to see into the future and figure things out, I don't have. I want to tell Annie this. I want to tell her she'd be better off without me.

Annie says we should keep driving West. I tell her we should turn around and go back where we came from and try to find the main road. She says that's crazy, that if we just keep driving we'll be sure to find a road or a town or something. I'm too tired to argue.

Last night when I thought we were going to die, I started to forgive Annie. The things we do to each other that seem so big and terrible at the time don't really matter that much in the end. Not sure if that's supposed to be a comforting thought or something else.

The earth is changing, like everything is falling away, receding farther and farther into the distance. That's how it looks, but the truth is, nothing is moving away from us – we're the ones who are moving away from everything.

Should have reached Lusk by now. I haven't said anything but I'm guessing Annie must know. I can tell by the sound of her voice, *"This doesn't make sense…"* The only thing she's said for miles.

The surface of the earth here is cracked, millions of cracks as far as the eye can see, spreading outward in all directions like a spiderweb or a bullet hole in a sheet of glass. The horizon is a flat line. Not a single telephone pole or power-line, not a single tree or bush. Nothing but a flat line all around us in every direction, nothing for the eye to hold onto. Hard to tell the difference between the earth and the sky. Maybe there is no difference.

That's stupid, of course. Everyone knows the earth is the earth and the sky is the sky. Though sometimes, things change places. Like a long time ago, millions of years ago, maybe billions, this whole area used to be covered by an ocean. Miles of saltwater over our heads, vast and terrible creatures moving all around us through the cold and dark.

The fucking car has died. We're stuck here. We should have just kept going. We should have never stopped.

It all started when we spotted something on the horizon four hours ago, some kind of outcropping of rock, miles away. It looked small, like one of those plastic mountains at the bottom of a fishbowl. The closer we got, the bigger it grew, until we saw how big it really was.

It looked like a giant had broken off a piece of mountain range from the surface of the moon and dropped it right at the center of all this flatness. Scalloped ridges and peaks rising into the sky, strange lunar shapes blasted by wind and sand.

Annie and I got out of the car to explore. Strange faded reddish-colored rock, coarse and grainy underfoot. Tried to climb high enough to look around but the rock was too steep, so came back down and got in the car to leave. Turned the key, a few clicks, then nothing.

I should have learned how to fix a car. I should have brought food and water. I should have brought a gun. I should have stayed on the main road. There are hundreds of things I should have done. And I haven't done any of them.

August 15

Slept in the car last night. Rough sleep full of strange dreams I can't remember now. Annie and I ate some crackers we had in the car and talked about what we should do. Annie thinks we should start walking. Walk where? In what direction?

Tried to climb the rock again this morning to get a better view of what's around us, maybe a building or a fencepost or some sign of people. Climbed as far as we could, but it was too steep; our feet kept slipping out from under us and there was nothing to hold onto.

On a ridge about twenty feet up, found names and dates carved on the rock.

BILLY AND THELMA 1970.
MARK AND REBECCA 1968.
JOHN AND LINDA, 1962.

Argued with Annie about trying to walk out of here, but something about all those names carved on the rock made me change my mind.

August 16

How the fuck could this happen? I don't understand.

Started walking around 10 o'clock, trying to keep the sun at our backs. Annie said that if we kept walking west we'd find something. Annie walking five feet ahead of me, just like the first time we went hiking in the woods. After three hours the sky above was a white blur and I couldn't find the sun. Annie said just keep moving. So I did, scanning the horizon for any kind of object. Three hours later I saw something, a dark blur against the sky that I thought was a storm cloud, but turned solid as we got closer. Another mountainous outcropping of rock, a smaller object on the ground near it. When we got closer we saw it was a car and started running toward it. We stopped running when we saw it was our car.

Don't know how long Annie and I stood there shouting at each other. Annie wanted to blame me. How could she blame me when she was the one leading the way? That was my fault too, according to her. If I'd just stepped up and led the way first, she wouldn't have had to.

After a while, Annie stopped shouting and looked like she wanted to cry. I should have tried to hold her and comfort her, but for some reason I couldn't and we went to sleep in the car again without touching.

August 17

Strange dreams again. The same one I've been having since I was a little kid. I'm in a big group of people, hundreds of us, men, women, and children camping on the ground, huddled around fires, wrapped in blankets. Some kind of mass migration or evacuation; we're trying to get away from something that's coming – we can't see it but it's very close. There are soldiers with swords and helmets telling us we have to get up and get our things and keep moving if we want to stay alive. I never see the thing that's coming for us, but I know it's there, right behind us, maybe just over the next hill, and I know we have to keep moving.

Not many crackers left, not much water either. Hard to tell what time it is – my watch stopped working today.

August 18

Found something strange. A small building made of sod, about ten by twelve feet, near the base of the rock. We found it circling around the rock, looking for a better way to climb up to the top. A rectangular opening where a door used to be, no windows, dark and empty, cool inside. Very old and crudely made; must have been built by settlers, though why any human beings would ever want to live here, I can't imagine.

Annie says we should sleep inside this thing tonight, but I didn't want to. There's something about it. It doesn't feel safe. How can I tell her that?

Annie says she's sick of sleeping in the car and waking up cramped and stiff. *At least we can stretch out here,* she says. I can't explain to her how much I don't want to do this. I think it's the door. Maybe I'd feel better if there was a door we could close. Or maybe not. Maybe that would make it worse.

August 19

Slept in the sod house last night. Strange dreams again, the old one about trying to get away from some approaching army. In the dream we need to move fast but there are so many of us and we're weighted down with so many things – clothes, pots and pans, food, small children. Some of us have started leaving these things behind so we can move faster. We leave them on the ground where the enemy will find them tomorrow, like offerings, but even as we do, we know these things will not slow them down. They are gaining and we can't get away from them fast enough.

Woke up from this dream before dawn, light coming from

the night sky outside the door, a perfect rectangle of sky and stars.

No more food left, and only a little water. If we tried to walk out of here now, we'd die. Our only choice is to wait here till someone finds us.

It's not too late. I really believe that. It's not too late for us.

August 20

Found more carvings on the rock today, higher up, older than the last ones.

JAMES AND NORA GREEN, 1945.

NATE AND KELLY JACKSON, 1939.

ZACHARY AND BEULAH CARTER, 1898.

What brought these people here? What happened to them?

Heard Annie cry out, a short, muffled sound like the ones she makes in her sleep. Found her staring at something on the side of the cliff. Two words carved in the rock among all the dates and names. *HELP US.*

August 21

Two days without food. The hunger pains are getting worse – I can only imagine how bad they are for Annie.

I think about what a small thing it takes to throw us off-course. Choosing one line on a map instead of another. Deciding to stop the car instead of keeping going. One wrong move. One wrong word.

Now I think I know what that falling star meant.

August 22

Three days without food. Looked around for some kind of grass or weeds to eat but the ground is nothing but hard-baked dirt. Remembered seeing dried grass in the walls of the sod house, broke off a piece with a rock and found dried grass running through the baked clay like veins and arteries. Rubbed the chunk of dirt between my hands till most of it crumbled away, then put the grass in my mouth and spit out the mud when it got wet. Tough and hard to chew but stopped the hunger for a while.

The whole time I felt eyes watching us, like we were doing something we were not supposed to do.

Annie and I sat tearing off pieces of the house and crumbling the dirt away between our hands. I looked at Annie and saw the whole lower-half of her face black with mud, hard to look at – saw her staring back at me and realized I must look the same to her.

August 23

Annie refused to eat the grass from the walls of the house today. When I asked her why, she whispered, *Because. They won't like it.*

August ?

Woke up before dawn again from another dream. and looked out the door at the stars. They looked different, like some were missing. Then I saw a few stars go out, one after another, from left to right across the sky. Then I realized. Something was moving across the doorway. Something huge, as big as a mountain, was blocking out the stars. Frozen with terror, I closed my eyes and waited. When nothing happened, I opened my eyes and all the stars were back again.

I think I know why we're still here. We're not ready yet. Whatever is going to happen is waiting for us to be ready.

August ?

The car is gone. I went looking for it this morning to see if there might be anything left inside that we can use and wasn't there. No tire-tracks, no oil stains, no marks on the ground at all.

When I told Annie that the car was gone, she looked me right in the eye and said, *What car?*

August ?

Last night Annie laid down on the ground looking up at the stars, and told me everything. The secrets I was afraid to hear and the ones she was afraid to tell. She told them all until there was nothing left. When we were through we both laid there on our backs, not looking at each other, not touching. I heard Annie say, *I'm ready now.*

August ?

Couldn't find Annie this morning. Thought about the car vanishing and started to panic. Heard a scraping sound and followed it till I found her high on a ledge with a rock in her hand, scratching something into the cliff. I saw the first four letters of my name and tore the rock out of her hand, screaming at her like a crazy man until she ran away crying. I didn't care. I had to stop her before she finished, because I knew what would happen if she did.

Found the rock she'd been using and started scraping away what she'd begun. I scraped and scraped until there was nothing left.

August ?

My name is James Thomas Franklin. I was born on January 12, 1962 in Frankfort, Kentucky. My mother was Sarah Johnson from Paducah and my father was Mitchell Franklin from Virginia Beach. I have a younger sister named Katherine who grew up to be a social worker in Washington. I met Annie Robbins in college, married her and moved to New York City when I was twenty four. I worked as a dishwasher, office temp, bookstore clerk, and part-time teacher and I have written and published five short stories and seven poems. I have tried to be a good husband, a good son, and a good brother. All those things will still be true when I am gone. They will not vanish with me, because that is not how things happen. Things do not simply vanish, even though they may appear to. Just because something looks like it's gone doesn't mean it really is. Nothing is ever really gone. Nothing.

Climbed to the ledge right before sunset and used my knife to carve our names into the rock, adding them to all the others, weeping as I did it because I know what it means, even though I still can't say it out loud.

They are coming.

Climbed to the top of the rock this morning for one last look, for one single sign of humanity that might tell us where to go, and I saw them. Annie is waiting for me below but I don't want to go down and face her. She's going to ask me what I saw and what's going to happen to us. What am I going to say? What am I going to tell her now?

I can see them. Coming from far away. They are running toward us on all fours. They fill the horizon like a swarm. Some of them are riding and the creatures they are riding on have human faces.

Please. Help us.

faces of the missing

I find the invitation in my mailbox on Friday. A plain three-by-five index card, the kind you buy in drugstores, the words written in Carter's bold scrawl.

AUGUST 12, 7 – 10PM
AVENUE X GALLERY, 211 LUDLOW STREET
'FACES OF THE MISSING'
PORTRAITS OF PEOPLE YOU SHOULD CARE ABOUT BUT
DON'T

I can tell Carter wrote it by hand because of how the ink is smeared by raindrops that still dot the surface. No stamp or postmark. That doesn't surprise me. I can see Carter delivering every single invitation by himself, riding the subway from borough to borough, thrusting them into the hands of doormen and security guards at hi-rise office buildings and luxury condos, cramming them into the mailboxes of artist friends like me.

IF YOU DO NOT ATTEND THIS SHOW YOU WILL REVEAL YOURSELF AS THE APATHETIC, COMPLICIT ASSHOLE YOU FEAR YOURSELF TO BE.

I read the angry scrawl and smile. Coming from anyone else, these words might be ironic or satirical, some kind of politically correct *attitude* dressed in dramatic language for effect. Not Carter. He means it. Every word.

When I get to the gallery at eight o'clock the wine is already gone, the usual sad cluster of empty bottles on a card table in the corner. More people than I expected, though most of them have stopped looking at the art and are busy looking at each other, talking in louder-than-necessary voices.

I work my way toward the wall to see the paintings. Some of them I've already seen in Carter's studio. Tonight there are at least ten or twelve I don't recognize, which means he must have done them all since my last visit a few days ago. This doesn't surprise me either. Carter works faster than any of us.

In the old days Carter used to spend a lot of time reworking the flyers of missing children he tears down from the walls of neighborhood buildings and light poles, making collages, layering them with paint and wax and broken glass. These days he mostly leaves them alone, mounting them on wood or sometimes just pinning them directly to the wall. *Let the faces speak for themselves,* he says.

Tonight the walls are also adorned with words he's painted in harsh, dripping red letters on rolls of meat-wrapping paper. *PROFIT. SALES. LIES.* On a few of the flyers Carter has painted a price directly over the kid's face. *$1,000. $2,000.* I told him last week that he was brilliant for painting the price of the work right onto the surface of the painting. *That's not how much for the painting*, he told me. *It's how much for the kid.*

I can hear Carter's voice in the next room, louder than all the rest, another voice trying to rise above it. I work my way through the crowd and find Carter going nose-to-nose with a young guy in a beard and thick black glasses. With his angry red face and the veins in his skull popping-out under his buzz-cut, Carter looks more like a Marine drill sergeant than an East Village artist. The guy in the glasses has clearly never had anyone get in his face the way Carter is. He's putting on a good show, still shouting and trying to look aggressive, but his body is already caving in, head bent backwards on his spine like he's facing into a hurricane – a few more seconds and his shoulders will be touching the wall behind him.

I see a couple of big guys in gallery t-shirts and grim faces moving toward Carter. Before they can reach him, he gives the glasses-guy a final *fuck you*, turns and stalks through the crowd that parts in front of him.

I follow Carter outside where he's already headed for the bar across the street. "Nice," I call after him. "Getting thrown out of your own opening."

"I didn't get thrown out," he says without turning around. "I *left*." He shoves open the door to the bar, letting out a blast of music and loud voices, then turns and looks at me for the first time tonight. "Well? Are you coming or not?"

I wait until the bartender puts the shots down in front of us and Carter throws one back before I ask. "So…what was that guy's problem?"

"Fucking piss-ant," Carter spits, his volume still on high. "'Comes up telling me about how I'm profiting from the suffering of all those poor missing kids and their families. I said, Yeah? And what are *you* gonna do for those poor missing kids and their families? Write another piece of *art criticism* for the fucking Village Voice?"

I see the bartender shoot a quick look over at us to make sure Carter isn't about to rip my head off.

"He said you were *profiting* off of your work?" I laugh. Among my artist friends, it's acceptable procedure to joke and bitch about each other's lack of financial success. It's like a badge of honor – if you're getting paid well for your work, it must mean you've sold out. Carter actually made some big sales five years ago when he was still doing large abstract work. *Wallpaper paintings*, he calls them now. An uptown gallery grabbed him and his paintings started appearing in penthouses and corporate offices all over the city. Then out of nowhere, he started working with the fliers of missing children and his gallery dropped him.

"I'm not profiting off of those kids," Carter says, lowering his voice, "But *somebody* is." He leans across the booth on his elbows, the wiry muscles in his arms growing tight. I know what's coming.

"You know how many kids go missing in this city?" Carter asks. "Just last year? Six thousand. Six thousand kids. How does that even *happen?* You're telling me this country can fire a rocket into space, land a go-cart on Mars, drive it around with a remote control, pick up rocks and split them open and find atoms from ice crystals that are a billion years old – and we can't find *six thousand* fucking human beings right here on this planet? In this *city?*"

"Maybe they don't all *want* to be found."

"Bullshit," Carter spits the word. "You know why they don't get found, don't you? Because *no one gets paid* if they do." This is a favorite theme of Carter's. "Why do you think no one steals police cars, Chris?"

I laugh out loud, "Police cars?"

"Yeah," Carter says, "You know why nobody steals police cars? If someone stole a police car in this city, you think the cops couldn't find it? They'd have it back in five minutes. Someone steals *your* car, how come they can't find *that?* Because. *No one gets paid* if they do. Car theft in New York City, Chris – it's a million dollar industry. *Multi*-million. Same thing with drugs. You think the government couldn't shut down the drugs coming into to this country if they really wanted to? They *get paid* not to do it."

"What's that got to do with all those kids?"

Carter drops his face into his hands and rubs his eyes so hard I'm afraid they're going to pop out of their sockets. When he looks up again his face looks weary and drawn in the red bar-light. For the first time tonight I can see he's sick. *The skull beneath the skin.*

"Those kids don't just disappear, Chris," he says. "It's an *industry.* You don't fuck with industry."

Carter sees things the rest of us never notice. The problem, according to Carter, is that no one pays attention. *It's right there in front of your face,* he says. *All you have to do is look.*

In the working class bars in Indiana where Carter and I went to college, anyone could tell which guys were beating up their girlfriends or wives. All you had to do was look for the black eyes or bruises. But Carter could tell which guys were *going* to beat their girlfriends, even if they hadn't done it yet. He used to position himself with his back to the bar where he could watch every couple when they came in. If the man walked in first with the woman behind him, that was the first sign. Carter would sit and watch until the guy did something. Sometimes it was just a look, or maybe the guy would shove his red face at the woman, drunken mouth twisting around ugly words you couldn't hear but had no trouble understanding.

Then Carter would get up and walk right over to them. I never heard what he said – I was too scared to get that close. Sometimes the guy would just get up and walk away. Those were the easy ones. Usually there'd be some kind of argument, with the guy doing most of the yelling; Carter would just stand there and say whatever he had to say until the guy walked away. Sometimes there'd be a fight but it was always over really quickly.

I never saw a girl turn on Carter the way you hear about some women doing when the cops come to take away the guy who's been beating up on them. Mostly they seemed grateful, sometimes more than grateful. They'd figure Carter had *won* them or something, like they were his prize for rescuing them, probably because that was what they were used to. But Carter wasn't interested.

Sometimes he'd take one of them home for the night, *just so she'll be safe*, but he never slept with them. That confused the hell out of them. They'd keep coming around, looking for him at the bar or on campus until they found him. Then they'd corner him at a table somewhere where they'd talk and talk about their lives and wait for him to say something that would explain it all to them because they figured he knew something they didn't, something important. I knew how they felt.

Sometimes, when it got to be too much for him, he'd call me to take them off his hands. That was how I met Kelly.

She was sitting on the couch in Carter's apartment, right on the edge, a glass of water in her hands. She looked up at me, and her gray eyes seemed enormous and busy like there was some kind of problem she was working on.

Carter was dashing around in the tiny kitchen behind her, running water and banging pans in an aimless deliberate way that told me how much he wanted her out of there.

"Chris," he said without turning around, "This is Kelly. Would you take her home please?"

Out on the street I took care to walk at a respectful distance away from her, as if we weren't really together, so if she needed to she could pretend that whatever had happened to her tonight hadn't really happened. I figured the details were the same as usual. Some people, it seems to me, invite the bad things that happen to them.

Not because they're ignorant or self-destructive but because they want to think the best of each other.

We'd just turned the corner by the Catholic church and were walking past the silent park when she finally spoke. "Why does he do that?"

"I don't know," I said. "He's a good guy." I knew the real answer was a lot more complicated but I had no way of explaining it to her, or to myself.

"I don't know how I let this happen to me," she said. I knew she wasn't talking about Carter now. Or me. Or maybe she was. The whole crazy, inevitable evening that had led her to this place. I knew it wasn't what she'd imagined for herself when she woke up this morning.

"It's okay," I said. "It happens to everyone sometimes."

"No," she said, the force in her voice startling me, waking me up. *Not to me*, was what her eyes said, and it was in that moment, in that look, that I gave myself to her. Here was someone who *knew* something, who knew it right down to her core. The way Carter did. The way I wanted to.

That was how Kelly and I ended up together. It's not the kind of story you tell your children when they ask how mommy and daddy met each other – that's a joke we used to share back in the days when we still talked about things like having children.

Walking home from the bar after saying goodnight to Carter, I look up at all the dark buildings with their lighted windows staring down at me. I wonder if Kelly's home, and find myself hoping she's not.

When I unlock the door and enter our tiny apartment all the lights are off. I reach for the switch but then I hear Kelly's voice in the dark. "Don't."

The only light is coming from the window, the electric gray of the city sky at night with Kelly's silhouette framed against it. Her long thick curtain of hair makes her look featureless, like a ghost or a nun. Then she turns her head and I see the outline of her nose, sharp as a hawk's, and the round high dome of her forehead. One arm detaches itself partly from the black outline of her body, then there's the sound of her hand patting the windowsill. "Come here."

I force a smile, walk over and sit next to her. The window is open and a cool breeze has started to roll in from the river, pushing through the humid night air, making Kelly's hair move a little. I can feel the warmth from her thigh next to mine.

"Listen," she says. I hear the smile in her voice. Beyond the hissing ocean sound of traffic and the blare of a radio playing Spanish music I hear a shuddering boom like compressed thunder, not from the sky, but from somewhere down below.

When Kelly and I first moved to New York we used to hear that noise at night and think that explosions were happening somewhere. It was just one of the many mysteries of the city to us back then. "Remember?" she asks.

The trapped feeling in my chest grows a little tighter, like she's trying to make me admit something I don't want to. "Sure," I say. "Sure I do."

"So," she finally says, "How was the show?"

"Good," I say automatically. The whole night – Carter fighting with the critic, nearly getting thrown out of his own opening, our conversation at the bar – unfolds behind my eyes and for a moment I think of sharing it with her, but all I can say is, "It was good."

Kelly sits silent for what feels like a long time, waiting for me to say more. Then she stands and walks to the bedroom door. "Are you coming?" she asks, and for a second I see Carter framed in the barroom door, glaring back at me over his shoulder. *Well? Are you coming or not?*

"Yeah," I say. "Soon." Kelly stands in the doorway for another moment, looking back at me, then goes inside. She leaves the door open, like always.

For the next couple of weeks I disappear into my studio, trying to be productive. Carter has that effect on me. It's not because I feel inspired; it's more like being afraid. Kelly says she thinks she disappears from my mind when I'm painting. *If I'm not right there in front of you,* she complains, *it's like I don't exist.* I want to tell her not to take it personally, that when I'm not around my paintings I forget about them too, what they look like, what it felt like to paint them, what I was trying to do or say.

When I unlock the door to my studio and flip on the overhead light and my paintings all leap at me out of the dark, it's not just that I don't feel connected to them – I don't even recognize them. It's almost like they were painted by someone else.

Today I'm walking down Avenue A when a patch of color catches my eye, high on a lamppost. I get closer and see it's one of Carter's flyers, the smiling face of a black child about six or seven years old, but with Carter's touch – a border of crumpled gold and silver aluminum foil that catches the morning sun. Just below the boy's face, bright red-painted letters: *HOW MUCH WOULD YOU PAY FOR THIS CHILD?* On the next block there's another one glued to the side of an abandoned building. *CHILD FOR SALE, SLIGHTLY USED.*

The next morning when I go out to buy milk for Kelly's coffee, the posters are gone. I see a piece of gold foil still stuck to the light pole and one ragged scrap of white paper. When I call Carter and tell him about it he doesn't sound surprised. "That's the way it works," he says. "I put them up, they tear them down, I put them up again." He chuckles, "It's a cycle."

"Who do you think is doing it?" I ask.

There's a long pause and for a moment I think he's hung up on me. Then his voice comes crackling at me through the phone again. "Who's *doing* it? Jesus, you *know* who's doing it, Chris. Open your fucking eyes."

Kelly says she's worried about the money. I should be too, but when I try to think about it lately there's something in the way, like the white spot that drifts in front of your eyes after a flash of bright light.

Kelly wants to know why I don't get a job. I want to tell her the reason but I can't because I don't want to scare her.

The last job I had was at a sandwich place on Second Avenue, chopping lettuce and tomatoes. I used to walk past it every day and see the men in white aprons and expressionless faces working behind the big plate glass window. Now I was one of them on the other side of the glass, wearing a white apron and plastic gloves, looking out at people walking down the sidewalk where I used to be.

One morning I stayed in bed and watched the clock get closer and closer to the time when I was supposed to be at work. I watched it reach the hour, then go past it. Nothing happened. No one called to find out where I was or when I was coming in. I waited until I couldn't stand it anymore, then I went down to the street and walked past the place. I looked through the big plate glass window at one of the guys I worked with. He looked up and didn't react at all. At first I thought he hadn't seen me. Then I realized that he was looking right at my face, not even a glint of recognition in his eyes. Fear rose in my throat and I turned and walked away as fast as I could. Because at that moment it occurred to me that I had never really worked there. I had never worn a white apron or chopped tomatoes and lettuce or worked side by side with those men on the other side of the glass. It had never happened. Which made me wonder – if I could be wrong about this, how much more of my life was I wrong about?

Tonight when I come home Kelly has a candle lit in the bedroom. The little flame cuts through me like a knife. I hear her running water in the bathroom, then some quiet, purposeful splashing. When she turns the water off, the silence rushes at me like a shock wave and I feel like running but I don't. The candle flickers when she opens the door. There's nowhere to go but here.

When Kelly walks through the bathroom door, the sight of her body shocks me and I realize how long it's been since I've seen it. If I watched her walk naked onto a crowded street I couldn't feel more surprised.

Kelly walks up and kisses me on the mouth. Her lips feel small and hungry. I pay attention to the part of me that's responding to this and try to keep it going all the way to the bed, when she rolls over onto her stomach, takes me into her hand and guides me higher. I'm shocked but I stay with it. I push hard but can't get in. She reaches for a tube of something on the bedside table and says, "We've never done this before." *No*, I can't stop myself from thinking, *but you have*, and I wilt instantly in her hand. She puts a little of what's in the tube into her palm and works patiently to bring me back but it's too late. I reach down to move her hand away but before I can she flings herself onto her back and sighs, the sudden motion of her body making the candle flutter and big shadows lurch across the walls and ceiling.

When Kelly finally starts talking I feel myself sinking down like a stone to the bottom of a deep river. I try to bring myself back before she can notice how far down I've gone. I think of truck drivers who burn their arms with cigarettes to stay awake on those long, all-night hauls and for a moment I picture my own arms covered with puckered red scars from the wrist to the elbow.

"I love you," Kelly says, the words rising up in the dark toward the ceiling. I know what she wants to hear but I can't bring myself to say it. It's not that I don't love her. Something else is happening to me that I can't explain or stop, and it's worse than just not loving her or forgetting how.

The room grows brighter as the candle flares higher the way it always does right before it dies. Kelly keeps talking. "Remember the night you came to get me at Carter's place?"

I feel myself sinking deeper. This is something we don't talk about.

"You think Carter saved me that night," Kelly says. "But he didn't. You did. You know that, right?" I can hear what she's trying to do but it's all just words to me. I didn't save her. I've never saved anyone. I'm not the type who saves people.

"Say something," she says. "Please. Just say something."

I know I need to do something now before it's too late but I can't think of what to say. I think and think until everything around me starts to disappear – Kelly, the bed we're laying on, the four walls around us. When those things finally start to come back, one by one, Kelly isn't one of them.

I don't know how long I've been laying here alone in the dark when the phone rings. It's Carter asking if I want to meet him at Veselkas for coffee. I roll out of bed and stumble downstairs. When I push the door open the sun is so harsh I have to shield my eyes against it with one hand.

I make my way down Second Avenue and find Carter standing against a wall with a terrifying look on his face, his eyes wide and wild. He's staring at something across the street but I can't tell what. I start to ask what's wrong and he raises his hand so fast that for a moment I think he's going to hit me.

"*Look*," he hisses. I look where his eyes are aimed across the street. I see a couple of Orthodox Jews standing by a truck, talking and gesticulating emphatically. A Latino woman in a waitress uniform smoking a cigarette in a doorway. A black child about six or seven years old standing on the corner holding a man's hand.

"What?" I ask, whispering without knowing why.

"It's him," Carter whispers. "Right there."

"Who? The kid?"

"Yeah. It's him. The one in my painting."

"What are you talking about?" I ask, feeling stupid and dishonest – I know exactly what he's talking about. I just don't want to admit it.

"The kid in the poster. That's *him*. I swear to God."

"Jesus, Carter – come on." I know it's too late to stop him or change his mind but I can't keep from trying.

"*Look* at him," Carter hisses. "It's *him*." I remember – Carter has probably spent more time than any other human being on earth studying the face of that child in the poster.

"But...he's with that guy," I say, still looking for some way to make it not true.

"*Of course* he is," Carter sneers at my stupidity. While we both watch, the man lets go of the kid's hand and steps inside the store. The kid stays by himself on the curb, studying something on the sidewalk near his feet.

Before I know it, Carter is hurrying across the street, his shaved head snapping quickly right and left, eyes blazing. I stand and stare like I'm watching a movie of some horrible accident I can't look away from.

I watch Carter bend down and say a few words to the kid who stares up at him, startled but seemingly not afraid. Then Carter reaches down, takes the kid's hand and starts walking back across the street toward me. For a moment I get the urge to run. But it's Carter who breaks into a run first, pulling the kid along with him and yelling, "*Come on,*" as they rush past me. I can't move – then I see the door to the store across the street swing open and the man step out onto the sidewalk. That's when something snaps and suddenly I'm running and running with a white light flooding my brain, blotting out every other thought. We dash into a narrow alley, when the full force of what just happened hits me.

"Carter…" I gasp, the breath burning a hole in my lungs, "What the fuck…"

"Shut up," he hisses at me, raising his hand and listening. I listen too. No sirens, no angry voices shouting.

Then we both turn and face the kid. He's standing there, looking at us. I'd thought he'd be screaming or at least crying by now but he's just staring at us with his big wide-open eyes, like he's waiting to see what's going to happen next.

"Don't worry," Carter says to the kid in a flat voice. When he walks to the mouth of the alley to look out, I follow him.

"What the fuck are you *doing*?" I try not to shout. I don't want to scare the kid any more than he already is. "Are you out of your fucking mind? You just kidnapped a kid. You can't just fucking take a kid like that." I realize with a feeling of shame that there are tears in my eyes and I rub them away before Carter can see them.

"I'm not taking him," Carter says. "I'm taking him *back*."

"What about his father?"

"His *father*? You think that was his *father*? Don't you get it…?" Suddenly he's doubled over coughing hard and deep like he'll never stop. When he rises up again there's a tiny smear of red at the corner of his mouth. I reach out to touch his shoulder but he shoves my hand away, angrily. *"Don't look at me,"* he snarls then starts coughing again.

I go back to check on the kid. He's standing in the same spot like he's been waiting for me to come back.

"Are you alright?" I ask. He keeps staring up at me. I kneel down where I can get a better look at his face. I see a tiny spot of brown in the inside corner of his left eye. "That man back there," I ask, "was he your father?" No answer. Just those big eyes with that fleck of brown. "Was that man back there your father?" I ask, a little louder than I mean to. For the first time, his lip starts to tremble and his eyes fill with water. *Fuck.* "It's okay," I say as softly as I can manage, "It's okay, don't worry."

Suddenly the sound of sirens rises up and fills the air around us. I look around for Carter and can't find him – then I see him already above us on a fire escape, one arm reaching down to help us up. *"The kid,"* he yells, *"Get the kid."*

We climb the fire escape and follow Carter up onto the roof where he leads us across three buildings to the end of the block, then down another fire escape to the alley below.

"Where the hell are we going?" I ask, out of breath again.

"Someplace safe," Carter answers.

A while later we're standing on a long-deserted stretch of concrete and bare earth between the train tracks and the East River. I can hear traffic on the highway above making a faraway sound like the ocean. There are a few rusted tin sheds here, and a stack of abandoned freight cars. It's to one of those that Carter leads us.

"What's this?" I ask as he turns a key in one of the padlocks.

"Just some storage," he says, opening the second lock, "He'll be safe here for a while."

Carter rolls the big metal door to the left with a rumbling, squealing sound. A terrible animal smell washes out of the dark and chokes me. I peer into the blackness but can't see anything.

"Go on," Carter says gently, putting his hand on the boy's shoulder. The boy hesitates for a moment at the edge of that black opening, then steps inside and vanishes from sight. I could never have made myself go into that place by myself, but I follow him inside.

My eyes slowly start to adjust to the dark. I can make out the shape of the boy standing near me. Then I see other shapes start to materialize around us, some small, some taller. Some of them are moving, some aren't. When I can finally make out their faces, I recognize them. I've seen them before, on the walls of Carter's studio and at the gallery. They're here. They're all here in the dark, waiting.

I call out for Carter and see him standing in the square of daylight, arms stretched across the opening, his face black with the light behind it.

"Don't worry, Chris," he says. "They won't find him here. He'll be safe. You'll all be safe."

"Jesus, Carter…"

"It's okay, Chris," Carter says as he starts to roll the big door shut. "I just need you to stay here and keep an eye on them for me. They need someone like you." He closes the big door with a rumble and boom and the light goes out. I throw myself at the door and push hard, yelling his name. "Don't worry, Chris," I hear his voice on the other side, "You'll be alright." I hear the rattle of the chain and the locks clicking shut, then Carter's footsteps getting farther and farther away. Then nothing.

I don't know how long I've been here. It's hard to tell in the dark. For the first few days I beat on the door and shouted until my hands went numb and my throat was raw. On the third or fourth day when I heard voices outside, I pounded and yelled louder than ever but the voices kept moving until they were gone. Now I know – no one will ever hear me. No matter how close they get. No matter how hard I try.

At first I thought that Carter wanted me to take over for him after he was gone. I think of how good that would be – to be as strong as the people who love us believe we are. Now I know that Carter must have realized what Kelly figured out about me a long time ago.

The children have started to disappear. At first I tried to comfort them but they don't seem to hear me, so I've stopped trying. I can tell which one is going to go next because of how the others move away when it starts to happen. The others don't watch anymore, but I did, the first time. The last thing to go was the eyes. After that I never looked again.

Every day there are fewer and fewer of us here. That's how I know Carter must be dead. Because you don't disappear when you run away or when someone takes you. You disappear when people stop thinking about you. That was Carter's job, to remember the lost and the helpless. Now he's stopped thinking about us forever so it's only a matter of time.

There's a small hole in the wall where the metal has rusted and a thin beam of light comes through. I put my hand against it and see the light pass through my hand, right through the bone and muscle and skin. How much longer do I have? Will I feel it when it happens? Or will it happen before I know it? Maybe I'm already gone.

something you leave behind

They were in *the dark mile* now, that lonely stretch of road through West Virginia where the lights of service stations and truck stops fall behind, and a vast darkness that feels swollen and dense rises up around you like a giant wave. She could feel it now, gathering its forces right outside the window of their small, rust-worn car. It was like that bridge over the Delaware River, the one she and her sisters tried to hold their breath all the way across when they were children. Each time, she was never sure if she could make it to the other side. She felt that way now.

Nine hours, seven more to go…

The hunger, as usual, had snuck up on her like some kind of silent predator and was sinking its claws into her.

"I'm hungry."

"Well, there's nothing out here…" Gary hadn't spoken in over an hour and his voice sounded rough and dry, like someone waking from a deep sleep. "We should be in Morgantown soon."

They'd left New York City at eight that morning on their way to Maysville. It was supposed to be a sixteen-hour drive but somehow it never ended up that way. The green-lit numbers on the dashboard never quite matched up with the directions on the map or the feeling of time ticking away inside her bones.

She peered out the window. A light from a farmer's house appeared, far off the road, and was snuffed out like a ship lost at sea.

"Why do we always do this?" she asked.

"What?"

"Keep going back."

"What do you mean? I thought you wanted to."

"Yeah… but we can't keep doing this forever…"

They'd talked about it before and it always ended like this, in silence. A Christmas of their own. No more sixteen hours on the road. No parents, no relatives, just the two of them alone in that tiny twelfth floor apartment on East 31st Street. Somehow the thought of that had once again forced them through the Holland Tunnel, past the factory fires of New Jersey, back out onto this dark stretch of highway where they'd found themselves so many times before.

They'd moved to New York City six years ago because they wanted to be new people. But somehow that had never happened. The raw energy of the city that they'd thought would push them on to greater things was instead like the waves of a rough sea that battered them from all directions and left them with little more than the strength to keep from drowning. They were drowning now.

She stared out the passenger window again, looking for a light, but there was no break in the blackness. When she opened the glove compartment to look for some mints or gum to stave off the hunger, the light bulb inside cast their reflections on the windshield, both of them still wrapped in their heavy coats and gloves against the cold leaking in from the faulty heater. *We look like astronauts,* she thought, two fragile bodies protected from the crushing cold and dark outside.

It felt strange to see the two of them side by side like that, even for an instant. There had been no photographs of the two of them taken together for a long time, not since he'd walked out on her a year ago. She'd eventually agreed to take him in again, even let him sleep in the same bed with her. But to pose together for a photograph was still more than she could do.

When Gary had left, she'd fallen into a deep and terrifying darkness, then bounced back with a strength and determination she never knew she had. She'd gone to see therapists, she'd read books with titles like *How To Win Back Your Man,* and had followed the directions inside, sending him brief love notes, tiny gifts wrapped in ribbon and colorful yarn. While she was engaged in this single-minded pursuit, she'd felt virtuous and on fire with a kind of focused energy she hadn't felt for a long time. But when Gary had finally told her that he wanted to come back, it wasn't *victory* that she'd felt – it was a strange sensation that whoever she'd fought so hard to win back, it wasn't this pale, uncertain-looking man sitting silently across the table from her every morning, the features on his face unfamiliar, soft and indistinct like a photo of something still inside the womb, not fully formed.

A small sign came hurtling toward them out of the dark. It went by fast but she could read the rusted letters. *Westville*

"There!" she said, "there's a place. Next exit." She heard him flick the turn signal, the steady *click click click*, then they were plunging off the highway into the thick darkness. The car came out of its long downward spiral and they found themselves driving past old brick row-houses huddled close together on steep, narrow streets. The windows of shops and storefronts were all either dark or boarded-over. One more place that time had passed by, leaving only the bones.

As they moved deeper into the dark streets, Janet noticed something flapping overhead. She looked up and saw a red, white, and green banner emblazoned with the words, *WESTVILLE HOLIDAY FESTIVAL.* It was, as far as she could see, the only trace of color in the entire town. She strained to see the date on the banner but couldn't make it out; for a moment she had a vision of the day of the festival arriving and no one showing up, the pale winter sun shining down on that lonely banner hanging over these same streets, cold and vacant as they were now.

Suddenly there was a blaze of light at the end of the street like the full moon emerging from behind thick clouds. She caught a passing glimpse of towers, steeples, massive stone walls bathed in cold white light.

"Jesus, what's that?" she asked.

"I don't know…" She felt the car pull to the left and realized he was driving toward it.

"What are you doing?"

"I just want to see what that thing is, don't you?"

"Gary…I'm hungry."

"I know, I know…But it's right here…"

She took a deep breath and blew it out; the feeling of irritation and nausea settled. "Alright. But make it quick. Please."

As the building emerged all the way into view, Janet was amazed to see how large it was; easily three blocks long, a sprawling expanse of stone walls and spires, imposing as a medieval fortress. Rising at the center was a clock tower, the hour hand frozen on the two, the minute hand on the eight. At the peak of the clock tower, a tiny red light burned dimly against the black mountainside like a dying ember. *Probably to warn off low-flying airplanes,* she thought.

As they rolled slowly past the massive building, their headlights lit up one of those old historic placards, the metal letters bleeding rust. *WEST VIRGINIA ASYLUM FOR THE POOR INSANE.*

"Oh my God…" Gary breathed out.

Janet didn't say anything – she was pondering the words on the sign. *The poor insane.* Was that an expression of sympathy for the unfortunates who'd passed their lives behind these walls? Or was it a particular type of madness, the kind that seizes people when everything else has been taken from them? They sat in silence, staring up at the empty building, the cloud of exhaust rolling up around them turning red in the brake-lights.

"Says it opened in 1864…" Gary muttered, leaning out the window to make out the rusty letters, "…closed in 1982…"

Janet thought she could see lights blinking in the hundreds of windows. A reflection? Or streetlights shining through from the other side? For a moment, she imagined someone or something moving inside, unseen figures passing back and forth in front of the light.

A dizzy feeling overcame her; she knew it must be hunger and motion-sickness. She looked over at Gary and saw him resting his forehead on the steering wheel, eyes shut tight.

"What's the matter?" she asked.

"I don't know," he said, eyes still shut. "I think…I think maybe I need to get out of this car for a while." He lifted his head up from the steering wheel, his familiar features washed away by the dim dashboard light. Finally, he took his foot off the brake and they rolled away from the great empty building and back into the dark streets.

"I don't think anything's open," he said. "Maybe we should just go on to the next town…"

"*No…*" she said. The thought of being back on that black highway was even worse than wandering these deserted streets. "There's got to be a place here, somewhere…" She could feel his reluctance, but he said nothing and kept driving in silence. As usual, it was up to her to decide.

It was like when she'd taken him to see that loft in Bushwick, a thousand square feet for sale above a grocery. *Raw space*, the ad had said; mildewed drywall and exposed pipes that sweated and dripped like stalactites in a cave. She'd tried to convince him that they could make something out of it, the two of them. If they borrowed money from their families, asked friends to help with the labor, in a year, maybe two, they'd finally have a place. A real place of their own, where they could start over. All they had to do was decide. "But how can we be sure?" he'd asked, the innocent terror of a child on his face. If they took this place, how could they be sure it was the right one for them? She remembered the fear she'd felt the first time she'd moved when she was five years old, and what her mother had told her. *A house is just a shell, something you leave behind.*

Later, she and Gary agreed that maybe this loft wasn't the right place for them. Maybe they just hadn't found the right place yet. So she'd let it drop, afraid to say what she was thinking, that maybe there was no such thing. No right place for them.

They rolled up to a four-way stop, a forlorn tinsel star hanging over the intersection; no other cars in sight, no people out walking in the snowy streets.

"Which way should we go?" he asked, peering through the windshield.

"How should I know?" she said, but what she wanted to say was *Decide. For once in your goddamn life. Decide.*

She felt the car roll forward, heard the tires crunching in the unplowed snow. A lighted window appeared ahead on the right. She saw people inside sitting at tables, eating and talking. A diner.

When she got out of the car, the ground seemed to pitch and sway under her feet, and she had to grab on to the car door to keep from falling. Gary came around and took her by the arm. It startled her, the feel of his muscle and bone pressing against hers – how long had it been since she'd let him touch her? But the ground felt unstable under her feet, and the sidewalks were uncommonly steep, throwing off her sense of gravity, so she gave him her arm and let him guide her across the street.

He held the door of the diner open for her and she stepped inside. The heat was like a slap in the face, and the smokey smell of burnt grease and coffee made her stomach clench. The other customers, mostly old and tired-looking men and women, didn't look up and kept eating in silence.

When they were seated at a little table in the corner, the waitress appeared, leaning over them. A thin, bony woman of indeterminate age, she took their order and then stood there quietly. When Janet realized the woman was still there, studying them, she felt the skin at the back of her neck tighten.

"Where are you two from?" the waitress asked in a slow West Virginia drawl.

For a moment, Janet wasn't sure what to say. What did it mean to be *from* some place? "New York," she finally said, feeling again, for some reason, that this wasn't the truth.

"Wow. New York City…" Janet looked up politely and saw the missing teeth and hollow cheeks of poverty, the dark shadows around the eyes coated with make-up. The woman's eyes blazed with an intensity that unsettled her. "Is that where you were born?"

"No. Actually, we're both from Kentucky," Janet said, somehow feeling again like she'd been caught in a lie.

The waitress continued to smile down at her, a feverish light in her eyes. "Well…" the woman spoke slowly, "Westville's a nice little town. A good place to settle down. Y'all oughta think about moving here." Janet realized the woman had not blinked once during their entire conversation.

"Yeah," Janet smiled, not knowing what else to say. "Maybe we will…"

Janet watched the waitress disappear into the kitchen, then clapped one hand over her mouth to hide a spasm of nervous laughter. "Oh my God! Did you *see* her? *Westville's a niiiiice little town!*"

Gary leaned close, mocking the waitress's somnambulistic drawl, *"Y'all should move here and stay… forever! And ever…and ever…!"* Janet covered her mouth and stifled a giggle; it felt good. He still knew how to make her laugh. At least they had that.

"Jesus, stop!" Janet laughed. "You're gonna get us thrown out of here." Gary sat back, smiling while Janet caught her breath and dabbed at her eyes with a paper napkin. "You should have been a comedian."

Gary kept smiling, but she thought she saw something behind his eyes shift or change.

"You think so?"

"Sure. You're really funny when you want to be."

"That's weird…" he said, staring out the window. "That's what I wanted to be. When I was a kid, I had all these comedy albums. I used to listen to them and think about doing that when I grew up.

After that, I wanted to be a rock star. Then, a famous writer…" Gary's words trailed off into silence. She looked up and saw all the humor gone from his haggard face. "But I'm not any of those things now…am I."

Janet felt a familiar shadow fall over the two of them, the first stirrings of alarm. She didn't want to talk about this. She was tired and hungry; they both were, and she knew it wouldn't end well. She looked around for the waitress, who was nowhere to be seen, then glanced impatiently out the window at the dim traffic light that looked like it was frozen on red.

"All those things…" Gary kept talking, "I really thought they were going to happen. But they didn't. Why not? Why didn't they happen?" When Janet looked back at Gary, he was gazing at her with an expectant face and she realized with a pang of anxiety that he was waiting for her to answer.

"Well," she spoke slowly, trying to keep her voice calm. "Sometimes…life just turns out differently than you expect."

He laughed his unhappy laugh, a harsh expulsion of breath. "Jesus, what's *that* supposed to mean? That doesn't mean anything, Janet. That's a fucking useless thing to say."

She felt the tears rise into her eyes so fast it startled her, and she reached up to wipe them away.

"I'm sorry," he said quickly. "Jesus, honey, I'm so sorry. I don't know what the hell is wrong with me…" He rubbed his eyes, and she saw how loose the flesh was on his face, how it stretched and sagged around his jaw and eyes. She'd noticed it before, but tonight it seemed worse, like he'd aged overnight. For a moment she thought that if she passed him on the street, she wouldn't recognize him.

"You're just tired." She spoke as calmly as she could. "Tired and hungry."

"Yeah...where's our food? What's taking them so goddamn long?"

She glanced back at the kitchen door, the hunger gnawing at her guts. The air in the room felt hot and thick and the walls seemed to tilt and throb when she moved her head. An old man sitting with an old woman at a table across the room was staring at her, his mouth hanging open and full of half-chewed food, his eyes a vacant blue like marbles in a doll's head.

When she turned back, Gary had covered his face with his hands. At first she thought he was just resting. When he lowered his hands, she was alarmed to see tears on his face.

"What's wrong?" she whispered. He shook his head and didn't answer. "Gary, please...what is it?"

He sat perfectly still with his eyes shut tight. When he spoke again, his voice was very small and fragile-sounding.

"Can I...can I tell you something?"

"Yes, of course."

He paused for a long time, pressing his lips together tightly, like he was trying to stop the next words from slipping out. "I'm afraid to tell you."

Jesus, she thought, *it's happening again. There's another woman.* Her guts clenched at the thought. *So soon? How could he...*

"You remember what you said, when I left? *You're not the same man I married.*" He paused and swallowed. "Those things I did, when I left. I used to wonder…how could I do that? How could I do those things to you? I tried to think, but there's nothing there…like it was someone else who did those things."

She felt a wave of sickness, a cold wall of resistance rising up inside her. "Jesus, Gary…why are you saying all this now? Stop. Just stop, okay?"

"No," he said, his voice becoming more urgent. "I mean…what if it *was?* What if it *was* someone else?" Janet heard a loud voice cry out from the kitchen followed by the sharp sound of breaking glass, then silence. Across the room, the old man was still staring at her with his vacant blue eyes. "You know how they say all the cells in your body die and get replaced by new ones…every seven years?" He leaned closer. "What if it happens quicker than that?"

She could see him breathing faster now, his eyes darting back and forth between the objects on the table. She'd seen this before, the way the words were rolling out of him in a kind of flood she knew neither of them had the power to stop. "I mean…" he said, "you wake up in the morning, you look in the mirror…and you look different."

"Gary," she said firmly, "that happens to everyone."

"No. Not like that. I mean…sometimes I look at my hand, and it's like…it's not my hand anymore. It sort of looks the same. But it's not. I look at it and I can tell. It's not my hand."

She tried to swallow back the feeling of helpless alarm rising in her throat. "Gary…you don't really *believe* this, do you?"

He looked up into her eyes, and she knew that she had never seen such a naked look of disappointment and heartbreak. She could feel a door starting to close between them. If she didn't say something now to stop it from closing, he'd be lost to her.

"Listen, Gary…if something like that was real, if that was really happening, why wouldn't we all know it? Why wouldn't we see it when it happens?

"Because," he said in a low voice, "it happens at night. When we're asleep. You wake up and there's all that dust on the floor. All that dead skin…"

She glanced down at the back of her own hands on the table between them, at the stark blue veins and parchment-like cracks around the knuckles, and quickly pulled them into her lap to keep from looking at them. She knew that panic was contagious; she could feel it starting its slow crawl up her spine. "But *why?*" she asked, "Why does it happen?"

"Because it *has* to. Because we're not strong enough. Or brave enough, or good enough to do the things we have to do. That person, the person we were, has to die. To make way for a new one. But it doesn't work. Nature's not perfect. So *we're* not perfect. Each time, we think it's going to be better. And it is, for a little while. Then it's not. Then *that* person has to die. And it never stops. It just keeps happening."

"Gary, that's…that's just crazy. You've got to know that, right?"

He paused, sighed deeply then, without meeting her eyes, spoke in a flat voice.

"Take out your driver's license."

She stared at him, a numb feeling of resistance taking over her body, but she found her hands moving to her purse, finding her wallet and removing the plastic card inside.

"Look at it."

She looked down at the youthful face on the card, the strange haircut and round apple cheeks, smooth and unmarked as a doll's. Many times, she'd looked at the face on that card and thought, *Who is that girl?*

"It's not you, is it."

"Of course it is…"

"No. It's not. Look at it. Look at the eyes." She did as he asked and saw the pale blue eyes, unmarked by age and sorrow. "Those aren't your eyes, are they?"

"You mean…they're darker now. I know that. That's just something that happens over time."

"But it didn't. It didn't happen over time. It happened overnight. I was there." He was staring at her closely, like he was waiting for her to understand. "Remember the night your dad died? How you said you weren't strong enough to take it?"

She did remember – the feeling of her own life leaving her body, how she was sure that this was what dying must feel like.

"If you were going to go on living, you couldn't be that person anymore. When you went to sleep that night, that's when it happened. I saw it. I was awake and I saw it happen." He glanced down quickly at the face on the card. "I didn't want you to see it.

So...I buried it." He swallowed and looked away. "I buried the others too."

A strangled moan drew her attention. Across the room, the old man with vacant blue eyes reached up with trembling fingers and began clawing slowly at his skin. The old woman sitting across from him moaned loudly, reached over and grabbed his thin wrists and tried to pry his hands away from his face. All around them, people at other tables kept eating in silence like this was a struggle they'd witnessed a thousand times before.

"...And it never stops," Gary was still talking. "Not till we get it right. I think that's why we keep moving around, looking for the right place. We think if we can just find the right place, maybe it'll stop happening. But it never stops. It's happening to me again right now." He looked up and she saw his eyes grow wide with alarm and pity. "It's happening to you too, isn't it?"

She stood up too fast and the room spun around her for a moment, but she kept walking through the other tables all the way to the bathroom. Inside, she locked the door, made her way to the sink and twisted the rusty tap. Filling her hands with cold water, she splashed it on her face, then rose slowly and looked at her face in the mirror, haggard and strange in the harsh bathroom light. She thought of what to say when she went back for him. *We have to get out of here. We have to get out of here now.* That's what they'd do. Get back in the car, back on the road and drive as fast as they could to another place. *There's always another place,* she told herself. If they just kept going, they'd find it.

When she got back to their table, his chair was empty. Janet hurried to the door and stumbled out to the icy sidewalk. In every direction as far as she could see, the narrow streets were empty. She stood in the middle of the street and called his name, the awful sound of her voice bouncing from the dirty brick walls.

Looking down, she saw footprints ahead of her in the snow, the only ones other than hers. She saw where they led, up the steep hill toward that giant cluster of towers and steeples and high stone walls bathed in eerie white light. For a moment she almost turned and walked back to the car, back out onto that dark highway where her reflection in the windshield would be the only one. But the thought of being alone on that dark road made her keep climbing.

As she drew closer to the stone walls looming ahead, she could see something dark sprawled in the snow ahead of her. It looked like Gary's coat. As she got closer, she recognized his shirt. A few yards further on, his empty shoes. Then the final thing, the terrible and familiar thing that lay limp and hollow in the darkness by the side of the road. The wind touched it and it stirred like a discarded plastic bag. She didn't look at it, but kept her eyes on the stone stairs and the massive stone doorway until she was standing right in front of it.

The huge oak doors were wide open now, and a light at the far end of the hallway shone like a distant star. A shuffling sound came from the darkness inside and the light was blotted out for a moment. Then a voice she thought she recognized came out of the dark. "Janet…"

She stood on the stone stairs, unable to move forward or backward. The voice was Gary's, and it wasn't Gary's, but it called out to something inside of her, something she couldn't ignore or deny.

"Janet, please…come in here. You've got to see this. It's beautiful. So beautiful…"

A hand reached out of the doorway into the light. She caught a glimpse of something wet and raw and impossibly smooth, like a newly born thing. She turned her face away, then felt a deep piercing sorrow, almost like tenderness. Closing her eyes, she reached out and took the thing that was offering itself to her, felt its terrible soft wetness in her fingers, so fragile she might crush it. Then it was drawing her in, further and further into the dark where she could no longer see what she knew had already started, the fact of her own flesh leaving her. She wondered if this was where it would finally happen, if she could just hold her breath and keep going, all the way to that cold white light and the place they were meant to be.

the truth about what happens after death: a short film in one reel

"Are you kidding me?" CJ stared at Jeff with a look of pure astonishment. "This is real? This is a real thing?"

The object CJ was holding in his hand was a 16 millimeter film reel with a white adhesive label. *The Truth About What Happens After Death.* There was no canister, no box, no illustration or accompanying text, no way to tell who had made it or what its purpose was. It had come to them along with two or three dozen others in the daily repair bin, films that had broken and needed splicing. Films like *American Colonial History*, *The Importance of Photosynthesis*, *The Human Circulatory System*. And now this one.

"Probably some kind of religious film," CJ sneered.

"How do you know that?"

"Come on. Those first two words – the Truth."

"So if it just said, *What Happens After Death*, it might be…what – a biology film?"

CJ was already threading the film into the viewer. "Let's see what we've got here…"

He flicked the switch, the small screen started to glow and the frames fluttered past. The title appeared, no music, which Jeff thought was strange. Then a name. *One Truth Association, Milwaukee, Wisconsin.*

"Wow," Jeff said. "The truth is in Milwaukee? So that's where they've been hiding it."

A soft-looking man in a suit that looked too blue appeared onscreen, sitting behind a red wooden desk. His hair was cut in a Marine flattop, his black tortoiseshell glasses heavy and angular. Those were the only hard-edged things about him; the face behind the glasses looked soft as a baby's, as did the two hands folded on the desk in front of him. The man opened his mouth and a garbled rush of sound exploded from the small speaker. Jeff thought he could make out a few words. *We…many…tomorrow…* CJ tried to adjust the volume but it didn't help – it was like trying to listen to a broadcast from outer space.

"Jesus, no wonder," CJ said. "This thing's shot." The screen flickered once and went white as the broken end of the film came flapping around and around the take-up reel. "There's the break," Jeff said, unnecessarily. "Probably more in there…"

CJ was still staring at the screen, an odd scowl on his face. "Who the hell is showing this thing? What kind of class watches a film called *The Truth About What Happens After Death*?"

"Maybe a religion class, like you said…" Jeff went over and took the big blue binder of scheduled showings down from the shelf and flipped through the pages. "I don't know. I don't see it here anywhere…"

"How'd it get into the return bin, then? *Somebody's* showing it."

Another thought stirred in the corner of Jeff's mind. He glanced up at the clock on the wall. "Shit…I've gotta be at the Health and Sciences Building in fifteen minutes."

CJ helped Jeff load the projector into the van, but had to stay behind to catch up on rewinds and repairs. Jeff had started working at the university film center when he was a student, and they'd kept him on after he'd dropped out. He liked driving the big white van around on campus, riding high above all the students walking to class. He liked rolling the heavy projector cart down the hallways and into the classrooms; it felt like he was doing something important.

He'd been showing most of these films for almost two years now, and he knew them by heart. Like the one he was showing today. *Emergency Childbirth.* The whole film was one long close-up shot of a woman's vagina stretching and pulsing in ways that didn't seem human, while her groans and screams ricocheted off the classroom walls. The first time he'd shown that film in a hot, crowded classroom, he'd felt faint, though later he swore to CJ that it was because of the heat. Sometimes students would run from the classroom or tumble out of their desks onto the floor, their faces wiped blank and white. Occasionally, a student or teacher would take him aside first and say something like, *Tell me the truth. How bad is it?* He'd lie and tell them it wasn't so bad, that there were just a few bad parts. The blood didn't bother Jeff as much as the afterbirth, a dark gelatinous mass that burst unexpectedly toward the camera like something malignant and alive. He knew by now when that part was coming – he knew when all the bad parts were coming, and exactly when to close his eyes.

After work, Jeff stopped at the food mart to pick up a six pack of beer. Martha wasn't home yet, so he sat on the sofa and put his feet up on the old wooden crate they used as a coffee table, enjoying the solitude. He was halfway through the six pack when the phone rang. Before he picked it up, Jeff knew it was his mother. The usual pang of guilt pieced his chest, followed by the same insane resentment – that he'd been about to call her, had been thinking about doing it for weeks; he'd just been waiting for the right time, and would have done it if she hadn't ruined it by calling him first.

What the hell is wrong with you? Martha had said to him. *What kind of son doesn't call his dying mother?*

"Hey sweetheart," his mother's voice came through the receiver, every bit as firm and strong as ever. It didn't sound like the voice of a woman who'd dwindled to eighty-five pounds. It fooled him every time, so that for a moment he almost forgot that there was anything wrong.

"Did you get that article I sent you?"

"Yeah. Yeah, thanks," he answered automatically.

"I know it's not exactly your cup of tea," she spoke with a

confidential wink in her voice, as if they were discussing someone else. "Maybe you can have a look when you've got some time. I know how busy you are."

He glanced over at the stack of mail on his desk, the brown envelopes with his mother's graceful, neat handwriting, some opened, some not. Four years ago she'd started sending him articles she'd cut out of her favorite magazines – Christian Living, Faith for Today. The articles were illustrated with child-like drawings, others with stock photography of smiling families, the kind (he'd tried to joke with Martha) that you see in laxative ads.

"How're you doing, Mom?" He steeled himself for the answer, knowing it would never be anything less than positive and cheerful, and that it was her relentless, assaultive cheer that he was steeling himself against.

"Oh, I'm doing great, just great," she practically sang.

"What's the doctor telling you?"

"Oh, he thinks I'm crazy."

You are crazy. He'd told her that once, had actually said those words, not joking, but angrily. A sixty-four-year-old woman with stage four cancer refusing treatment and living alone. What else can you call that but crazy?

She had another explanation. "I prayed on it," she'd told him. "I asked the Lord what he wanted me to do."

So the Lord said he wants you to skip chemo, stay home, and read the Bible all day? Had he really said that to her? He'd been drinking, so it was hard to remember.

"Oh, don't worry about me, sweetheart," she'd chided him. "I've got plenty of things to keep me busy."

"Mom," he said, "Do you want me to come home? I mean…do you want someone there with you?"

"Why?" she said, and he felt his heart crack a little. "I'm just fine. Don't worry about me."

He hung up the phone, his heart hurting, went to the kitchen to get another beer, then took the bottle of Jim Beam down from the top of the fridge and poured some in a glass jar. He drank it down, felt the burn go down his throat and into his belly, then closed his eyes and waited for that slow feeling of relaxation and release, but the tightness in the back of his neck wouldn't go away.

I've got plenty of things to keep me busy, she'd said. Like what? What could his mother possibly have to do all day? He tried to remember. Prayer groups? Volunteering at the library? Was all her time really accounted for, like she claimed? Or did she look at all the empty days lined up in front of her and wonder how to fill them?

One thing he knew had not changed was his mother's weekly appointment at the beauty shop. Every Monday afternoon at two, he'd look at the clock and know exactly where she was: sitting in one of the high chairs at Ultra Beauty Hair Salon, looking at herself in the big mirror while one of the Ultra ladies trimmed and styled her beautiful long hair. At sixty-four, his mother's hair was still luxuriously full and auburn-colored, and she was proud of it. His mother wasn't a vain woman; it was just that she'd been given something special and was simply doing her part to take care of it.

Since his father had died when he was thirteen, his mother had never dated another man, so he'd never had to experience that particular type of jealousy. Then she'd found Jesus. Like any lovestruck fool, she'd drop his name into every conversation, then grin and glow like an idiot. He'd thought it was Jesus he was jealous of. Lately he'd begun to think it was something else, some other invisible thing she wrapped herself in that kept her apart from him, the thing whose name she couldn't say.

When he looked at the clock again, it was after midnight. Martha was still not home, so he turned on the TV, flipped through the channels and landed on one of his mother's favorite programs, a baby-faced televangelist who hosted a late-night Christian talk-show. He started to change the channel, but decided to watch, just to see what it was like. One of the guests was a successful gospel singer whose face had been burned off in an airplane crash. His head was a puckered mass of raw purplish flesh, like someone had tried to carve a human face in a rotting gourd and placed it on top of an expensive suit. The singer's voice was still strong and pure and, according to the televangelist, a testament to his faith and the healing power of the Lord. Jeff watched, unbelieving, as the singer walked through the audience singing in a beautiful rich baritone while the audience members blanched and recoiled from him.

At one point, the televangelist peered earnestly into the camera and said, *People, if you think those flames were hot in that airplane that day, just imagine what an eternity without Jesus would be like.*

Drunk and angry, he wanted to throw something at that soft, unctuous face. Before he knew it, the bottle was actually leaving his hand and flying toward the screen that exploded, showering the room with shards of broken glass and filling the air with the harsh stink of burnt electricity and spilled beer.

He'd tried to explain it to Martha. He was sorry about the TV, but if she'd only seen it, if she'd seen what he saw, she would understand. "You would have thrown something too," he said.

"Jeff. You need to go see your mother."

"Why?" he'd said, hearing instantly how horrible it sounded. He tried to soften it. "I talk to her."

"It's not the same thing. You need to go see her. What are you afraid of?"

He got up and went to the refrigerator for another beer, hesitated at the door, then went back and got another one for her. When he came back into the room, she was standing by the broken TV, gazing into the shattered screen. He took a step closer and held out the beer toward her. She didn't look up and kept gazing into the dark jagged hole in the glass.

"It's not working," she said.

"It's okay," he said, "We can get another one."

"No…" She looked back at him and her eyes were wet and grim. "I mean, it's not working."

The rest of what she'd said he didn't hear. He knew from the expression on her face that what she was saying was serious, was in fact terribly important. But it was like something had broken in his brain and no sound could get through. He could see her mouth moving, and could almost make out some of the words she was saying. *"We...you...no..."* He looked away before he could see any more.

Jeff went to work early the next morning. Whenever things were going wrong, work always helped. Rewinding the films, splicing the films, packing the films, labeling the films. Solving problems. Fixing things that were broken. It all helped him tune out the bad thoughts.

When Jeff arrived at work, CJ was out showing a film, so he had the back room to himself. He could tell CJ had been busy; the repair bin was empty now, except for one reel. He recognized it immediately — it was the one they'd been talking about the day before. Why hadn't CJ touched it yet? *The Truth About What Happens After Death.* Again he wondered — what kind of class watches a film like that?

Rolling the creaky desk chair up to the splicer, Jeff loaded the reel onto the viewer and threaded the film onto the take-up reel. Then he flicked the switch. The film began to rattle and the small screen glowed.

The image on the screen was different, no longer the pale faced man in the bright blue suit. It was what appeared to be some kind of illustrated chart, the generic outline of a man's naked body, faceless, sexless, suspended on a black background. The arms were extended like that drawing by Da Vinci that he'd seen a thousand times, palms open and turned toward the camera like it was ready to receive something. The distorted voice continued to blurt and crackle, *"We....who....no one...."*

He looked again at the human figure with its arms spread wide and suddenly saw it from a different angle, like he was looking down at it from above. He no longer saw a triumphant rising angel, but a human body laid out for a crucifixion or a dissection.

The screen tuned white again and the broken end of film started flapping around and around. He sat there and let it flap for a long time before he finally turned it off.

Gazing at the small, sharp blade of the splicer on the table in front of him, a memory came to him from when he was five or six, sitting in the doctor's office waiting for a nurse to bring the needle and give him a shot. He remembered the cold feeling of dread pinning him to the big wooden chair, until he realized that he could just leave, just stand up and walk out. When his mother's back was turned, he'd slipped away, down the dim, medicinal-smelling corridor toward the heavy glass doors. He was amazed to walk out into the bright sunlight and find the familiar world going on as usual. He could still see the cracks in the sidewalk passing under his feet, the bright flowers planted on either side, the large people moving around and above him. He felt invisible, indestructible.

It wasn't until later when another kind of realization came to him. At home, sitting alone in his room with his toys and pictures around him, he suddenly understood that he was going to grow up. The beautiful world around him now, the one he knew and loved – he was going to have to leave it. And there was nothing he could do to stop it from happening. No matter how fast or how far he ran, it was going to happen to him.

Terrified, he walked through the house, looking for his mother. He found her in the tiny alcove outside the kitchen that she used as her office. On the big white bulletin board behind her head she'd pinned some cardboard Easter decorations, happy toddlers clutching Easter baskets, a smiling yellow chick winking one eye, a cross covered with white lilies. It frightened him how something so bright and pretty could feel so useless. He remembered sobbing uncontrollably, *I don't want to grow up,* saying it over and over, gasping and choking on the words. He wanted her to tell him that it was alright, that he didn't have to, that she could save him from it.

Oh, honey, she'd said, *It's not that bad, really. There's just a few bad parts. That's all.*

Driving home from work, Jeff turned the car radio on, but instead of music, there was nothing but static. Some kind of problem with the station. He tried tuning in to the next station, but again there was nothing but static. He kept trying. All the stations were the same. The damn thing wasn't working, he decided, so he turned it off and drove the rest of the way home in silence.

When he finally pulled up to the apartment house and got out of his car, he noticed a strange odor in the air. It was the same stink of burnt electricity from when he'd broken the picture tube. This time, the odor was outside and seemed to be coming from everywhere, like the smell of rain right before a storm.

Sitting in the half-empty apartment, he noticed how many cracks there were in the walls and ceiling. One crack, in particular, ran across the ceiling directly above his head and seemed deeper and more dangerous than the rest. He wondered, had it just happened? Or had it always been there?

The phone rang. He felt deep in his bones, the way he always did, that it was his mother.

"Jeff?" It was his mother's voice, but different. The strength had leaked out of it somehow, the uncanny assurance. It wasn't there anymore.

"Mom, you okay?" He could hear her breathing. Her breathing sounded wet, and for a moment he wondered if she might be crying. He hadn't heard her cry in years. "Mom, what is it?"

"It…it's not working."

The chill he'd felt before raced up his spine so fast that it nearly stopped his heart. "What? What's not working?"

He heard a few more ragged-sounding breaths. When she spoke again, her voice sounded smaller, like a frightened child's.

"It's not working…"

When he arrived at his mother's house, he was shocked at how run-down everything looked. The grass had grown long and was patched brown by the sun. Mail had piled up in the mailbox and overflowed onto the ground, a few wrinkled bills and flyers caught in the scrubby bushes like debris left by a flood.

He knocked once and waited only a moment before he tried the door. It opened without trouble, and he stepped inside. The terrible odor of illness hit him full in the face. It was an odor he'd smelled before when he'd last visited a few months ago, but it was only a faint trace in the air then; now it was overwhelming.

"Mom?" he called out, stepping further into the house. In the kitchen he was surprised to find a pot of soup simmering on the stove, the gas flame beneath it a faint flicker of blue. He turned it off immediately. "Mom?" he called out again, louder this time.

He walked to her bedroom door, afraid of what he might find, but her simple twin bed was empty and neatly made without a wrinkle.

He went back to the kitchen and stood by the table. He felt dizzy and wanted to sit down, but was afraid that if he did, he might never be able to stand up again.

He closed his eyes and tried to think. For a moment it felt as if the house had disappeared around him, all the walls, floor, and ceiling above him had melted into thin air, but when he opened his eyes, it was all still there. He tried to imagine what he would say to the police. He'd tell them about finding the pot of soup simmering on the stove, how he'd made sure to turn off the gas flame – that was the right thing to do, wasn't it? Should he have left everything exactly as he'd found it? Was that important?

No signs of a struggle. The words came to him as if someone was speaking in his ear. He imagined policemen standing in his mother's kitchen, one of them writing things on a notepad. *No signs of a struggle.*

He stepped around the table and was about to pour a glass of water from the sink, when he saw the magazine on the floor. It was one of those religious magazines she was always cutting articles from and mailing to him. He recognized the font on sight. It was lying open to an article she'd started to cut out and then stopped. He looked closer and saw that the cuts were irregular and sliced right through the words on the page, dissecting sentences. He looked around for the scissors but couldn't find them anywhere.

He walked to the bathroom and looked inside. There was something in the sink. At first he thought it was an animal, one of his mother's cats, until he remembered they were all dead. He stepped closer, looked down into the sink and saw that it was full of his mother's hair, long auburn-colored tufts of it piled high in the white porcelain. The scissors were perched at the edge of the sink, carefully balanced like someone had just left them there.

The rest of the day was a blur of phone calls. None of her friends or prayer group members had seen her or heard from her. He left his number but called them back later to ask again, then again, until they started to sound annoyed or alarmed. By the time he finally called the police, his mind had already started to shut down, so that he could barely remember letting the officers into his mother's house, the answers he gave them, or what he did while they inspected all the rooms.

It wasn't until later, when he found himself sitting alone at his mother's kitchen table in the dark, that the panic hit him. What was he supposed to do? He'd done everything he could, hadn't he? What was he supposed to do now but wait? It occurred to him that maybe this was what his mother had felt. She'd been waiting too, for a long time. Longer than him. Maybe she was through with waiting.

In the morning he woke up not knowing where he was, until he recognized the curtains on his mother's kitchen window, the pattern of the wallpaper. He tried to turn his head and pain seized his neck. He'd slept all night in the hard kitchen chair. His mind was exhausted, his whole body painful and stiff.

He made another round of phone calls to her friends and the police. Nothing. It was his day off, he remembered gratefully. He was about to go home and sleep in his own bed when his phone buzzed. It was Maryanne from the film center.

"Jeff, you've got to get up to the Humanities Building. Room 107. There's some kind of problem with the projector."

"Who's up there? Isn't CJ supposed to be doing that?"

"CJ left."

"What? He left? Why?"

"I don't know. They said he just left. The teacher said he started showing the film, then something happened and he just left."

"You think he's okay?"

"I called his home number a few times. He picked up the third time. He didn't sound good."

"What did he say?"

"I don't know. He just said it wasn't working. That's all. Listen, I know it's your day off, but I really need you to do this. Please. You've got to get up to that classroom and fix whatever's wrong."

For a moment, he thought about saying no, telling her he was sick. He felt sick. But he couldn't face a day of waiting. Work would take his mind off of it, the way it always did. Whatever had happened, he would still have to get up every morning, put on his clothes, and go to work. Nothing that had happened would change that.

On his way to the Humanities building, he noticed that there seemed to be no students on campus. The sidewalks were empty, no one walking between classes, no one gathered in front of the dorms. He wondered for a moment if school was closed, if there was some kind of holiday he'd forgotten about.

When he parked the van and got out, the air felt charged with the heavy silence that comes right before a storm. The same smell of burnt electricity had followed him. He looked up and saw that there was something wrong with the sky. It was a false sky, like an image projected over something else he wasn't allowed to see. He turned his eyes away and didn't look up again.

When he reached room 107, the door was closed. He opened it and saw that the lights were still out, only a faint underwater-green glow from the heavy window shades that were all drawn shut. A group of twenty or more students were seated silently at desks scattered around the room. None of them were speaking or moving.

The teacher, a woman with a soft, pale face starting to show signs of age, was standing about six feet away from the projector, looking at it worriedly as if she was afraid to get too near it. When Jeff came in, her eyes flickered toward him and he realized with a shock that she'd been crying.

"What's the problem?" he whispered, not knowing why.

"It's not working," she said in a broken-sounding whisper.

"What…what's not working?"

She kept staring at him with those wet, wide eyes. *"It's not working…"*

Swallowing back the wave of cold he felt rising in his throat, he stepped closer to the projector to have a look. The white adhesive label on the film reel was facing outward, and he recognized it immediately. He didn't have to read it to know what it was.

Turning back to the teacher, he asked, "What class is this?" She didn't answer, and he asked again, "What class is this?" The teacher covered her mouth and shook her head quickly, looking at him over her hand with wide frightened eyes.

His heart beating faster, he turned back to the projector and saw that the film had been broken. He pulled out a length of film to re-spool it onto the take-up reel, but it was dark in the room and hard to see.

"Can you turn on the lights, please?" he asked. The woman said nothing and only nervously shook her head again. His eyes were getting used to the dark now. He looked around the room at the students sitting silently at their desks. He'd thought they were all boys when he'd first come in, now he could see that some of them were girls and that their hair had been cut off – hacked off, he thought, very close to their skulls. Their faces had the same terrified look that the teacher's had.

When he got the film threaded again, he hit the play button and the projector rattled to life, the bright light blazing onto the screen. One by one, he saw the students fold their arms on the desks in front of them and lower their faces. Sound erupted from the speaker, a terrible metallic voice that didn't sound human. He could see the teacher standing in the far corner of the room, her face pressed against the wall like a frightened child. *It's not so bad,* he wanted to tell her. *Just a few bad parts. Just a few bad parts. That's all. Then it's over.*

The harsh metallic voice blaring from the projector was louder than ever now. He closed his eyes and saw it all. The horrible blackness rising inside the broken picture tube. The sun and the clouds projected above his head, flickering and stuttering. His mother's long beautiful hair falling in pieces from the sky. For a moment he wanted to run from the room, as fast and as far as he could.

The voice from the projector howled and raged. He opened his eyes. He turned and looked.

the sea in darkness calls

John first noticed the green window when he was praying. He was not a particularly religious person, but had been driven to his knees by a series of actions and consequences over which he was realizing he had little or no control.

He was on his knees in the spare room of his brother's house where he'd come to "get himself together" in the aftermath of a long and painful divorce. It was the latest in a series of such visits, the first when he and his wife had separated, the second when he was trying to stop drinking, and the third when his ex-wife Kathy had left the state without warning, taking their two children with her.

"I don't see what the big deal is," Kathy had said when he'd finally reached her on the phone. "Billy's going to college next year and Kaitlin's going right after him." Behind her words, the hateful unspoken message. *Your time with them is up. And you missed it.*

At first he'd thought of jumping onto a bus for the four-hour drive to Allentown, where Kathy had taken the kids to her sister's house. He pictured the scene in his mind; him standing alone on the front porch in the rain, pounding on the door, Kathy, Billy, and

Kaitlin huddling in the kitchen or the hall closet, Kathy scowling a warning and raising one finger to her lips. *Shhhh. Be quiet. He'll go away.*

After he'd calmed down a little, he told himself that things were not as bad as he imagined. Kathy was not a kidnapper. She probably just needed some time to think, some time away. There was no need for him to go running after her like some kind of desperate character in a bad movie.

So he'd come to his brother's house by the sea to clear his head and plan his next steps, but after almost three weeks he still had no idea what they might be. He'd already spent what little money he had on the divorce and had nothing left for a lawyer, if it was going to come to that. He hoped it wouldn't.

This morning he'd woken up in the spare room of Danny's house where he'd slept so many times before. The same chocolate-brown futon that smelled of mildew, the same ash-grey cinderblock walls. It was where he and Kathy had stayed with the kids when they'd come for weekends at the beach during happier days. A poster from a circus Danny had treated them to when the kids were younger was still on the wall, its corners curling and mildewed from the damp sea air.

It was the poster that had driven him to his knees this morning. An old-fashioned print of a pretty girl riding atop an elephant being led by a clown, once all bright reds and yellows, washed-out now by years of harsh sunlight. The girl was smiling, even the elephant looked pleased. He thought about how someone had made this image and put it out into the world for a reason; it was an advertisement for happiness.

That's all I wanted, he said to himself, *I just wanted everyone to be happy.* A surge of grief washed through his chest and suddenly he was sobbing. "I just wanted everyone to be happy." He said it out loud, and the words brought on a second wave of wrenching grief that felt like it would tear him apart.

He found himself on his knees, both hands covering his wet face. "*Please…*" His voice sounded loud and strange inside his hands. He said it twice more before it occurred to him that he was praying.

He took his hands away from his face and looked out the window at the row of clapboard beach houses that hid the ocean from view. A flash of bright green drew his attention. It was coming from inside the house directly across from Danny's. At first he thought it was a TV screen. Then he realized it was another window, and that he was seeing straight through the house to the ocean on the other side.

The small, square patch of green looked bright and warm. As he looked at it, he felt some of the heaviness start to lift from his chest. After a few minutes he almost felt peaceful. He stayed there on his knees, staring at the green window inside the house across the road, until the smell of coffee brought him to his feet and into the kitchen.

Danny was standing at the counter, sawing away at a bagel with a long bread knife. He turned and flashed that same big, optimistic grin he'd greeted John with every morning. "Hey, bro. Coffee's ready."

John followed Danny out onto the small deck where they sat as they had every morning, sipping their coffee and watching the gulls wheel over the rooftops of the houses across the road. *My beach view,* Danny liked to call it.

The first time John had come here with the kids ten years ago, Kaitlin had been excited but Billy was just old enough to show a little disillusionment. "Where's the beach?" he'd said, staring out from Danny's deck with a glum expression.

Unfazed, Danny had leaned down to Billy and said, "Listen. Hear that?" John had listened too. The sound of the waves was audible like the sound of blood in your own body if you stay quiet long enough. "If you close your eyes," Danny said, "you can pretend you're right on the beach."

That's right, John thought. *If you close your eyes, you can pretend anything.*

Kaitlin had wrinkled her nose and asked, "What's that *smell?*"

"That's the ocean, honey," John told her, taking a deep breath. "Isn't it great?"

"I think it stinks," Kaitlin said. "It smells like dead stuff."

"That's right, sweetheart," Danny said, swooping in with a first round of beers for the grown-ups. "It *is* dead stuff. Lots and lots of dead stuff. Seaweed, plankton, fish…"

"Sharks?" Kaitlin said, her eyes getting wider, "Dead sharks too?"

"Sure. Dead sharks too."

"What about whales?"

"Absolutely. Dead whales. Lots and lots of dead whales."

"What about people?" Billy spoke up.

"Billy!" Kathy hushed him. Danny looked at Billy for a moment, a serious expression on his face, then spoke in his best pirate voice.

"Sure. Dead people too. All the sailors who ever drowned. All the little children who ever got dragged out to sea by big, hungry waves."

The kids had stared at him. Kathy did too, her look of disbelief changing to anger.

Danny drank down the last of his beer, threw his arms wide and shouted, "Okay! Who wants to go swimming?"

Later that night, John had begged Kathy to keep her voice down. *I don't care if he's your brother. What kind of asshole says that to a little kid?* He'd defended Danny, of course, which had only made her angrier and louder.

John could smell the thick ocean breeze now, sitting on the tiny deck with Danny. It was the same deck where they'd all had bagel breakfasts and crab-claw dinners together in summers past. It looked so small now, barely big enough for Danny and himself. It was hard to remember how they'd all once been able to fit on it.

"Remember that time you told the kids about all the *dead* things in the ocean?" John said. "Man, I thought Kathy was gonna kill you."

"Yeah…she killed *you* instead."

John felt the blood rush to his face. Danny had heard. Of course he had. The house was small and the walls were thin. Which made John wonder – had Danny had heard him crying this morning?

"So," Danny said, "You thought about your next move yet?"

"I don't know. I was thinking about joining the foreign legion, but I think they closed down."

"Very funny." Danny took a long sip of coffee and squinted at the gulls diving overhead. "I mean, have you thought about what you're gonna do if Kathy doesn't…you know…"

"No. What?"

"Hell, John, I mean…how long has she been gone now? A month?"

"No. Not a month. Twenty two days. She just needs some time. You know how she gets."

"Yeah, " Danny sighed. "I know. It's just…"

"What?" John felt anger start to rise, slow and steady.

"It's just…you're my brother. I don't want to see you get hurt, that's all."

"I know," John sighed, "I'm just doing the best I can." This was something he'd said a lot to Kathy. *I'm doing the best I can.* Kathy didn't believe it anymore. He hoped Danny still did.

"Well," Danny said, glancing down into his coffee mug, "you know you've got a place here. As long as you need it."

"I know," John said; then, doing his very best Bogie voice, "Danny boy, you're a schweetheart."

"No. *You're* a schweetheart." They'd been doing this since college-days, trading Bogie voices back and forth until one of them laughed. This time John laughed first.

When Danny left for work, John went for his morning walk on the beach like he'd been doing every day. As he passed the row of houses, he glanced at the one right across the road and remembered the green window. He thought about getting closer and trying to look inside, but didn't want to frighten anyone, so he kept moving.

He passed through the short alley between houses, climbed the sandy hill, and the ocean opened up in front of him. That moment was always a little startling, even frightening, like the first time his father had shown it to him when he was a child. An echo of that first feeling still remained and came to him now, unbidden.

The boardwalk was crowded, even at this early hour. Ancient-looking men and women wrapped in heavy clothes moved slowly on canes or walkers, their bored-looking care-workers trailing along beside or behind them. Other men and women, younger but well on their way to old age, jogged fiercely into the wind, their faces lifted defiantly to the sun that had baked their skin an alarming shade of mahogany brown.

When the boardwalk got too crowded, John stepped down onto the beach and headed toward the water, where the sand was firmer underfoot and easier to walk on. He turned left and started walking with the ocean at his right side, the sand stretching out in front of him as far as he could see.

As he walked along the edge of the sea, John heard a voice. It was an echo of his own voice from a few days ago, strained and agitated.

Let me talk to the kids.

"They're asleep," Kathy had said after a long pause. It was the pause that told him she was lying.

"It's eight o'clock," he'd said, speaking slowly to keep his voice under control. "Put them on the phone."

Another pause. "They're tired, John. They've had a hard day. They don't need to be upset."

"Upset?" He heard his voice rising on the surge of rage in his throat. "What do you mean *upset?* Put them on the god damn phone!"

"That's what I mean," she'd said. "Call me when you're feeling better, okay?" Then she hung up.

Don't fucking hang up on me! Don't you ever fucking hang up on me like that!

He could feel the words burning in his throat, pushing for a chance to get out. He let them out now under his breath, relishing the feeling. Then he looked up and saw a young couple walking toward him, looks of suspicion and alarm on their faces. The man took the woman's arm and led her away from the water, cutting a wide berth around him.

His face burning, he turned his gaze away and saw something on the horizon. An oil tanker, long as a football field but miles away; it looked as small as a child's toy on the vast grey mirror of the ocean. The light was playing tricks with his eyes so the miniature ship looked grainy and ghostly, almost like he could see through it.

He saw another ship in his memory, smaller and closer. It had been there one morning years ago when he'd brought Kaitlin and Billy down to the beach. A small blue and white boat running parallel to the shore just beyond the breakers. He could feel Kaitlin's small hand in his.

What's that boat doing there, Daddy?

He could see men moving around on deck, others standing at the rail staring down into the water. At first he'd thought it was a fishing boat. Then he saw the orange vests and the white letters NYPD painted on the side and remembered what he'd seen the night before…

Kathy and the kids had gone to bed, worn out after the long drive. He'd been sitting up late by himself, drinking and trying to unwind, when the news came on. He'd watched through a haze as the images rolled by on the screen: the same blue and white boat running parallel to the shore, yellow police tape fluttering in the wind, the sunburned police chief squinting into the sun and saying words like *rip tide.*

Two children had drowned, an eleven year-old girl and her friend. He was glad that Kathy had gone to bed and hadn't seen the news. The police had closed the beach the day before but had decided to open it the next day. The sunburned police chief encouraged parents and their children to *exercise caution*. That would not be good enough for Kathy. She would insist on keeping the kids out of the water, maybe for the whole trip. His anger rose at the thought of it. Leave it to her to ruin everyone's good time.

So the next morning he got up early, woke the kids and got them into their swimsuits and out the door before Kathy could wake up and stop them. He pictured her face, the angry things she'd say. He could always plead ignorance. At least they'd get in one good swim.

The yellow police tape was gone, so was the news van and the reporters with their cameras and microphones. But he hadn't expected the boat to still be there. It unnerved him to see it so close to the shore. Close enough, he told Danny later, to wade through the breakers and touch it.

"What's that boat doing there, Daddy?" Kaitlin wanted to know.

"Oh, nothing," he said, "They're probably just looking for something."

"What are they looking for?"

"Dead bodies." John turned to look at Billy. He was facing the ocean, squinting out into the harsh glare on the surface of the water. "That's a police boat," Billy said. "They're looking for someone who drowned."

A quick feeling of panic rose in John's chest. *He's not supposed to know things like that,* he thought. *He's only ten.*

"I don't know," John said, trying to sound casual. "Maybe they're looking for something else…"

"No," Billy said. "They're looking for bodies."

"Really?" Kaitlin sounded more fascinated than frightened. "Can we go in now, Daddy?"

He looked at the grayish-green water as it rushed at their feet and retreated, hissing, then out further where it got deeper. *There are bodies out there. Dead bodies.* Billy was right. He glanced out at the police boat, at the men climbing over its deck, and felt a flash of anger. Why did they have to be here today? Why did they have to ruin this for him?

"Daddy, please…" He felt Kaitlin tugging on his hand, breaking into his thoughts. He looked down into her little round face, hopeful and impatient. "Daddy, aren't we going in? You *said.*"

John looked to the right along the shore and saw a man standing alone far up the beach, staring out to sea. The man wore a bright blue windbreaker that ballooned and billowed in the wind and made him look like some kind of strange bird ready to take flight. Following the man's gaze, John realized he was staring at the police boat. The man was too far away for John to see his face clearly, but for a moment it looked like he might be crying. *Oh, God,* John thought. *God, no…*

Kaitlin tugged his hand again and he felt a flash of anger. "Daddy, you said we could go in. You *said.*"

He looked down the beach in the other direction and saw other parents venturing into the water with small children, laughing and splashing. He glanced at his watch. Kathy would be awake soon. Then she'd come looking for them.

"Sure, sweetheart. Sure we are."

Taking her hand, he led her down to where the cold gray water rushed at them and retreated. The first wave that broke across their legs was freezing cold, and he felt his muscles cramp instantly. Kaitlin didn't seem to mind and squealed in delight as another wave rose to meet them.

John looked around for Billy and saw him still standing behind them on the shore, squinting out at the police boat that was almost directly in front of them now. *"Come on,"* John yelled at him, *"Cowabunga, dude!"* Billy flinched, embarrassed by his Dad's use of surfer lingo, then walked slowly toward the water and waded in.

John glanced out past the breakers. A diver had surfaced near the boat and was talking and gesturing to the men on board. *Jesus,* John thought, *what if they find something?* He glanced down the beach toward the man in the blue windbreaker and saw his mouth contorted in a silent howl.

Kaitlin's squealing tore at his nerves and he snapped at her. "Stop! Don't do that!" She quieted down, but when another wave came at them and lifted her up she started squealing again, louder than before.

John heard another voice raised in anger behind him. Kathy's voice. He turned and saw her walking swiftly toward them across the sand, her face a mask of anger. Gripping Kaitlin's hand tighter, he said, "Come on, sweetheart," and drew her deeper into the water, away from the shore. He felt the waves sucking the sand from under his feet, making him lose his balance and stumble. He didn't want to fall. Not today, not here.

Then he felt it. Something long and soft drifting and grazing against his skin underwater, twisting around his leg. Long hair.

Panic and horror rose in his throat, choking him. He felt the thing below the water wrap itself around his legs, and he kicked wildly to get it off. He didn't realize he'd cried out until he heard Kaitlin calling, "Daddy! Daddy! what's wrong?" A strand of dark green rose swirling to the surface and he saw what it was. Seaweed.

He saw Kaitlin staring up at him, fear in her eyes. Kathy was staring at him too, frozen at the water's edge, the anger in her face giving way to alarm. *"What the hell is wrong with you?"* she called out.

"Nothing," he said. "It's nothing." With shaking hands, he tore the slimy strands from his legs and threw them away as far as he could, while out beyond the breakers, he saw the diver in the water wave to the men on board, then slip beneath the surface again.

Kathy had ended up keeping the kids out of the water for only one day. She'd relented the next morning but kept watch from her beach chair, yelling at him whenever she thought he'd taken the kids out too far. He obeyed but tried to ignore her contemptuous, disapproving gaze at his back.

Kaitlin, who'd been so fearless at first, running to meet every wave, now seemed to hold back a little, and clung to him fearfully whenever a wave came rolling toward them. On their third morning, she'd stood stiffly at the water's edge.

"What's wrong, honey?" he'd asked.

"I don't want to go in." Her voice was quiet but he could hear the trace of fear in it, and immediately felt a flash of anger toward Kathy.

"Why not?"

"I just don't."

"Sweetheart," he said, kneeling in the sand beside her. "Don't be afraid. There's nothing to be afraid of." She didn't look at him but kept staring out at the vast gray-green ocean before them. "Sweetheart," he tried again, "you know Daddy will never let anything bad happen to you, don't you?"

He saw a scowl pass over her small face, though whether it was at the waves or at what he'd just said, he wasn't sure.

"Okay…" she finally said. Then, holding his hand, she let him lead her into the water.

They'd been happy for a while, hadn't they? For a few precious summer days, when she had trusted him. Even Billy had dropped his suspicious reluctance and played soccer with him on the sand. They'd both played with him and trusted him, and while those days lasted he had been happy too, really happy for a while.

Standing on the same beach now, he watched other parents playing with their children. He saw one man leading a little girl by the hand into the waves. The little girl had long brown hair and squealed and clung to her father every time a wave rushed at them. Sadness pierced his chest, and he turned and walked back toward the boardwalk, little broken shells buried in the sand cutting into his bare feet.

By the time he made it back to Danny's house it was almost dark. When he saw that Danny's car wasn't back yet, he almost kept walking. He didn't like being alone in the house with Vicky. But he hated feeling like a coward even more.

Vicky was standing at the stove, stirring something in a pan, a half-empty glass of white wine on the counter next to her.

"*So*, John," she said without turning to look at him. "How *are* you? How was your day?" There was something in her tone that set his nerves on edge, a sing-song friendliness like she was speaking to a child.

He wanted to keep walking past her, back to his room where he could be alone. *Vicky thinks you're rude to her sometimes,* Danny had said one morning. *She says you act like you don't like her.* So he positioned himself stiffly against the counter, acutely aware of his own body, unsure of what to do with his hands.

"Fine, Vicky," he said. "How was yours?"

"Oh, you know," she sighed, moving toward the refrigerator and opening it. "Same old shit." Bringing out a bottle of Chardonnay, she filled her glass and then held the bottle out toward him. He shook his head and forced a polite smile. "*Oh,* that's right," she said. "Sorry…"

No you're not, he thought.

"Well," she said, turning back toward the pan and stirring it. "Must have been beautiful out there today. Sure wish I could spend all day hanging out on the beach. I guess that's what vacations are for, right?"

Is that what you think this is? A vacation? He started to walk back to his room when she spoke again.

"So, heard anything from Kathy?"

"She's fine."

"Really? Good. What about the kids?"

"They're fine."

"Well, that doesn't surprise me. Kathy's a good mother."

"Excuse me," he muttered, and walked out of the kitchen and back to his room, closing the door behind him.

The room had a claustrophobic, animal smell. *His* smell. Walking over to the wall, he yanked the window open and sat heavily on the futon, letting the soft sea air wash over his skin while the blood pounded like a drumbeat in his ears.

Outside the light was failing, draining all the color from the sky and the houses. In a few more minutes it would be dark. The lights were already coming on in the houses across the road. He could see people moving back and forth inside the windows; a woman with curly gray hair and bare brown arms working at a kitchen sink, and in the next house, a group of young people laughing with beer bottles in their hands.

He turned his gaze to the house right across the road. It was dark except for a flicker of greenish light in the downstairs window. Probably a TV or computer screen. But the longer he looked the more he was certain – it was the same window he'd been looking at this morning, and he was seeing straight through the house to the ocean on the other side. How could it be so bright? He decided it must be some kind of trick of the light, an optical phenomenon. The reflective quality of the water or the sand crystals trapping the last of the sunlight.

A loud knock on his door startled him and Danny's voice boomed from the other side. *"Chow time, bro!"*

Vicky had lit citronella candles to keep the mosquitos away. Their cloying, medicinal scent clung to John's nose, and he pushed the candle in front of him to the other side of the table.

"So," Vicky said, spooning salad onto her plate, "you like having your blood sucked, John?"

"Actually, no, Vicky. I don't like having my blood sucked."

"Those are there to keep the mosquitoes away," she said, measuring each syllable slowly.

"Really? I thought you were just trying to set the mood."

While Danny talked on about things that had happened at work, John looked over his brother's shoulder at the house across the road, trying to see into the window. But the angle was wrong, and all he could see was darkness. Danny was still talking when John finally spoke up.

"Who owns that house? The one right across the road?"

Danny looked at him, an expression on his face that John couldn't read, then looked down and kept eating. "Nobody."

"You mean it's empty?"

"It is *now*," Vicky chuckled, taking another sip of wine. John thought he saw Danny throw her a warning glance, but it was growing darker so he couldn't be sure.

"Did you know you can see the ocean right through that house?" John said. "It's pretty cool, actually. I was looking at it all morning." He stopped when he realized how this sounded. *I was looking at it all morning…*

When Vicky had gone inside, Danny leaned forward and spoke in a low voice. "John, I was thinking…how would you like to borrow the car and go to Allentown? You know, see Kathy face-to-face? Figure things out?"

John felt a twinge of panic in his chest. "I don't know, Danny. I think it's probably better to do that on the phone…"

"No offense, bro, but I don't think it's the kind of thing you can do on the phone."

John saw a flash of the same picture he'd imagined before, of himself standing alone on the front porch of Kathy's sister's house, pounding on the door and calling out to be let in. The feeling of panic in his chest started to grow.

"You could see Billy and Kathy," Danny said. "You'd like to see them, right?"

"Sure I want to see them."

"Okay, then," Danny smiled, "It's settled. You take the car Saturday morning, have it back Sunday night. No worries."

Back in his room John turned out all the lights and lay down on the futon. He could hear Danny and Vicky's voices through the walls. Their voices had an anxious, angry edge. He could fill-in the words himself. *You're letting him take the car? How do you know he'll bring it back in one piece? What makes you think he'll bring it back at all?*

He swallowed back the anger in his throat. He was imagining things again. What made him think they were talking about him? But what if they were? He'd made mistakes, he knew, and there were consequences for those. That's what they all said at the meetings. You have to pay for your mistakes. He'd listened and wanted to say *yes. But when does it end?*

A small flapping sound drew his attention – the circus poster on the wall, moving in the current of air pouring in through the window. He saw how the corners were curled and stained by the destructive elements of sunlight, water, and air. The pretty picture was rotting away before his eyes.

The same thing was going to happen to him. It was happening already.

A terror he'd only felt vague hints of before suddenly rose up fully formed inside of him. It was going to happen. It was going to happen and there was nothing he could do to stop it.

The room tilted and he was clinging to the side of a bottomless chasm, trying to keep from sliding down. It wasn't until he felt the ache in his hands that he realized he was digging his fingers into the mattress.

He walked over to the window, gripped the frame with both hands and drew deep breaths of the sea air into his lungs. When he could breathe again, he opened his eyes.

There in the house across the road, the green window was blazing bright. He stood staring, unable to believe what he was seeing. But there it was. Surrounded by the darkness of night, one small square of sunlight.

He rubbed his eyes and looked again. It was still there. He could see the sun's rays glistening on the waves as they swelled and rolled. And what should have felt frightening, a rip in the fabric of the world, instead felt peaceful, almost comforting.

As he stood gazing, he saw another motion different from the rhythm of the waves. Human figures passing quickly across the frame and then disappearing. He stood still, afraid to breathe, waiting for them to reappear. When they did and he saw how small they were, he knew they were children.

They vanished from the frame and his body was flooded with a terrible yearning. The mystery of the sunlit beach in the window no longer felt important. All that mattered was those small bodies that flickered back and forth across that bright green space like moths flying in and out of a light. He wanted them.

When the sunlight woke him in the morning, he didn't remember laying down on the bed or how long he'd stood at the window waiting and watching. He got up, stiffly, walked over to the window and looked across the road at the empty house. He could still see the beach through the window on the other side, but it no longer looked strange or miraculous. Daylight flooded everything with ordinariness.

He wanted to tell Danny but he didn't dare to. What would he think? That he was drinking again? Or that something had gone wrong with his mind?

He thought again about that bright square of daylight shining in the middle of the night and felt no fear, no confusion. It was other things that confused and frightened him. People's faces on the beach and on the street. The thought of coming face to face with Kathy again after all these weeks. The sound of her voice on the phone.

Danny had urged him to call Kathy to let her know he was coming to see her and the kids. He took a deep breath and punched-in her number on his cell phone. She sounded confused and alarmed when he told her.

"You're doing *what?*"

"I told you. I'm coming there. I'll be there tomorrow."

"I don't think that's a good idea, John."

"Why not?"

"It's just not, okay?"

"No," he said, trying to keep the anger out of his voice, "It's *not* okay. I haven't seen the kids in a month, Kathy, did you know that? A month. I need to see them."

"It's just not a good idea, John." She paused. "It's not going to be like you think."

"What do you mean?" he said, the anger starting to rise in his voice. "I need to see them."

There was a longer pause and for a moment he thought the line had gone dead. Finally, she spoke again.

"Alright. Do what you have to do." Then she hung up.

Danny made dinner the night before John left. Steamed clams and crab claws, grilled corn on the cob, bottles of non-alcoholic beer buried in buckets of ice. It made John nervous. It was the kind of meal you make for someone who's not coming back.

"What's the occasion?" he asked, watching Danny moving back and forth from the grill to the table and back again.

"No occasion," Danny smiled. "Do I need an occasion to cook for my family?"

John glanced at Vicky sitting on the far side of the deck in a lounge chair, her face lifted toward the sun, her eyes hidden by sunglasses. *My family.* Was this the picture Danny had in mind when he said *my family*?

Later, after the sun had set and the table was littered with broken crab claw shells and empty bottles, Danny raised his drink and said, "Well, *bon voyage*, bro."

"You mean *bon chance*, don't you?"

"Sure," Danny shrugged. "*Bon chance…bueno suerte…*break a leg…whatever."

John was looking over Danny's shoulder again at the house across the road. The sky wasn't dark yet but it would be soon.

"What are you looking at, John?" Vicky's voice was slurred. John hated the sound of it. Danny had gone inside to take a leak. John glanced toward the door, wishing he'd come back.

"How come you're so interested in that house, John? Any naked girls move in over there or something?"

"No. No naked girls."

"Well," Vicky smiled, bringing her wine glass to her lips, "There *used* to be. Shit, that guy knew how to party. Till his money ran out. All that booze and blow. Loud music every night. Funny thing is, he never used to be that way. Till he lost his girls…"

"His girls…?" Suddenly, John could see it. The police boat just offshore, the man in the blue windbreaker standing alone far up the beach, his face a distant, ruined blur.

"Yeah, you remember," Vicky continued. "First his girls drowned, then his wife left him. I used to watch him wandering around over there in that big empty house…"

"*Vicky…*" John looked up and saw Danny standing in the doorway glaring at her.

Vicky raised her hand to her mouth like she was trying to hush herself, then her shoulders started to shake. "Jesus," she said, and John realized she was laughing. "All that great big ocean right there in his front yard. And the asshole goes and hangs himself…"

"Vicky – goddamn it…" Even in the dark, John could see Danny's mouth trembling. Standing quickly, he hurried past his brother and down the hall to his room.

John locked the door and sat on the floor right in front of the window, looking across the alley for the bright green window. But it wasn't there. Only darkness.

He closed his eyes and concentrated on the sound of the waves, thinking of the green window shining in the darkness. *Please*, he thought, like he had the first time. *Please.* And when he opened his eyes, there it was. The little figures he'd seen passing back and forth were there too. This time they were not running but were sitting in plain sight playing in the sand, their backs turned. But he knew them. He knew them. He watched and his heart filled with a longing that lifted him up until it felt like he was there with them in that bright warm place.

The drive to Allentown was longer than he remembered, and he stopped twice to check the map and make sure he hadn't gone too far. The sky was a molten iron gray rimmed with red, like he was driving into a tornado or a forest fire. When he pulled up in front of Vicky's sister's house and opened the car door, he felt the first drops of rain hit the back of his hand. By the time he reached the front door his shirt was soaked.

He rang the doorbell twice before he started banging on the door.

He'd promised himself that he wouldn't do this, that he would not pound on the door or call out her name, but that promise felt useless now, as useless as the sound of his own voice coming back to him in the rain.

He tried the doorknob; to his surprise, it turned in his hand and the door swung open. Stepping across the threshold, he listened for a moment. Hearing nothing, he began to move through the house, his heart pounding harder in his chest. "Billy? Kaitlin? Sweetheart, it's Daddy…"

He thought of how long it had been since he'd heard her call him that. Kaitlin had stopped calling him *Daddy* when she'd turned thirteen, about the same time he'd left. That was going to change, he decided. That was all going to change, starting now.

He climbed the stairs to the guest room where they usually slept and it was empty, no sign of their clothes or luggage. He opened the closet door and froze when he saw what was scrawled in black marker on the wall.

FUCKYOUASSHOLEIHOPEYOUDIE

He stared at the black letters, feeling everything drain out of him. It wasn't Kathy's handwriting he was looking at. It was Kaitlin's.

John had turned around and driven back from Allentown without stopping; the four hours behind the wheel he could only remember in jagged pieces like a bad dream.

Danny's face had looked worried when he'd opened the door. "What happened, John? What's wrong?" John couldn't answer at first. He took the glass of water Danny handed him, and when he closed his eyes to drink he saw headlights and the white lines of the highway flying toward him out of the dark.

All he wanted was to lay down, close his eyes and hear nothing, see nothing, feel nothing for a while. When he finally finished telling what had happened, he looked up and was shocked to see Danny crying.

"I'm sorry, John. I'm sorry," Danny's voice sounded small and strangled. "You can't stay here. Vicky's been really patient. You've been here a lot, John. A lot of times. That's why I gave you the car. I was hoping…" John stared at Danny's wet, red face, his mouth twisted out of shape, unrecognizable. "Vicky's been really patient, John. She's been patient with me too. You know what I mean. I can't blow that, John. I can't."

Danny stopped to wipe his eyes. When he spoke again, his voice was steadier but still fragile-sounding. "You can stay here tonight. You've got someplace to go, right?"

John could only nod his head. *Yes. Yes I do.*

The green window was still blazing bright inside the house across the road, just like he knew it would be. As he sat staring at it, finishing the last of the bottle of vodka he'd found in the kitchen, it all became clear to him. These past three weeks, the months and years of anger and separation, the ugly black letters on the wall. None of it was true. This, the green window shining in the dark, the beautiful figures that moved and called to him from the light and the fierce and powerful yearning inside him that answered them. That was true. And if it wasn't, it was all he had.

It was a short walk across the alley to the empty house. When he climbed the wooden steps and approached the sliding glass door, he could see the green window flickering inside, closer than ever. Then his whole body went numb with fear. A man's face, pale and hollow-eyed, stared back at him. He cried out and struck at it, and the face shattered into pieces of glass that fell at his feet. His hand was cut but the pain felt distant, unimportant. Only the green window mattered, and the small familiar figures waiting for him on the other side.

The closer he came to it, the brighter the light grew until he had to shut his eyes. He felt for the windowsill with both hands, gripped it and pulled hard until he felt it slide up. Then he climbed through.

The moment he was on the other side he knew something was wrong. The air here was not warm but icy cold and felt thick and hard to move through. As he walked, the sand rose up around him in grainy, swirling clouds, and his limbs moved slowly and heavily as if he was dragging them behind him.

By the time he reached the small figures in the sand, he understood they were not his children. When they began to turn their heads, their long hair swirling around them in the thick, green air, he covered his eyes. He didn't need to see their faces to know what they were. He didn't need to feel their cold, damp fingers on his wrist to know where they were taking him. He had known that for a long time.

the last testament of jacob tyler

My name is Jacob Tyler. Let there be no mistake or controversy about my identity – Jacob Tyler is my true Christian name, no other false name or names that I have provided my current employers, for reasons which will soon be made clear in the story I am about to relate.

My personal effects, such as they are – a pocket watch and my Tyron rifle – I bequeath to whatever man discovers my remains and gives them a Christian burial. These items – in particular, my rifle – I would have preferred to leave to a son. But in this, as in much else, I have been disappointed – cursed, some would say. So to the man who takes this rifle from my hands, may it serve you better than it has served me.

Any property holdings that were once mine – namely twenty-five acres in lower Dutchess County, New York – have long since been liquidated and passed from my hand. And it is in that place, where I lost my name and every other good thing that holds a man in the circle of human society, that my story must begin.

All my life I have earned my living at the barrel of a rifle. It is true that no sportsman will ever earn his living by settling in one place – not until beavers and turkeys grow from the ground like corn.

Until the age of thirty I did right well for myself as a hunter of wild game, providing food for the tables of wealthy men from Manhattan to Albany, and later as a trapper for Mr. Astor's company. When the fur trade dwindled and the price of game did also, I hired out my rifle for other enterprises, such as protecting properties in dispute or returning escaped slaves to their owners. I know some men, good hunters, who refuse such work, but I have never seen the point of such scruples. Say what you will, as long as there are slaves, there will be those who escape and those who hunt them down. It seems to me that such work is best done by professionals – I am, as I have said, a hunter and trapper by trade, and those skills have served me well.

Still, by the autumn of 1845, I was unable to find work – none that suited me. A man too long out of work will grasp at the first thing that looks like salvation – as will a man who has spent too much time alone.

My wife's maiden name was Kathleen van Cortland. Like all women, the advantages she promised seemed at first to outweigh the disadvantages. Her sharp tongue that I took at first for wit and her quick temper that I mistook for passion soon made their true selves known to me.

The property I have mentioned came to me through marriage. It had been in my wife's family – as she was fond of saying – for the better part of a hundred years. It was in its day a decent piece of land, yielding a good crop of wheat as well as milk and apples. But in the absence of any male heir, it had lain fallow for many seasons.

I had been married but a fortnight when a man approached me in the tavern where I spent my evenings and began to make offers to purchase the twenty-five acres. When I told my wife of this she became much incensed and made it known that no amount of money could bring her to part with her birthright. I asked her what good was a birthright that cannot put food on the table. She then made bold to say that it was not the land, but I who was to blame. "This land will give back what a good man puts into it," she said, and went on to revile me for my drunken and wasteful ways. Not wishing to hear more, I left her at her raging and went to the tavern, where I drank many glasses of brandy to still the angry voices in my head.

You might well ask why I did not exercise my right as lawful head of the household and sell the property without my wife's consent. Indeed, I could have done so. However, I would then be free of the property but not of my wife – and the misery she had caused me before would be nothing compared to what she would inflict upon me afterward.

It was about this time that my wife fell victim to consumption and soon took to her bed. Doctors came and went and she spent her days and nights in the most dreadful fits of coughing until I thought she would choke. The only thing that gave her any relief was a tonic that the doctor had prescribed for her, of which she took four doses every day. This alone seemed to provide her with some repose.

As my wife's illness increased, so did my hours at the tavern, where my debts likewise grew. The man who had wanted to buy the twenty-five acres continued to press me with his offers which, in my circumstances, I was more and more loathe to refuse.

It was when I was preparing my wife's nightly dose of medicine that the idea came upon me. Taking the bottle to the kitchen, I poured a third of the tonic into the basin and replaced it with spring water. If the taste was any different, my wife did not seem to notice, but I could hear her wracking cough grow worse throughout the night.

The next day I poured out a little more of the medicine and replaced it with spring water. Indeed, my wife's fits grew worse and worse till I could scarcely bear to hear them.

I congratulated myself for my own cleverness – there would be no poison left behind, nor any sign of wrongdoing whatsoever, only the illness that God Himself had seen fit to visit upon her. In this manner I told myself that no action of mine would bring about her end – I was merely allowing nature to take its course.

One night as I was preparing my wife's nightly dose, her hand suddenly flew out and clutched my wrist with an iron-like grip. Her sunken eyes remained shut and her breathing was shallow and weak, but her grip was as unbreakable as a vice. I could feel the strength of her intent, though whether it was entreaty or accusation, I could not be sure.

After a few long moments had passed, I felt her grip release, and I fled the house for the tavern, where I spent several hours waiting for that which I felt would not be long in coming.

I waited until midnight had passed before I returned home. There was such a pall of silence within the house that I fully expected to find my wife's lifeless body in the bed where I had left her. When I entered the darkened bedroom I could hear what surely were her last labored gasps of breath – so far apart they came that at first it seemed she was no longer breathing at all.

Hearing her struggle so, and knowing that the end I had worked for was near, a feeling of victory rose within me – fed, no doubt, by the brandy I had consumed – along with a feeling of – dare I say it – sympathy, almost a tenderness. I turned and fumbled to light the candle that sputtered and sent wild shadows swelling across the walls. *Are you ready to die?* Those were the words that had formed themselves in my brain and were now on my lips, ready to be spoken, when I turned and saw my wife sitting bolt upright in bed, her lips curled back from her teeth and her eyes wide open with a look of malevolent fury that was not human. I cried out in terror and dropped the candle to the floor where it instantly went out, plunging the room into blackness. I now felt ten times the terror as before and scrambled desperately to strike a light – but not before I heard my wife speak out in the darkness in a terrible voice I could scarce recognize as her own. *"Are you ready to die?"*

Hearing these words I had meant to speak myself coming from my wife's lips, and in such a terrible, inhuman manner, I might have fainted away in terror, but I could not, so overwhelming was my desire to strike a light – if I was going to die, I wanted to see the agent of my death.

Somehow my trembling hands managed to light the candle. When I did, I was amazed to see my wife once again lying in bed on her back, her eyes still wide open but with no light left in them. One touch at her throat confirmed it – she was dead.

It was the work of less than a week to sell my wife's property for a greater sum of money than I had ever seen. I have often heard it said that the more money a man has in his possession, the quicker he loses it. Once my debts were paid it did not take long for me to incur more, and life once again became difficult. Moreover, rumors had begun to circulate that my wife's death may not have been entirely due to her illness; indeed, word reached me that certain members of my wife's family who were no doubt behind these rumors were planning to bring the matter before the law.

It was for those reasons that I made plans to leave Dutchess County. I had read in the newspapers of a property dispute in the Kansas territories where a man who was handy with a rifle could earn decent pay. But my resources had dwindled to such an extent that a journey of that distance was beyond my means. Imagine, then, my great pleasure when I learned that Governor Seward was seeking armed men to help put down an uprising among tenant farmers in Delaware County. Delaware County – scarce two days journey! It was – so I thought then – a gift from the Almighty. So it was on a cold October morning that I cleaned my rifle, put my remaining money into my boot, and set out with a group of twelve other men for the village of Andes.

On the second morning of our journey we were joined by twenty men of Sullivan County looking to cast their lot with us. It was then we were required by Sheriff Henricks, who rode with us, to sign a document swearing allegiance to the Governor of New York and agreeing to the terms of payment we had been promised. It was thus that "Jacob Tyler" became "Jonathan Brown" and I rode the rest of that day with a feeling of lightness and well-being in my breast, as if, by the stroke of a pen, the past and all its ills had been erased.

By mid day we were already deep into the Catskill Mountains, as dark and difficult a range as I have seen in this part of the country. We followed the meandering Easophus and before sunset we came upon the first homes of the residents of Andes, pleasant-looking white clapboard houses set back off the road. The men, women, and children who witnessed our approach did not come forth to greet us but watched from their porches and windows with caution and, it appeared to me, some degree of suspicion as we rode past.

"You can hardly blame them," said Jonas Petersen, a young man of Sullivan County who rode with us. "It's not *them* we've come to protect."

Petersen was one of those young men whose education was greater than any practical use he had for it. Thus anyone in his company was subject to the excess of fact and opinion that could not remain inside his head. It was from him that I learned the nature of the conflict we had been called in to resolve.

"Even the rich must pay their debts," Petersen said as we passed along the road through the village. "The men who own this land but do not work it owe great debts to men who are even wealthier than they. In that sense, they are just as trapped as these poor families you see staring at us from their meager homes. The men who own this land can turn to these poor men and women to exact the money they need to pay their debts. But for these people, there is no one lower to turn to. That is why they have taken up rebellion."

I asked Petersen if he was prepared to use violence against those for whom he felt so much sympathy. He looked at me with some alarm and said – as though he was explaining something to a child – that Governor Seward had brought us here to prevent violence, not to be the cause of it. When I saw that he actually believed this, I nearly laughed, but seeing the look on his young face, I decided to say nothing more, and we rode the rest of the way in silence.

If young Petersen had weak and ill-formed notions about our purpose, there were none in Sheriff Henricks' mind. The rebels we were about to face were desperate men, he warned, and would not scruple to use violence to achieve their goal. When I asked where this army of rebels might be found, he said without pause, "All around you." I cast my eye about the room at the local men nursing their tankards of ale, and at the tavern keeper counting his coins.

"They do not appear to be as fearsome a foe as I have been told," I said.

"And what have you been told?" he asked, fixing me with a cold glare.

"Merely that a few farmers have taken up arms against their landlords and wealthier neighbors."

"And what have you heard of the Indians?"

I confessed that during the ride from Dutchess County I had

heard some of the men speak of "the Indians" although I knew of no tribes in New York that still made war against white men.

"They are not true Indians," Henricks said with much disgust in his voice. "They are cowards who put on savage dress and mask themselves with the hides and antlers of dead animals to hide their identity. They meet in secret and roam the roads at night to frighten the landlords and their own neighbors who are in sympathy with the forces of law and order."

"I would like to see these Indians," I boasted. The brandy had made my blood run hot. Besides, I wanted Henricks to see that I was not afraid of the childish tricks of a few poor farmers.

"You will see them," Henricks said, still unsmiling. "Tonight."

So it was on the evening of our arrival that Sheriff Henricks ordered us to assemble with our horses and firearms in the field behind Hunting Tavern. After muffling our horses' hooves with burlap and rope, we proceeded down the road that led into the woods north of town, taking care to go slowly so as not to raise any alarm.

Our goal was an abandoned barn about a mile from town, where an informer had told Henricks the Indians would meet. Before setting off, Henricks cautioned us to be wary of ambush. Looking about me as we rode, I was reminded of why I had never liked hunting in the mountains because of how the land rises up on every side and lets no light pass through the trees – in that darkness, there could be a hundred of the enemy crawling near and you would never see them until their hand was at your throat.

After we had ridden for a half an hour, a light came into view, a small white flame hovering motionless in the darkness. Drawing closer, we could see it was a solitary candle burning in the window of the barn we sought, a black, dilapidated structure that squatted alone in a clearing. Henricks raised his hand and signaled two dozen men to spread out in a wide circle to prevent those of us who were going in from becoming surrounded. The rest of us then dismounted and proceeded to make our way on foot through the trees toward the barn and that solitary candle. I thought it odd that these rebels had placed a candle in the window of what was supposed to be a secret meeting place. It did not bode well.

Henricks himself approached the barn door, rifle in hand. After waiting for us to gather around, he gave the door a mighty kick. It swung open and Henricks leapt inside with a shout and the rest of us rushed in behind him, quickly deploying along one wall so as not to shoot our fellows in battle.

Within a moment it became clear – we had been deceived. The barn was empty. There was only that one candle burning and, for some reason, a lingering smell of tar. Henricks walked over to the candle that had been set on the rotting windowsill and touched it with curious fingers. It was at that moment that one of our party cried out in a voice that was terrible to hear. Looking about for the source of his alarm, I thought at first that we must be under attack, but saw nothing moving in the shadows around us. I then looked at the man who had cried out and saw his gaze fixed on a point high above our heads. When I followed his gaze, I did not cry out, but came as close to it as I had in my life.

There above us in the rafters of the old barn was a man, or what had been a man. His limbs had been bound and stretched so far apart that he looked like a bird stripped and splayed for gutting. And now we could all see where the smell of tar had come from. If you have seen drawings in the newspapers of men who have been tarred and feathered – those comic figures of fun, like creatures from children's books – then you have not seen the bulging, blinded eyes, the skin burnt black by the molten pitch, the places where the skin itself has been torn away by the victim's struggles.

It was at that moment when we heard cries of alarm and gunshots from outside. We swiftly ran out – glad to quit that barn and its horrible tenant – and saw two men running toward us, their faces white with alarm. They related how they had been standing watch when a face suddenly appeared between the trees, a face one man described as *like a scarecrow* and the other described as *a withered corpse*. Both men claimed to have discharged their firearms in the direction of that terrible face which remained motionless, looking at them, then melted back into the darkness.

As these two men were relating this story, there arose all around us a terrifying clamor like the howling and braying from the throats of a thousand unseen animals. I saw more than one of the younger men looking wildly about, naked fear in their eyes. Henricks shouted at us to stand fast. We followed his command until that terrible clamor died down and finally ceased altogether. Afterward came a silence that seemed even more threatening than the awful din that had preceded it.

Before departing, Henricks ordered the barn burned to the ground, so we rode the first half-mile back to town with that conflagration at our backs, obliging us to watch our own shadows writhing ahead of us on the ground. Whether Henricks ordered that poor man be cut down or left him hanging there to burn, I do not know to this day.

After we had stabled our horses and returned to our quarters for the night, I asked Petersen if he was still in sympathy with the rebels, now that he had seen their handiwork. The young fellow seemed shaken but still undaunted in his opinions, stating that the rebels were decent men driven to indecent acts by terrible circumstances. It occurred to me that one might say the same of any man, and I thought to engage young Petersen on this point, but he had already taken to his cot and turned his face to the wall.

The following morning, I noticed that our tavern keeper was not to be found in his usual place. I later learned that he was the informer who had led us to that barn – and the same unfortunate wretch we had found hanging in the rafters.

Henricks was not daunted by the loss of a single informer. In a village where every soul knew someone or something worth telling, new informers were all around.

After breakfast, Henricks ordered ten men including myself to accompany him to the village stables. Upon arriving we found no one but a young buy of twelve or thirteen who looked upon us with great suspicion and, it seemed to me, fear.

"Where is your master?" Henricks inquired.

The boy said nothing but continued to stare at us with the wide eyes of a frightened animal.

"Speak, boy," Henricks raised his voice. "Where is your master?"

"Gone," the boy finally stammered.

"Gone where?" Henricks demanded.

"To Bovina – to shoe a horse."

"So," Henricks said, "The horses in Bovina have no one else to shoe them?"

To this the boy made no reply. I was sure that Henricks was about to lay hands on the lad – then he spoke more quietly. "Come. There is something I want to show you."

Henricks led the boy – who came with some hesitation – out of the stable and into the sunlight where he stood squinting at the other members of our militia standing by with their rifles in their arms.

"Do you see it?" Henricks asked. The boy looked around, even down at the dirt at his feet, a look of confusion on his young face.

"You do not see?" Henricks said. "Then you must look closer." At that he grabbed the boy by the hair and plunged his head into the trough, holding it deep underwater. The boy thrashed and kicked but Henricks' grip was iron. Finally, he pulled the boy free from the water, still holding him by the hair.

"Do you see it yet?" Henricks asked. The boy was gasping and choking and could not answer. "Then look again." He plunged the boy's head back underwater and held it there while the boy flailed and kicked. When he pulled the boy from the water again, the lad's face was blood-red and water poured from his nose and mouth.

"Where is their meeting place?" Henricks shouted into the boy's ear. "Where do the devils meet tonight?" Without waiting for an answer, Henricks shoved the boy's head underwater again and held it there longer than before. The boy's thrashing grew weaker and weaker and when Henricks pulled him up again he seemed already half-drowned.

"You want to breathe?" Henricks said. "Tell me where they are meeting tonight. Then you can breathe." I saw the boy's lips moving but could hear nothing. I saw Henricks put his ear close to the boy's mouth and close his eyes, nodding slowly. Then Henricks rose up and spoke in a gentle-sounding voice, "Now you can breathe." He then patted the boy on the shoulder, put his pistol to the back of the boy's head and shot. A black hole opened in the boy's forehead with a great spray of blood, a look of surprise on his young face – then he slumped forward into the trough, sloshing water that Henricks took care to step away from before it could wet his boots.

I confess that I was startled by Henricks' action. In my time I had seen men do terrible things with some goal or result in mind, but what Henricks had just done seemed unnecessary, wasteful, even more so when I asked if the boy had told him where the rebels would meet. "No," he admitted, then added, "Now we don't need to look for them – they will come looking for us."

If I was startled by Henricks' action, young Petersen was completely undone by it. I found him alone in the inn, a half-empty bottle of brandy in his hand. He sat staring into the cold hearth with his back to me so I could not see his face. I called his name three times before he finally spoke in a hollow, ragged-sounding voice.

"He will die for this."

I cautioned Petersen that he could be shot for such speech, and that he was no match for Henricks when sober, let alone drunk as he was now.

"It's not *me* he needs to fear," Petersen said in a voice so low I could barely hear it. Suddenly he turned and fixed me with a red-eyed stare and spoke in a hollow-sounding voice. "Are you ready to die?"

The shock of hearing my wife's last words to me from Petersen's lips was like a cold hand at my throat. I had to close my eyes for a moment and shake my head – it was a strange and cruel coincidence, nothing more.

"Death will come when it comes," I finally said. "It matters little if I am ready or not."

"How can you know that?" he asked, a look of great earnestness and intensity on his face, "If you are not ready to die, how can you know it doesn't matter? How can you know what death wants?" He took a long draught from the bottle, emptying it, then turned back to stare into the cold hearth. "Every man with a gun thinks he can make death his slave. But death will not be any man's slave. Not his. Not yours."

After this drunken speech Petersen's eyes closed and he laid his head on the table, where I left him to sleep until nightfall.

That night Henricks ordered us to assemble once more behind the inn at moonrise. This time there was no muffling of our horses' hooves, no orders to move quietly. We rode for a half hour north of town to a quarry where flint had once been taken from the ground, now a deep bowl in the forest floor. Henricks ordered several men to descend into the quarry where they struck tents and built a campfire that they lit and left blazing. Then Henricks ordered us to climb high into the trees around the quarry's edge and be ready with our rifles. We smeared our rifles with mud to avoid reflecting the firelight – some of the men darkened their faces too. Then we waited.

The moon had almost climbed to its highest place in the sky above when I heard them coming – at first, nothing more than the distant snap of a twig. Then I saw them moving through the trees below. Dark shadows, the moon illuminating a grotesque painted mask, a set of antlers, then more and more of them until it seemed the whole forest floor was alive. They poured down the sides of the quarry and I thought of a herd of deer I had once trapped in a dead-end gulch and shot, one by one, as they'd struggled to leap the steep walls and climb over each other as they fell. The figures below moved closer to the empty tents and the campfire, their grotesque faces illuminated in its reddish glow.

Then Henricks gave the order and the trees all around exploded with volley after volley of rifle fire. Figures below fell to the earth and were trampled by more figures running to escape the hail of bullets from above. I shot one man in a red and yellow robe with a painted scarecrow face who was waving a scythe and shouting, then another with a pair of bull's horns on his hooded head who fell to the ground screaming and writhing like a snake until I shot him again. Altogether I shot fifteen men.

When Henricks shouted the order to cease-fire, the forest was full of the haze and stink of gun-smoke, and the quarry below was carpeted with bodies, some of them still moving. We climbed down from the trees and walked among the bodies, shooting the ones who were still alive.

Before we left, Henricks ordered two men to douse the bodies with coal oil and set them afire. From the cries that rose from that smoldering mass, I knew we had left some alive, despite our best efforts. So I stood and fired my rifle in the direction of those cries until either the bullets or the fire had silenced them.

When we had done with this work, Henricks led thirty men, including myself, north along the Kings Road where he believed some of the rebels had fled. He left behind a contingent of twenty men to make sure that the fire did its work. Petersen was among those left behind at the quarry. His face, when I last saw it, was ghost-white in the firelight. I didn't know if he had fired any shots tonight and, seeing the haunted look on his face, I determined never to ask him.

We rode north along the Kings Road halfway to Delhi, encountering not a soul along the way. Finally, Henricks gave the order to turn and go back. As we rode, I became aware of the darkness ahead growing thicker and heavier, the way the sky feels just before a storm. I cursed the mountains around us that blocked out the moon, the trees that crowded close and let no light through. When I saw a dark figure coming toward us, moving in a halting and unnatural way like a scarecrow being pulled along on strings, I raised my rifle, and all the men around me did the same.

Then we saw – it was Petersen, but a horrid, changed version of the man we knew. His head had been laid open with a great wound from which the blood flowed, soaking his white shirt red. Black, scorched marks covered his hands and face, and the smell of burnt cloth and flesh hung heavy upon him. As we ran to meet him, he stumbled to his knees and by the time we reached him he was laying full on his back in the middle of the road, staring up at the moon and the trees with a look on his face that was terrible to see.

"Where are the others?' Henricks demanded.

"Dead," Petersen answered in a choked whisper.

"Dead?" Henricks said. "How? Not *all* dead…"

"All dead," Petersen rasped out. "They came…they came out of the fire. Still burning. With their masks and pitchforks. And their scythes. Still burning. They are coming."

"Who?" Henricks demanded, although by now he knew the answer as surely as we all did.

"The men," Petersen said. "The men we killed tonight."

"They are *dead*." Henricks spoke loudly and deliberately like someone trying to wake a child from a bad dream.

"They are dead," Petersen said, "and they are coming."

With that, a sudden rushing sound rose up from the dark road ahead of us, like a great wind moving through the trees. And with it a smell of smoke, tar, and burnt things.

When I looked back down, Petersen had ceased breathing. Suddenly, there came a hideous torrent of noise out of the darkness ahead of us like the one we had heard before, like cries from the throats of a thousand unseen animals. At that, several of our men broke ranks and took off running through the trees. Henricks shouted at the deserters who did not stop, and took a shot at one, although he missed. He then ordered us to retreat to a barn that stood just off the road where we bolted the doors, positioned ourselves at the windows and made ready to face what was coming.

There is nothing like hot-blooded action to push back fear, so it was by making these familiar preparations for battle that the doubts and terrors of just a few moments ago began to seem small and distant. I now believed, as Henricks surely did, that another rebel force had discovered their slain brethren, taken vengeance on Petersen and his fellows and were now on their way to engage us. Petersen had been drunk, destroyed by his own fear and weak will, and his words were the ravings of someone who could not face the truth. I checked my rifle, wiped the sights clean with my thumb and fixed my gaze on the road, waiting for a target.

As I stared into the darkness, I saw a flickering glow through the trees that grew brighter and closer. *Torches*, I thought – then I saw. The figures that approached by the hundreds were not carrying torches. It was they themselves who were burning. God help me, they were all burning.

In a second they were on us in a great howling rush of wind. Doors and walls burst inward in a shower of sparks and the nightmare figures stepped through, laying about with their scythes and pitchforks, butchering men like pigs at a slaughter. All around me, men screamed and fired their guns uselessly. I saw Henricks firing his Colt again and again at one of the burning devils who lifted him by the throat with one hand and forced a pitchfork through his chest, pinning him to the wall while the poor man kicked and squealed in a thin, shrill voice that was horrible to hear.

A tall robed figure appeared before me, burning antlers rising from its head, its face the skull of a great stag painted red and black with the skin dried and cracked like leather. It was on me in one stride, grasped the back of my neck in a grip like iron and pushed me to the floor, pressing my face down into the dust. I could feel its great head lean closer, hot breath and heat from the smoldering skin licking at the back of my neck. Then it spoke into my ear through the burning cloth and leather in a voice that I knew. It was my wife's own voice.

"Are you ready to die?"

It was then that I screamed as I had not screamed since I was a child. I screamed like a sick man emptying himself of the poison that burns his insides. Something left me then. I don't know what, but something went out of me, and with it, the feel of that hand – of *her* hand on my neck. I did not feel it release me – one moment it was there; the next moment, it was gone.

At first I believed I had been dreaming – then I woke at dawn and saw the terrible slaughter all around me, the scorched and blackened bodies of men where they had fallen. I rose and walked away from that burning ruin, away from those black mountains, away from Delaware County. I went as far as my money would carry me and put as many miles as I could between myself and that cursed place. I finally reached the Nebraska territories where a land company hired me to watch over a large property and keep all unwanted persons from entering. And so I come to the end of my story.

And yet, it is not really over – not yet. Every day I sit here with my old Tyron rifle across my knees, looking out over this strange, unbroken horizon, and wait for them to find me. Let them. Let them come. I am ready now. Still, when I dream of dark glades and vales and hills pressing close on every side, I am relieved to wake and find this flat and empty landscape that stretches out all around me. Because if there is something coming for me, as it surely must, I want to see it when it comes.

the professor of history

The professor of history is hosting an open house on Halloween night. He has kept this tradition for over thirty years. Some of the parents who bring their children here can remember peering up at this old house through the eyeholes in their own dime-store masks many years ago.

The professor of history does not decorate his house for Halloween. No fiberglass spider webs, no styrofoam tombstones with funny epitaphs. The house itself is the decoration. One hundred years old and three stories tall with many windows, all of them dark but one, hidden in a grove of ancient oak trees with thick limbs that have grown into tangled arterial shapes.

The professor of history appears at the door and welcomes the children and parents who have gathered here on his front porch. He is an old man somewhere in his seventies, short, with a pot-belly and a fringe of white hair that rises like wings from the sides of his head. He has a grandfatherly smile and a gentle voice, sweet and melodious. There is, in short, nothing frightening about him.

The boy who has come to this house for the first time tonight is disappointed. He had expected a more imposing presence, someone taller, more sinister. The professor of history is about as sinister as Santa Claus.

Tonight the boy is accompanied by his father for the first time. Last year it was his mother. It hits him somewhere in his stomach that "last year" really means *the last year*. There are other children here with their fathers, their mothers not visible, but he and his father are different. They are alone now, the two of them, and he imagines that anyone who looks at them long enough can tell.

The first thing the boy notices inside the house is the books. Books bristling from shelves on every wall, books stacked on tables and cabinets, books lined-up in neat rows along the floor. The boy has never seen so many books in one home. A little girl asks the professor of history if he has really read all of these books. He chuckles and tells her no, but his wife has. *These are my wife's books,* he tells them. *She read them all. Every one of them.*

The boy stares at the books and is struck by a sudden memory of his mother reading to him at bedtime. In the memory, he can see the book open in front of them, her pale, slender hands turning the pages, but her face, which is hovering right behind him, he cannot see or even bring to mind.

Years ago, when he must have been four or five, a woman had told him, *You have your mother's face.* It confused him, even frightened him. How could he have his mother's face? If the face that he wore belonged to her, what had happened to his own face, the one he was born with? And if the face that he wore was his mother's, whose face was she wearing now?

The boy follows the professor of history through the dining room and past a long wooden table big enough for a banquet. He sees several bowls of candy and a punch bowl full of apple cider. In the center there is a pumpkin with a smiling face painted on it, topped with a straw gardener's hat that looks like something a woman might have once worn.

The professor of history leads his guests into the front hall where they gather near the foot of the stairs and wait for the story they have all come to hear.

In the story the professor of history tells, there was a girl who lived in this house long ago. There was a boy who she was in love with but the girl's father did not approve and forbade her from seeing the boy. To the girl, this was exactly like dying. The boy had become part of her; they had become part of each other and she could not imagine life without him. *That is what love is.*

It occurs to the boy that he does not know what this boy and girl knew. He does not know what love is. He remembers hearing his parents' voices raised in the kitchen on that last night, their ugly, incomprehensible words. *You don't know what love is.* His mother had yelled this. Or was it his father?

When he woke the next morning the house had looked different. Then he realized what had changed. Every picture of his mother was gone. Her face that had smiled down at him from every wall was now absent. Later when he finally said that he wanted to see a picture of his mother, his father glared at him until he felt afraid and went back to his room.

Later than night the boy had looked up to see his father's silhouette filling the doorway, swaying back and forth and blocking out the hallway light. "You want to see your mother?" The boy could not speak. He watched his father move toward him, toss something onto the bed, then turn and stagger out of the room.

The boy waited till he heard his father's footsteps shuffling further and further away. Then he turned on the bedroom light and picked up the object. It was a photograph of his father, younger and smiling with the ocean at his back, a woman's body standing close to him. Where the woman's face had been was a jagged hole where someone had taken a sharp object and gouged it out. The boy stared at the hole for a long time until he could see something slowly coming into focus, like an object in deep water rising toward the surface at a tremendous speed. He pushed the picture under the bed and left the room. When he came back for it the next day, it was gone.

The professor of history continues with his story. *One night the boy came to the house in the middle of the night…*

Here the story changes from year to year. Sometimes it's the boy who kills the father. Sometimes it's the father who kills the boy.

The boy listens to this story and imagines all the other versions that the professor of history doesn't tell hiding behind the one he tells tonight, the one in which the father kills the boy. The boy is sure, somehow, that this is wrong, that it was the boy who killed the father.

The boy can't help but glance at his own father and wonder how he is hearing this tale of violent, passionate love and its consequences. Which part does he imagine himself playing? Or has he turned off the professor's voice and is only thinking ahead to the armchair and the glass of whiskey and the TV making its soft hushing noise like rain?

When the story is over, the professor of history shows his guests the bloodstains on the hallway floor. The children all crowd around, jostling to see. The boy looks hard and sees what looks like a faint, brownish discoloration in the wooden floorboards. It reminds him of the rusty water-stains on his bathroom ceiling at home. It's disappointing, not what he expected. Still, there is something there.

The professor of history leads the group back to the banquet table. The children all grab fistfuls of candy while the professor of history offers the adults a glass of the orange wine his wife used to make. The boy drops a half-dozen peppermints into his trick-or-treat bag and wonders if this means it's over, if this is all that is going to happen tonight.

On the way out the door, the boy finally asks the question he's been wanting to ask. *Is your house really haunted?* The professor of history smiles and says something the boy will remember, even after he's grown up and looking back on this night. *That depends on what you mean by 'haunted'.*

Later that night the boy waits for his father to fall asleep in front of the TV, then slips past the flickering glow and the stale smell of whiskey and out the door. There is no one on the street at this hour, only jack o-lanterns, all gone out except for one that glowers at him with a weak and dying light.

The boy keeps walking until he sees the professor of history's house rising in front of him, its many windows dark now. He is sure that what he saw and heard here tonight is not all there is. He knows there must be more. Something else is going to happen.

The boy goes to the tall window to the left of the front door and looks inside. He stares into the blackness until his eyes start to throb. Then he sees a small light floating through the darkness, flickering on and off. It reminds him of a firefly. The light comes to rest and hovers motionless in the blackness. The boy stares at the light until his eyes ache, waiting for it to move again.

Another light appears from the same direction and moves across the room, coming to rest about a foot above the first one. Then another. And another. The boy watches until the little lights form a kind of chain that arcs upward in the dark. In their combined light he can now see what they are. Candles, each one lighting the way up a long staircase. But the boy does not remember a staircase being in this room. He keeps staring until he understands what he's seeing. Not stairs. Books. Hundreds and hundreds of books, the wife's books, that the professor of history has used to build a staircase that reaches from the floor all the way up into a darkness that the boy's eyes cannot penetrate.

The professor of history enters the room carrying a single book and a glass of the orange wine. The boy watches the professor of history move a chair to the foot of the strange staircase, where the candles lead upward like runway lights into a darkness that is already growing thicker and heavier like the sky before a storm. The professor of history smiles and opens the book. He sits. He waits.

The boy feels something like a cold light growing brighter and brighter inside his chest, rising to fill his head, but cannot look away from the spot at the top of the strange staircase, where the darkness has started to gather and swirl like a cup of ink poured into dark water.

Years later, when his own children are still young enough to beg for stories, they will ask what he saw step out of that black cloud at the top of those stairs on that Halloween long ago, and he will describe for the hundredth time how the professor of history's wife stepped out of the darkness, out of another world, and began her slow, ethereal descent. He will tell them how she wore the straw gardener's hat he'd seen on the pumpkin earlier that evening, how her plump, smiling cheek bore a single smudge of potting soil. He will tell how each candle flame shone through her body as she passed in front of them on her way down to her husband waiting faithfully below.

What he will not tell them, what he will never tell them, is what he really saw. How what had stepped out of the darkness at the top of those stairs had worn his mother's face, familiar but changed, her mouth a jagged black gash, the eyes gouged-out lightless pits. He will not tell them about the broken way she walked, like a crippled bird or an insect. He will not mention the dark and faceless thing that walked beside her whose arm she clutched, or the horrible way they were joined together that made their walking ugly and strange as they descended. It was not the kind of thing you tell your children.

And when they ask, as they always do, *Daddy, did you really see a ghost?* he will not know what to say.

the smell of red clay

They'd been telling ghost stories all night in this run-down bar on the north edge of town. Only five blocks from the apartment where the woman he'd said he wanted to spend the rest of his life with was waiting for him, but here he was, crowded into a grimy red vinyl booth with a group of people he barely knew – Jerry from accounts receivable with his spiky black hair and hyena laugh, some glum-looking guy from shipping named Billy, and two women he'd never even seen before. Jerry had invited him to go drinking every Friday after work, and every Friday he'd said the same thing. *I have to go home.* He'd said it regretfully but gladly, loving the sound of it. Home. Tonight he couldn't even say the word.

It was the week before Halloween, and the dark wood-paneled walls were covered with cardboard witches, ghosts and skeletons, the kind you find taped to the windows of elementary schools. Their faces were cartoonish in that simplistic, unthreatening way he'd always hated. The one closest to him, taped just a few inches from his face, was a witch whose skin was not the typical green, but an inexplicable purple. The witch was stirring a large black cauldron from which a number of creatures – snakes, bats and spiders – were peeking with comical expressions, as if they thought it was funny to be boiled alive.

He was here because of another story, one Carla had told him just a few hours ago. It had started, as many stories do, with a simple question, one he asked every night when he came home from work to the small apartment they'd been sharing for almost six months. What did you do today? He thought of it as one of the little rituals of domestic life, although they were not married – not yet, he liked to say. On most days she'd tell him about some jerk at the restaurant who'd given her a lousy tip or made a pass at her. And while he made a point of acting appropriately concerned or pissed off, he actually liked hearing about the men who'd made passes at her – it proved to him that he was living with a desirable woman, which somehow meant that he too was desirable.

Carla was the first woman he'd ever lived with. It had not been an easy sell. *You don't want to get mixed up with me* was what she'd said the first night he'd told her that he loved her. That was how it went. He'd said, *I love you,* and she'd said *You don't want to get mixed up with me.* He didn't take it too badly – if she'd said *That's nice* or *You're sweet,* that would have been a death blow. Instead, *You don't want to get mixed up with me* meant he'd struck a nerve, had drawn blood.

When she finally gave in and told him that she loved him, she'd actually bowed her head, her dark curly hair hiding her face when she said it. Everything about the way she moved and spoke looked like defeat, and he felt a quiet rush of victory inside, knowing he'd won.

That was when he started following her. At first he didn't realize that was what he was doing. When he drove past the restaurant where she worked, he thought it would nice to surprise her so he pulled into the parking lot. Then the thought crossed his mind that maybe this was a bad idea, maybe she'd be too busy, so he waited in his car until he saw her come out of a back door and walk toward a white Camry. He started to get out, then he worried that maybe she wouldn't like him surprising her like this, maybe she'd think there was something creepy about it, so he waited until she'd started the car and turned onto the highway before he pulled out behind her. He followed her for a mile or two, watching the familiar shape of her head with its long curly hair silhouetted in the oncoming headlights before he finally pulled over, blood pounding in his head, and watched her tail lights moving farther and farther away from him until they vanished in the dark.

He stayed behind her a little longer every time, but he always stopped before he saw something he didn't want to see.

He was aware, dimly, that she'd had another life before him and that he'd somehow taken her from it. When she talked about Steven, the guy she'd been with before him, his head would fill with a rushing white noise that blotted out the stories she was telling him, while he nodded and smiled like a patient, confident lover who was not threatened by these things. That was the picture that he wanted her to see – not the other picture of himself on his knees on the cold tile floor of their bathroom with the contents of her purse spread out in front of him; the round black compact with the cracked mirror, the pack of Marlboro Light cigarettes she'd told him she'd stopped smoking, the brown leather woman's wallet where he finally found the photo he was looking for. He stared at the broad, sunburned face, the bright toothy grin under the bushy blond mustache, the blue eyes that looked bright but a little too small and close together.

Tonight when he'd asked *what did you do today*, she didn't answer right away, and he felt it coming, felt it in his body, and he tensed his stomach muscles like a fighter expecting a blow.

"I saw Steven today," she finally said.

At the sound of the name from her lips he felt a quick stab of pain in his gut. "Oh yeah?" He tried to sound casual.

"I told him about you and me," she said. He kept moving around the tiny apartment, keeping busy, not looking at her. He could tell by the way her voice kept coming from one place that she was standing against the little white stove, her brown eyes following him as he moved.

"He took it pretty hard," she said, and he realized then that the sadness in her voice wasn't for him, that when she spoke she was seeing that big blond head bowed, those broad shoulders slumped in defeat, maybe even shaking with manly sobs. But where had this touching scene taken place? Instantly, he shoved that question as far as he could into the back of his mind. He didn't want to see the picture that was starting to develop.

"That's too bad." He forced the words out of his mouth. *Don't say anything else,* he thought. *Please stop talking. Stop talking now.*

"Yeah," she kept on. "I think he felt better by the time he left."

That was when the image leapt full-blown into his mind, the one that would not go away, of what she had done to make him feel better.

The things she said next were swallowed by the roaring sound that filled his head. As he watched her mouth forming words he couldn't hear, he realized he could see through her skin and flesh and the solid wall behind her, through the flimsy wood of the dresser and into the drawer by the bed where the gun was. Carla's mother had given it to her when she'd first moved away to college. He'd never owned a gun before, never even held one. She'd said it made her feel safer. Just knowing it's there. When he realized that the roaring sound in his head was coming from the drawer in the bedroom, he grabbed his keys from the kitchen counter and walked out the door.

For two hours he drove around in a kind of vibrant daze. A hole had been ripped in the fabric of the world. That was why he finally found himself at this bar on the edge of town with these people he barely knew. He wanted to burn out every trace of his old self and see what was left. There was a hole in the universe and he was going to jump through it.

He'd been drinking shots of bourbon and chasing them with ale. After the third shot he looked up at the raindrops scattered across the plate glass window and saw how a certain number of drops each captured and held the color of the red neon beer sign, how the lights of cars moving past washed across the glass like wind rippling across a field of tall grass.

They were telling ghost stories. He couldn't remember who'd started it, but they were well underway now. Each storyteller would lean forward, gripping their glass and lowering their voice in appropriately hushed, dramatic tones.

Jerry was telling a story that he recognized right away as a rip-off of a dozen bad slasher movies, the kind where a bunch of teenagers are stalked and butchered by a knife-wielding maniac.

"Hey Jerry," he said. "We're supposed to be telling ghost stories, not gross stories." A ripple of appreciative laughter went around the booth, and he congratulated himself for managing to be so witty and drunk at the same time.

"Hey," Jerry said, taking mock offense. "You saying my story wasn't scary?"

"He's saying there weren't any ghosts in it," said Linda, a big blond girl with a husky laugh that he liked to hear.

"Okay, okay," Jerry said, rapping the table with his beer mug like a judge's gavel. "Who's got a story with a real ghost in it?"

"I do," Linda said eagerly. "I've got a real ghost story." He watched her assume the storytelling position, leaning forward across the booth on her elbows.

"So," she began, "there's this couple, right? One night they go out parking, in the woods by the river. So they're making out and stuff when the girl hears this scratching sound coming from outside the car. She asks her boyfriend to go see what it is. He doesn't want to, but she's really scared, so he finally gets out of the car to check it out. She sits there waiting for a really long time. Then she hears that scratching sound again, except this time it's coming from the roof of the car. So she gets out to see what it is, she looks all around and there's nothing there. Then she looks up and sees her boyfriend, hanging from a tree with his throat cut – and it's his feet swinging back and forth making that scratching sound on the roof of the car."

"Hey," Jerry said. "Where's the fucking ghost?"

"Shut up, goddamn it," Linda whined, punching Jerry in the arm. "I'm not finished yet!" Jerry rubbed his arm and grinned. Linda took a deep sip of her beer and started again. "So…a few months later, she's out parking with this other guy…"

"Fucking slut," Jerry chuckled under his breath. Linda ignored him.

"She's making out with this new guy, when she looks up and sees somebody standing out there in the dark, right outside the car. She looks closer and sees it's her old boyfriend, standing there with his throat cut and blood all over his shirt, just staring at her through the glass. All of a sudden he points his finger at her and starts screaming, just screaming at her through the window, so she starts screaming too. The guy she's with, he can't see anything – he thinks she's crazy, so he drives her back to town and kicks her out. And she never sees him again."

Linda leaned back and lit a cigarette. The booth had become very quiet. Even Jerry wasn't saying anything.

"So," Linda continued, "from then on, every time she's out with a new guy, wherever she is, she looks up and there's her dead boyfriend, just standing there staring at her and screaming."

"So," Jerry finally said. "That's it? That's the ending?"

Linda leaned back, took another long sip from her beer. "I don't know," she smiled. "Is that how it ends, Carla?"

He watched the dark-haired girl across the booth reach over the table and stab her cigarette out in the overflowing ashtray, then mutter in a flat voice, "Fuck you, Linda." Jerry laughed one of his shrill hyena laughs like this was the funniest joke he'd ever heard.

A minute later, Billy was stumbling through another story that sounded like a bad copy of the one Jerry had told, which had sounded like a bad copy of a bad movie. He tried to shut out the sound of Billy's voice and focused instead on the dark-haired girl sitting directly across from him. She was listening, but it didn't look like she expected to be entertained; it was like she'd given up on that possibility and was listening for something else, something she didn't really expect to hear. Her arms looked thin and hard under the sleeves of her white muslin shirt, and when she flicked her long black hair out of her face and over her shoulder, she did it with no awareness of him or of what effect she thought it might have, but simply because it needed to be done. He wanted to see what her face would look like looking directly into his.

When he finally asked her for a cigarette, his voice a little more slurry than he would have liked, she stared at him. "Why are you asking me?" she said in a flat ironic voice. "I'm not the only one here with cigarettes."

"Because," he said, his mind racing for an answer, "yours taste better."

"How do you know?" she asked. He thought he saw the beginnings of a smile at the corner of her mouth, but he wasn't sure.

"I don't know," he said. "They just look like they do."

"So," she said, "mine look like they taste good. Is that what you're telling me?"

He knew if he backed down or looked away now he'd be lost, crushed down to a tiny speck. So he kept looking right at her and let a smile rise to his face.

"Yeah," he said. "Yours look like they taste good."

When he heard the slow howl of disbelief and drunken glee rise up all around him, he realized that the others were listening but he didn't care – the group's witnessing what he and this girl were doing, their drunken delight and approval created a kind of safety zone that made it easier for him to take the next step.

He drove her to a place he knew, a country road far from the lights of town. He was surprised and a little proud of how he'd got here so quickly, how he hadn't wasted time with too much warm-up conversation but had driven them both right here, like a man who knew what he wanted.

Her tongue tasted like vodka and bitter nicotine, and a third flavor that was her own. He'd heard stories about people who had died, or almost died, how they floated free of their own bodies and looked down at the operating table or the car crash and seen themselves, apart from themselves. That was how he felt now, like the old laws of the universe suddenly didn't apply to him.

He watched her silhouette take shape against the vague light coming through the passenger window, heard the flick of a cigarette lighter and saw her bring the flame close to her lips. He was a little startled by the way her face looked in the light from the little flame, her cheekbones casting shadows up over her eyes that were suddenly cavernous and black.

"You want one?" she asked. She spoke quietly but it sounded loud to him – it was the first time either of them had spoken since they'd started.

"Sure," he said, and in the pause that followed, he felt all the self-consciousness, all the awkwardness he'd expected to rush in and drown him rise up for a moment then suddenly fade away. Here they were, two strangers with every reason to feel uncomfortable, but as he sat listening to the rain peppering down on the windshield, watching the tip of her cigarette glow bright orange and then dim again, he realized it was because he didn't love her, didn't even know her – that was what made this feeling of freedom and power possible.

"So," he broke into the silence. "What did you think of those ghost stories back there?"

"What do you think of them?" she replied. "That's what you want to tell me anyway, right?"

He looked at her and tried to figure out if she'd just given him a shot. For a moment he considered denying it, saying, *No, I really want to know what you think*, but that wasn't the reason he'd brought it up. She'd been right about that.

"I thought they were bullshit," he went ahead. "It was like they were just repeating stuff they'd heard somewhere else, you know, from movies they'd seen. They weren't real."

He stopped talking for a moment and let what he'd just said hang in the air between them. Part of him was afraid he'd sounded like a pretentious asshole, while the other part of him felt that this was what was required to make an impression, to be a man with definite tastes and opinions, a man for whom certain things are acceptable while other things are not.

"I liked the one Linda told, though," he said, feeling generous.

"Oh yeah?" she said. "Why?" It was a question he hadn't expected.

"I don't know. There was just…something about it."

She nodded and looked out the window at the darkness outside. "So," she said, "how did you picture it?"

"What do you mean?"

"When her boyfriend gets killed," she said. "How did you picture that happening?"

He thought hard for a moment, not sure of what she wanted. "I don't know," he said. "Probably one of those knife-wielding maniacs. You know, like in Jerry's story."

"Yeah, well…" she said, still looking out the window as she spoke. "There wasn't just one guy. There were four."

He stared at her silhouette against the passenger window and tried to understand what she'd just said. Something in his mind had stopped working.

"We were out parking," she said. "Sort of like this. All of a sudden, there were these four guys. They just sort of came out of nowhere and got in the car. It happened so fast. I mean, we didn't even know they were there. It was all dark and everything. They just…came in."

He could hear the raindrops popping on the roof of the car, the heated metal under the hood ticking as it cooled. What was she saying? Was she fucking with him? He stared at her face in the dark, looking for a sign.

"We didn't have any money," she said. "We never did. That pissed them off. So…they took me in the back seat."

He sat there in silence trying to figure out how to be, how to receive the things she was telling him.

"They made him watch," she said. "They had him turned around with his head pressed over the edge of the seat. They were doing things to him too. I think they were cutting him. I don't know. He was yelling a lot. He kept screaming my name, over and over, the whole time. Sad thing is, it got on my nerves. I wanted to tell him to shut up. I don't know, maybe I did." He heard her sigh, a harsh, ragged sound. "There were four of them, so it went on for a long time. I wanted it to be over, so after a while I started doing things, you know, to make them finish quicker. That's when he stopped screaming my name. He just started screaming."

He wanted to get out of the car, get out of the car and start running. Away from her and the things she was saying. But his arms and legs felt frozen.

"After a while," she said, "he stopped screaming. You know what he said then? Kill me. 'Cause he couldn't stand to watch any more. I called him a coward. You fucking coward. That's what I said. Then…they shot him." She paused for a moment. "You know how they say gunshots aren't so loud, how they just sound like balloons popping or something? Well, not up close, not in a car like that. Up close they're loud. Real loud."

He stared at the profile of her face, black and still against the window streaming with rain. He looked for some kind of sign that she was crying, but it was too dark to tell.

"Do you want me to take you somewhere?" he asked in the softest, kindest voice he could manage. He wanted to sound kind. More than anything, he wanted to be rid of her.

"I'm not finished yet," she said. "Don't you want to hear the rest of the story?"

He glanced down at the green numbers glowing on the dashboard. 1:17. He could tell her he had to be back in town by two. He could tell her the truth, say no, he didn't want to hear any more. *Stop talking*, he thought. *Please, stop talking now.*

"So," she continued, "the next time I was with a guy, maybe three months later…" Suddenly she turned to look at him. "Is that bad? I mean, it's all bullshit, right? Wait three months to fuck another guy, you're a slut, six months, it's okay – what do you think? You think I'm a slut?"

He realized, with a feeling of panic, that she expected him to answer, so he gave the only answer he could. "I don't know." It sounded false and hollow in his ears, the kind of answer that deserved to be ripped apart, but it seemed to satisfy her.

"So," she continued, "three months later, I'm out with this other guy, in a car, like this. I look up and there he is, standing right outside the window, staring at me. I didn't recognize him at first. Then he raised his arm and pointed at me. I saw him open his mouth real wide and he started screaming, just like that night in the woods – that's when I knew it was him. So I started screaming too. The guy I was with, he couldn't see anything – he freaked out, started the car and took off. I turned around and saw him running after us. His face was all lit up red in the tail lights, his mouth was hanging open with that goddamn sound coming out of it..." She took another drag on her cigarette and when the tip flared in the dark, he thought he could see it tremble a little before it went dark again.

"When I saw him running after us like that, that's when I knew he was dead. I mean, I already knew, but the first time you see someone like that, you think maybe you're wrong somehow. Maybe they're still alive. But when you see them running like that, when you see the way they move...then you know."

He looked at the numbers glowing green on the dashboard. 1:37. All he had to do was turn the key and start the car, drive her home. If she wouldn't tell him where home was, he could drop her off at a gas station, someplace with a phone. He willed his hand to reach out and turn the key but he couldn't do it. It felt like he was paralyzed.

Suddenly he hated her. She was fucking with him, trying to freak him out. Or she was crazy. Either way, he was done with her.

He realized with a start that she was staring at him. She spoke in a slow, hard voice. "You're sorry you brought me out here, aren't you? I'll bet you wish you'd never seen me."

"No," he said, and the sudden false tenderness in his own voice disgusted him. "No. Of course not." The anger he'd felt just a moment ago was gone. In its place was a hollow space inside his chest filling slowly with something weak and cold. He was a coward. He would always be a coward. "I'm sorry," he said in a small, defeated voice. "Go on. Please."

A little patch of fog that had formed on the windshield while they were making out was still there, just above the dashboard, and she reached out with one finger and drew a line through it, slowly.

"I met this guy at work," she said, her voice softer now. "He was really nice. We talked all the time, about everything. He told me he loved me, before we even did anything, you know? I guess I loved him too. I mean, why wouldn't I? He was so nice. One night he took me back to his place. He had a really nice place, too. We went to bed and…it was great. I mean, he was just so sweet. I was just lying there in his arms, feeling like everything was going to be all right. Then I looked up and there he was, standing right there at the foot of the bed, staring at me. I tried not to scream – I really tried. But then I saw his mouth start to open – it looked all black inside. I begged him not to do it. Then that god damned sound started coming out of him. So I started screaming too. I couldn't help it."

"Then what happened?"

"Then?" She looked up at him, almost surprised. "I met you."

The green numbers said 2:01. He could start the car, drive back to the lights of town, let her out somewhere. He could go home, wake Carla and tell her he was sorry, tell her everything was going to be all right.

He heard upholstery and clothing sliding against each other, felt her shift her position and turn toward him in the dark. "You're a nice guy," she said, her voice suddenly closer. "You don't think you are, but you are." He felt her hand touch his thigh and he jumped.

"I've got to go," he blurted the words out. The rain had stopped. He felt the silence and darkness outside pressing against the windows of the car like it might crush them.

"What's the matter?" she said. "What are you afraid of? It's the noise, isn't it? That noise inside your head? I hear it too, sometimes." He backed away from her, cold terror rising up his spine. "Don't worry," she whispered. "It'll go away. I can make it go away." He heard her voice coming closer to his face in the dark, her hand sliding up the inside of his thigh. He started to push it away.

Suddenly she was scrambling backwards across the seat and away from him, her eyes staring wild with terror at the window behind him. *"Oh God!"* she was shrieking. *"You bastard! Why don't you die? Why don't you fucking die?"*

He grabbed her by the shoulders and shook her. "Stop," he shouted. "Stop it!" all the while fighting the horrible urge to turn around and face what she was seeing in the window behind him. She kept screaming and flailing at him with her thin arms. One of them struck him hard in the mouth. Pain and rage flooded his brain, pushing out the paralysis that had been holding him. He hit her across the face with his open hand, but she kept screaming and thrashing like she couldn't hear him, like he didn't exist, so he hit her again, feeling the sting in his hand and the hot surge of adrenaline through his veins. *"Shut up,"* he shouted in a voice he barely recognized as his own. *"Shut up, you bitch! Crazy fucking bitch!"* He heard her clawing at the handle, then the door behind her swung open and she tumbled out weeping into the dark.

Cursing, he opened the driver's door and stumbled out in time to see her running deep into the woods. He started running after her, following the trace of her white shirt disappearing in the darkness ahead of him. Trees rushed at him and he dodged to avoid them, all the while trying to keep his eye on that glimmer of white growing smaller and smaller between the trees. Soon he couldn't see it at all.

He staggered to a halt, his breath ragged and burning in his throat and chest. He started to call her name then realized with a small feeling of horror that he couldn't remember it.

The woods in front of him were a thick impenetrable blackness. When her name finally came to him, he called out and the sound of it was just as awful and hopeless as he was afraid it might be. He looked up and saw the rain clouds reflecting a faint light from the town that was not so far away. That thought and the dim gray glow above gave him the little bit of courage he needed to start walking forward.

It was so dark, he could feel a tree materializing out of the blackness before he could see it, so he walked with his right hand raised in front of him, like a blind man. He could still feel the sting in the palm of his hand where he'd hit her. He'd never hit a woman before.

He walked deeper into the darkness, surrounded by the cold green smell of the river he couldn't see and another smell he remembered from long ago, the raw metallic smell of red clay. He'd grown up with it in the fields and riverbanks near his home; he remembered how it stuck to his shoes and marked his clothes with rusty blood-colored stains his mother had said you could never wash out. It was sticking to his feet now; he could hear the slight sucking sound as he walked.

When he realized how far he'd come into the woods he stopped walking. He stood still, trying to fight back the panic rising inside him, and listened. The blood was pounding so loud in his ears, he had to wait until it slowed down – when it did, all he could hear was water dripping from the branches onto the thick carpet of dead leaves all around him. Then, another sound, more rhythmic, slow and steady. Something was walking toward him.

He turned back toward where he'd left the car, walking fast, fighting the urge to break into a run. He strained his eyes to see some sign of a clearing ahead, and for a terrible moment he thought he'd gone in the wrong direction. When he finally saw the car materialize out of the darkness in front of him, his breath caught in his throat like a sob and he broke into a run. Something caught his foot and he fell hard on his face, knocking the breath from his lungs. He scrambled to his feet, slipping in the mud and wet leaves, ran the last few yards and clawed at the door handle, praying that he hadn't locked it. That was the moment when he was most afraid – reaching out to take hold of the door handle, feeling the whole dark woods rushing up behind him.

He slid into the driver's seat and turned the ignition key, taking comfort in the sound of the engine revving as he stepped on the accelerator. He threw it into reverse and backed out fast toward the road, tires spinning and spewing wet gravel and mud. He knew that the scratching and clawing sounds he heard on the roof were only low-hanging tree branches, but the sound made him want to scream.

He felt the rear wheels bounce hard over the edge of the asphalt road, then the front wheels, and he was free and clear on the highway. He threw the car into drive and stepped down hard on the accelerator. It was only then that he let himself look behind in the rear view mirror, but he saw nothing but the thin gray ribbon of highway disappearing behind him and the black woods on either side.

All the way back to town he had the feeling that someone or something was following him. He checked the rear view mirror and saw nothing, no headlights on the dark, winding road behind him. After several miles, a horrible thought came to him, like one of those stories they'd been telling at the bar – that whatever he felt behind him was in the car with him. He twisted around once to look in the back seat and saw nothing, but the feeling would not go away.

He looked down at the green numbers on the dashboard. 3:45.

He wanted to go home. Home, he thought. He would go home and find Carla. He'd tell her he was sorry, tell her that he loved her, that everything was going to be all right.

When he pulled into the small gravel lot behind the old white apartment building, the windows were dark. He turned the key and entered quietly. The front room was empty. He made his way carefully to the back bedroom and paused in the doorway, peering inside. Even before his eyes adjusted to the dark, he could tell the bed was empty. It hadn't even been slept in. He walked toward the small bathroom, put his hand on the doorknob and said, "Carla?" No answer. He opened the door slowly, fighting back a sudden surge of panic at what he might find. Empty.

He turned on the bedroom light, the sudden illumination more harsh than comforting, and looked for a note, but there was nothing. He went over to the old battered dresser, pulled the drawers open and saw that Carla's clothes were still there, neatly folded. He ran his hand over them as if to make sure they were really there, touched a hardness that felt out of place but familiar. His hand slipped beneath the soft blouses and pulled out the gun he'd forgotten was there. He stared at it in his hand for a long time then closed the drawer.

He went back into the front room and turned on the lights and felt a freezing terror grip his throat at what he saw – blood-red footprints all over the carpet, red fingerprints smeared across the doors and light switches. Then he looked down and saw the last traces of red clay still on his hands, the rusty stains on his shirt and pants, the dank, earthy smell of it all over him.

He sank down to the floor in the middle of the room, looking at the red stains all around him, blinking in the harsh light. A thought came to him and would not go away, that not only was Carla not here, she had never been here. And he had never been here either. None of it had been real. The roaring white noise in his head had come back louder than before and he squeezed his eyes shut, willing it to go away.

The sound of gravel crunching and popping under someone's tires brought him back, and his hand flew up to the light switch and plunged the room back into darkness. He peered out of the window and saw a car he didn't recognize parked at the end of the driveway, its headlights dark.

He opened the screen door carefully, slipped out into the dark and crept along behind the bushes, keeping close to the side of the house. Whatever had followed him from the woods was very close now. He could barely feel the gun hanging at his side, like it had become part of his hand. When he stood and stepped out of the bushes he could no longer feel his own body, as if the space where he had been before was hollow.

The car windows were fogged up, but he could still see two heads in the front seat, very close to each other, one with familiar curly hair silhouetted against the streetlight pouring in from behind. In the reflection in the passenger window he saw what they would see – a figure with hollow eyes standing outside in the dark, blood-red stains all over a white shirt, one arm raised and pointing, mouth open as if at any moment it might start screaming.

a face in the trees

The first time Alma saw Kalutara it was from the air. Looking down from the window of the airplane, she could see dark ridges of jungle vegetation that looked more black than green, then the multi-colored rooftops of houses that made her think of toy blocks scattered by a child's careless hand.

"Look, sweetheart," she said. "Want to see?"

Alma noticed the thin white wires trailing from her daughter's ears. "Sweetheart…" She touched Mia lightly on her arm. The girl removed one ear-bud from her right ear and looked at her mother with sleepy eyes. It had been a long flight for both of them.

"What…?"

"We're here," Alma said. "Look."

Mia leaned across her mother to peer down through the small window, and once again Alma breathed-in the sweet animal scent of her daughter's skin and hair, and felt the warmth of her young body pressed against hers. Rubbing her hand up and down Mia's bare arm, Alma looked down and saw goose-pimples on the pale, smooth skin.

"Are you cold, sweetheart?" Alma said. "Do you want Mommy to get your sweater?"

"No," Mia said. "I'm not cold."

"Here," Alma said, wrapping her arm around the little girl's shoulders and pulling her close. "I'll warm you up."

"I said I'm not cold, Mommy," Mia complained, but didn't pull away. Alma drew Mia closer, then she felt that dropping sensation in the pit of her stomach as the plane began its slow descent toward the colorful rooftops and dark green trees below. They'd both be warm soon enough.

You're going to love Sri Lanka, she'd told Mia back in New York. *It's really beautiful there.* Mia had dutifully examined the pictures Alma showed her and asked only one question. *Are there any other children there?*

The truth was that Alma had plenty of pictures of Sri Lankan children. The free clinic she'd helped to establish in Matara six years earlier provided care for children with varying degrees of malnutrition, even leprosy. Those were not the kind of pictures she wanted Mia to see.

Alma was glad this was going to be a short visit, not a six-month stay like before. Just a month, maybe two, long enough for her to examine the potential site for the new clinic and facilitate negotiations with contractors and local authorities. Meanwhile, there were beaches and boat-rides and plenty of things for her and Mia to do together. It was going to be wonderful. More than wonderful – it was going to be perfect. Alma was going to make sure of that.

The judge who had finally awarded Alma sole custody of Mia had done so, Alma thought, reluctantly. Mark's attorney, a young woman with platinum blond hair and too much makeup, had argued that Alma's job made it impossible to provide a stable home for her child. Coordinating non-profit humanitarian relief programs around the world might be admirable, the attorney had conceded, but the world's poor and needy were not a mother's only responsibility.

Mark had said it less diplomatically in one of his angry emails. *You're not going to drag my daughter off to another one of your fucking third world countries.* Now, whenever she had a vision of Mark's stricken face in the courtroom when the judge had read his decision, or the angry look he'd given her afterwards, all she had to do was look down at her side and see Mia's small body next to hers, smell her skin and hair, and think, *This is worth it.*

The streets of Kalutara were a slow-moving riot of poverty, color, and chaos. Mia clung to Alma's arm on the cab ride from the airport, eyeing people on the street with fascination and suspicion. "Look, sweetheart," Alma said, pointing out the beautiful saris that the women wore. She loved the easy, natural way they wore them, how the bright garments almost seemed to be part of their bodies, like the wings of large, colorful birds.

When they got to the house and saw a woman in a red sari standing silently in the doorway, Mia clung even harder to Alma's arm. When they reached the doorway, the woman put her palms together in front of her chest, lowered her eyes, and spoke in a quiet, dark voice, "Vaanga. Vanakkam."

Alma returned the gesture. "Thank you. Hashani, this is Mia. Mia, say hello to Hashani. The way I showed you."

Mia hesitated for a moment, staring up suspiciously. Then she brought her palms together in front of her chest and said the word Alma had taught her. "Vanakkam." Hashani smiled, deep wrinkles exploding around her dark eyes.

After helping the driver unload their luggage, Hashani went into the kitchen and started preparing dinner. The house was soon filled with the heady smells of cardamom and cumin. Mia kept her distance from the strange new woman until Hashani noticed and handed her a small piece of baked dough. Mia nibbled at it suspiciously, then ate it all.

"Mung kavum," Hashani smiled.

After that, Mia seemed more curious than fearful, and followed Hashani from room to room as she went about her duties. When Hashani brought the big bowls of steaming, fragrant curry to the table, Alma thanked her but did not ask her to join them. The woman disappeared silently into the back part of the house. She saw Mia's eyes follow her, frowning curiously.

"Mommy," Mia asked, "Why isn't Hashani eating with us?"

"Because," Alma smiled, "That's not the way they do things here." Mia held her spoon limply and stirred the curry slowly without eating. "What's the matter, sweetheart?" Alma asked.

Mia shrugged. "I'm not hungry."

Alma knew it had been a long day for her daughter, stealing out of the city under the cover of darkness, then an eighteen hour plane ride to a strange place.

"If you want to go lie down now, sweetheart, that's okay."

Alma got up and walked Mia back to her bedroom. She'd brought posters of Mia's favorite movie characters, but there hadn't been time to put them up, so the walls were still blank and cold-looking. A thin crack ran in a crooked trail across the ceiling over the bed in the shape of a lightning bolt. It made Alma think of storms, earthquakes, and falling plaster.

Alma sat, rather heavily, on the edge of Mia's bed and patted the mattress with one hand. Mia crawled in next to her and curled up at her side. "Mommy," Mia said, "are there hurricanes here?"

"No, sweetheart," Alma said, realizing sleepily that she wasn't sure if this was true or not. She pulled Mia closer to her side, stretched her legs and felt her muscles begin to relax. Strange words and phrases circled in her head, signs that part of her brain was already dreaming. When Mia spoke aloud, it startled her.

"Mommy. I want to go home."

And there it was. The thing Alma had been dreading. She was dismayed by the flash of anger she felt. *You're with me*, she wanted to say. *I'm your home.* Instead, she simply held Mia closer and stroked her hair until she felt the child's body relax in her arms. Then fatigue and the long day took her, and she fell asleep with the image of that lightning-bolt making a white, jagged trail across the inside of her eyelids.

In Alma's dream the skies were black and filled with birds. When they drew closer and began to strike her face and hands, she saw that the birds were scorched leaves, pieces of burnt paper and black ash. There was a fire somewhere. It was getting closer, but she couldn't tell which direction it was coming from. She looked for Mia but couldn't find her. The air grew thicker and thicker with flying soot and ash. Alma knew that by the time she saw the fire, it would be too late to outrun it.

Alma woke to the smell of smoke. She was startled at first to find Mia sleeping peacefully next to her, then remembered that she'd fallen asleep in her daughter's bed. The dream had vanished, but the smell of smoke was real.

Alma got up and walked to the kitchen, but the smell was fainter there. She followed it down the hall to the door of Hashani's room. Alma was about to raise her hand to beat on the door, when she recognized the pungent scent of incense. She heard Hashani's voice muttering on the other side. Probably some kind of religious ritual. But there was something odd about the woman's voice, something troubled and troubling. For a moment, Alma thought she recognized the sound of crying, and for the second time she almost knocked on the door. But the thought of intruding and embarrassing the poor woman stopped her, and she turned and walked down the hall to her own room.

Later at breakfast, Alma watched Hashani closely, but the woman went about her chores with the same stone-faced deliberation, making Alma doubt what she'd heard earlier.

The truth was that she couldn't afford for anything to be wrong. Alma had to make sure that construction was underway on this new clinic before the rainy season arrived. She hated leaving her daughter with a stranger, especially so soon after arriving here. But the woman's references had been good, she was supposed to be professional and reliable.

A white car was waiting in front of the house. A young man in a white suit and wire-rimmed spectacles was standing by the car and smiled as she approached.

"Mrs. Randall?" When she nodded, his smile grew even bigger. "I am Doctor Kumar."

Alma tried to hide the surprise on her face. "From the university? It's a pleasure to finally meet you in person."

"You are shocked," he smiled. "I look more like a doctor's son than a doctor, it is true?"

"There's no crime in being young," Alma said.

"Then we agree," he smiled. "Please…" He opened the car door for her to get in, came around and sat next to her, spoke a few words in Sinhalese to the driver and the car pulled away from the curb and into the flow of traffic.

"I didn't realize you were coming to meet me," Alma said.

"In this part of the country, it is considered improper for a woman to be traveling unaccompanied," Dr. Kumar smiled. "That is my very good fortune."

The car rumbled and bounced over the rough road. Alma glanced out the window at the buildings that looked like they were made of plywood and cardboard, some painted sky-blue and lavender like Easter eggs. It looked like the least little wind could blow them all away. Men on mopeds and bicycles flashed by and were gone.

"Who will be at the meeting this morning?" Alma asked.

"Everyone except the representative from the Provincial Council. He will not be there."

"This is the third of these meetings that they've missed, is that correct?"

"That is correct."

Alma felt annoyance rising. "Don't they *want* this clinic?"

"Oh yes, they want the clinic. The thing is, the Provincial authorities want to prove that they are just as important as the Central Government."

"And that's why they're not coming."

"That is one way of putting it."

Alma turned her face away and looked out the window so Dr. Kumar couldn't see her expression. Political infighting and petty power struggles were all part of the process – she knew that. She'd faced the same kind of thing before in Matara and had still managed to get the job done.

But this time was different. Last time, she was alone – now she had Mia. She'd promised Mia they would be going home in a month. Now she could see that month stretching into two months, then three, then four, five, and six. She'd promised Mia a good time here, not a mother who was always gone, not endless days and nights in the company of a stranger.

"So," Dr. Kumar said, "The house. It is to your liking? Your belongings have all arrived?"

"Yes, thank you," Alma said. "The woman. The one you hired to help me…"

"Yes. She is also to your liking?"

Alma stopped. She didn't know how to ask what she wanted to know. "Yes," Alma finally said. "Yes. She seems fine."

When Alma returned to her house later that night, tired and discouraged, she was surprised to see Mia standing outside by herself, clutching her favorite doll close to her chest. As Alma got closer, she could see her daughter's eyes were wide and glassy-looking, her lips twisted into an eerie smile.

"Sweetheart," Alma said, "what are you doing out here?"

"Hold my baby…" The child's voice was an eerie, raspy whisper.

When Alma bent down to take the doll, Mia suddenly threw her arms around her neck, snarling like a wild animal. Alma felt the girl's wet, sharp teeth gnawing at her throat, and pushed her away.

"Stop!" she cried out, "Jesus, Mia, what are you doing?"

Mia kept staring up at her with the same wild-eyed expression. *"I am Mohini, the Lady in White. You hold my baby, then I drink your blood and eat you."* The child's voice, raspy and deep, made Alma's spine crawl.

"Sweetheart, stop talking like that – you'll hurt your throat." Mia kept staring up at her mother, the crazed expression starting to fade.

"Where did you *hear* that?" Alma asked.

"Hashani," Mia said in her normal voice. "Hashani told me a story."

Taking Mia's hand, Alma led her daughter inside. The lights had not been turned on yet, and it was dark and quiet inside the kitchen. No smell of onions or curry.

"Wait here, sweetheart," Alma said. Then, realizing she still had Mia's doll in her hand, she gave it back to her. Mia took the doll and looked down at its plastic face with a disapproving expression, as if it had said or done something wrong.

Alma walked quickly down the short hallway to Hashani's room. Once again, she could smell the scent of incense seeping through the closed door. For a moment she hesitated as she had the last time, then knocked firmly. No answer. She was about to knock again when the door opened. Hashani stood in the doorway, looking at Alma with a blank expression.

"Why was Mia outside by herself?" Alma asked.

Hashani kept looking at Alma strangely, as if this question did not make sense.

"I don't want my daughter outside by herself. Do you understand?"

Hashani nodded and kept looking at Alma as if she was waiting for something.

"Mia said you told her a story. About…the White Lady. Did you tell her that story?"

"Yes." No apology or defiance in the woman's voice. Her face was unreadable.

"Well…I don't think that's the kind of story you should be telling a young child. I mean, I know it's part of your culture…" The more Alma spoke, the more frustrated and ridiculous she felt. "Don't leave my daughter alone like that again," she said, then added, "Please." She waited for an answer but Hashini said nothing, so Alma just stood there, taking the unwavering gaze from the woman's eyes.

Later, when Alma was kissing her daughter goodnight, she heard Mia's voice, small and soft in the dark. "Mommy?"

"Yes, sweetheart."

"I'm sorry. I'm not really Mohini. I would never really eat you. Don't be scared. Please don't be scared of me, Mommy." Alma thought she could hear tears in Mia's voice. She sat down next to the child and gathered her up in her arms.

"Of course not, sweetheart. Mommy's not scared of you. Don't worry, it's okay." When words failed her, she kissed Mia's forehead again and again until she could feel the child relax in her arms.

But when she finally stood up to leave, she knew – it was true. She had been afraid of Mia. For that one split second when she didn't understand what was happening, she had been afraid of her own daughter. And Mia had seen it.

Dr. Kumar knew all about the White Lady. "Oh yes," he said over tea after one of their lengthy committee meetings, "there are many stories like that. Mohini, the White Lady. Kalar Kumaraya, the black prince. Mahasona, the shape-shifting demon…"

"Where did you hear these stories?"

"My brothers. They told me. They were older, so it was their job to frighten me. They heard these stories from my parents, from my aunts and uncles. It was their job to frighten all of us."

"Why?"

Dr. Kumar's friendly smile flickered out. Alma noticed his eyes dart nervously around the room before they came to rest again on his teacup. "My parents, their brothers and sisters. They grew up in a very difficult time. They call it the *beeshanaya*. The terror. Many people, men, women, and children, were kidnapped and killed in the war. My mother's two older brothers were taken that way."

"I'm sorry," Alma said. "This was all mostly…before your time, I imagine?"

"Not entirely…" Dr. Kumar frowned. "When I was a student at the university… It is a very beautiful place. Very clean and modern. The war, the attacks and kidnappings…we thought of them as something that happened far away in the north, in the country." Dr. Kumar paused. "There is a fountain at the university, at the center of the campus. A round pool. Very beautiful, very peaceful. The students enjoy relaxing and sharing their lunch around it. One morning we woke to find that there were severed heads all around the pool. The Tigers had come in the night and put the severed heads of their enemies all around the pool so we would wake and see them."

"My God…"

"Yes." Dr. Kumar shrugged. "It was a very difficult time for everyone. And these stories…" Dr. Kumar took a sip of his tea, grimaced as if it was cold and bitter, then set it down again. "People want to keep their children safe. They tell them these stories to keep them home at night. A lady in white who drinks the blood of careless travelers. A man who can change into a black dog. Ghosts who hide in the trees and wait to attack you. These things, I think, are easier for children to picture and understand. Sometimes I think they are easier for all of us to understand."

When Alma returned home that night, she found a note in Mia's careful childlike script saying that she and Hashani had gone to the market. It felt like all the heat of the day was trapped inside the house.

As Alma went around opening the windows, she was surprised to see something balanced on one of the windowsills outside. She looked closer and saw that it was one of her dinner plates, and that it held small pieces of what looked like fried food, all carefully arranged.

Puzzled, she brought the plate inside and was about to throw the food away when a faint sound caught her attention, a muffled humming. At first she thought it was or some kind of motor or engine, maybe the sound of water groaning through the pipes of the house. She listened more closely and heard that the sound had a *human* quality, like a voice, or many voices all together.

Alma followed the sound to the door of Hashani's room, then slowly pushed the door open. The voices rushed out, each one reaching like a long tendril bending and twisting through the air to wrap itself around her. When Alma saw that the voices were coming from a small, old cassette-player on a table in the corner of the room, she walked over and punched the off-button. Silence fell, almost as deafening as the voices.

Alma heard a strangled breath behind her. She turned and saw Hashani standing in the open doorway, her normally stoic face contorted in shock, embarrassment, and fear. Before Alma could apologize, Hashani pushed her aside and began frantically stabbing at the buttons on the cassette player with trembling fingers. The strange sounds exploded, flooding the room, and Alma fled into the hallway where the voices followed her, Hashani's among them, like the cry of a trapped animal in pain.

Dr. Kumar arrived around seven. He spoke with Hashani in her room for almost an hour while Alma played with Mia outside. When it grew too dark to see, he came to the front door and signaled for Alma to come in.

Alma took Mia to her bedroom. When she came back out to the kitchen, Dr. Kumar had made tea. He set two cups on the table and motioned for her to sit down. His professional smile was in place, but his face looked weary and a little pale.

"Is she alright?" Alma asked.

"She is alright now," Dr. Kumar said, carefully stirring some cream into his tea. "Hashini is a good woman. But she is troubled. She has worked for my family for many years."

"She cries," Alma said. "Every night."

"Yes, I imagine she does…" Dr. Kumar put his tea cup down and folded his hands carefully before he began to speak. "You should know this. Hashani had a daughter. A beautiful girl. She would be a grown woman now. She was killed in the war. Kidnapped and murdered."

"Oh my God, I'm so sorry…"

"Yes. It is very sad." Dr. Kumar scowled down at his hands, gathering his words. "Hashani believes that her daughter's ghost follows her. She believes that her daughter's ghost is very angry with her."

"She really believes that?"

"It is a common thing. Many people here feel the same thing. People who have lost their loved ones. Have you heard her chanting?"

"Yes," Alma said, remembering her first night in the house. "Yes, I have."

"She is chanting so that her daughter's ghost will not be angry with her. She is afraid because it is not working. Hashani needs the monks to come and chant the *pirith*. But she cannot afford it. Many poor people cannot. So they chant themselves. All night they do this. Or they play tapes of the monks chanting instead. This is the tape you heard. But this is not working either."

"How do you know?"

"Hashani told me. Many nights she has played it. And every night she sees her daughter's ghost in the trees outside her window. Have you found food outside your house?"

"Yes. Today."

"That is for her daughter too. Hashani cries because her daughter's ghost will not eat the food she gives her."

"What will she do?"

"If she cannot afford the *pirith*, she will call the *yakadura* to trap the daughter's ghost and bury it. Maybe destroy it."

"She would do that? To her own daughter?"

"It is what you would call a last resort. It is not a thing anyone would choose to do," Dr. Kumar shrugged again. "But the living must go on living."

Alma glanced down the hallway at the closed door to Hashani's room.

"She asked me to convey a message to you." Alma looked up, startled by Dr. Kumar's words. "She wanted to say this to you herself, but her English is not the best, as you know, so I offered to say it for her." He cleared his throat and continued. "She wishes to thank you for your kindness, and asks for your forgiveness. She hopes that, since you are a mother yourself, you will understand."

After Dr. Kumar left, Alma went to Hashani's door and knocked gently. A moment later, the door opened slowly and Alma caught a glimpse of Hashani's dark eyes looking up into hers, then she sat at the edge of her narrow bed, hands folded in her lap, waiting. When Alma reached into her pocket, pulled out the roll of money and held it out, Hashani looked at it with alarm.

"Here," Alma said. Hashani did not move, so Alma crossed the short space between them and laid the bills in the woman's lap.

Hashani stared at them for a long moment, then looked back up at Alma, a stricken look on her face.

"I leave now?" Hashani said, "Or in the morning?"

"No! No," Alma said, realizing what the woman thought the money was for. "I don't want you to leave. This…" she nodded toward the roll of bills on Hashani's lap, "This is for your daughter." Alma pointed toward the cassette player, quiet now in the corner. "For *this*," she said, "For her. For you."

Alma saw a flash of understanding in the woman's eyes, and had to look away. She waited in silence. When she realized what she was waiting for – the outpouring of thanks, the tears, the clasping and kissing of hands – she felt foolish and ashamed, and turned to leave.

She glanced back at Hashani on her way out the door and saw her still sitting on the edge of her bed, the money still in her lap, her face lowered. For a moment, Alma wanted to go back and sit down beside her, take the woman's hands in hers. *The thing you're afraid of,* she wanted to say. *The thing you think is your daughter. It's not her. Do you understand? It's not her.* Instead, she turned and left Hashani sitting in silence.

The next day was Christmas. Alma had done the best she could to create a Christmas for Mia. An artificial tree she'd found in the market stood in the corner of their front room, decorated with gold tinsel, sparkly blue and red balls, and big red bows that looked like butterflies.

After dinner, Alma brought out the package she'd been keeping in her luggage and handed it to Mia. "Merry Christmas, sweetheart." Mia opened the package and stared at the bright purple, patterned cloth folded inside. "It's a sari," Alma said. "Just like the girls here wear. Do you like it?"

For a moment Mia didn't respond, and Alma's heart froze. She couldn't bear to see Mia disappointed. Not on their first Christmas together like this. Then a big smile broke out across Mia's face. "It's beautiful, Mommy!" Mia said, lifting the sari out of the box. "I love it – thank you!"

Alma felt a wave of relief and gratitude wash through her. "I'm glad you like it, sweetheart," she said. "Maybe tomorrow Hashani can show you how to put it on."

At midnight, thousands of firecrackers started going off like gunfire in the streets outside. Mia moaned and stirred, but Alma pulled her closer, and they both lay still until the loud racket outside finally dwindled and ceased.

The following day, Alma was supposed to fly out to inspect the clinic site seven miles inland. Alma knew that today was the day Hashani planned to go to the temple and request the pirith ceremony for her daughter's spirit. Alma couldn't take Mia with her, so she'd asked Hashani if she would mind taking Mia with her to the temple. She'd felt guilty asking, but there was nothing else she could do.

"Can't I go with you?" Mia asked. "Please?"

"Sorry, sweetheart. There's only room for two people in the helicopter. And I don't know how to fly a helicopter, do you?" Mia scowled and shook her head. "Okay, then. I'll be back in time for dinner. Hey, maybe Hashani can show you how to put on your sari."

Mia disappeared with Hashani into the back room. Five minutes later when they both came back out, Alma was stunned by how beautiful Mia looked wrapped in the purple cloth. Hashani had also fixed Mia's hair in a traditional knot at the back of her head.

When they walked out the door together, Alma saw Mia's hand slip into Hashani's and felt a tug of something like jealousy at her heart. But this was good, she reminded herself. After all, she had responsibilities, and Mia could not always be with her – it was good for her to learn that.

An hour later Alma was sitting in the passenger seat of the helicopter she'd chartered to take her to the clinic site. The pilot was a friendly Muslim man who'd greeted her warmly and promised a quick flight.

The helicopter engine and rotors thudded loudly, a physical rhythm she could feel pounding in her head and chest like another heartbeat. The landscape rolled slowly beneath them, the same stretch of white sand and black-green masses of jungle she'd looked down on from the plane when they'd first arrived. Alma tried to pick out their house from the many others below, but she could not. She did spot a gleam of gold that she knew was the roof of the temple, and wondered if Mia and Hashani had reached it yet.

Suddenly there was an explosion of harsh static from the pilot's radio, frantic-sounding voices shouting things Alma couldn't understand. The pilot clawed at the microphone and shouted back in Tamil.

"What is it?" Alma tried to raise her voice over the noise, but the man either couldn't hear her or couldn't answer. In another moment, she saw the reason. Below them, the ocean was rolling in over the land like a dark green curtain being drawn closed. Horrified, mesmerized, she watched the long, dark line moving slowly and inexorably from right to left like the shadow of night passing over the earth, setting everything it touched into motion. Houses, cars, buses, a thousand other objects too far away to identify, all suddenly set into boiling, churning frenzy wherever the great moving line of the sea touched them. She kept waiting for the dark green shadow to stop moving but it would not. It looked like it was going to keep going forever.

The pilot was still shouting into his microphone, tears streaming down his face from under his sunglasses. Alma looked down and saw the dark green wall overtake the gold roof of the temple below. It turned slowly and then went spinning away, a shiny piece of flotsam surging and churning among all the rest. That was when something broke inside of Alma, and she started screaming. She screamed and screamed while the dark green line below kept moving, slowly, mercilessly, erasing the world.

Alma could not remember her return to earth, or those first frantic hours that passed like the fragments of a nightmare. When the images began to break through, it was worse than anything she had ever seen, awake or asleep. Every sight, every sound cut into her, things she saw and things she imagined, until she could no longer tell the difference between the two. Empty pairs of shoes littered the streets like fallen leaves, young boys gathering and sorting them in piles. Riderless bicycles, bent and twisted, perched on the rooftops of the houses that were left standing. The rear-half of a bus protruded from the smashed face of a concrete building, its motionless wheels ten feet from the ground.

Alma stayed in Kalutara another two months, haunting the hospitals, temporary camps and medical tents. The first dead child a relief worker showed her nearly tore her in two – by the twentieth, she could no longer feel her own heartbeat. The few stories of people finding missing loved ones still alive came and then stopped. There would be no more miracles, she knew.

The streets were full of people with nowhere to go. Some sat in the ruins of their homes and wept. Others stared into space. They were all around her. The haunted eyes. The stunned faces. The lost and hopeless people of the world. She was one of them now.

Mark had come and left without seeing her. She'd learned that he was staying in Colombo, working with the same agencies she'd worked with. Their only communication was a single text he'd sent the day he left.

How does it feel to be a murderer. Burn in hell you fucking bitch.

When Alma saw the airplane that would carry her back to New York City, she comforted herself with the thought that the plane might crash; then there would be no need to go back and face the empty apartment that was now hers alone.

Just before she boarded the plane, a movement from above caught her eye. She looked up and saw them hanging in the trees. Caught between her and the blazing sun, harsh slashes of color, red and blue, yellow and purple. Empty saris. Animated by the ocean breeze, they trembled and waved at her from on high.

The plane did not crash. It was one of many things that kept going as if nothing had happened. Traffic lights, subways, time-clocks, people on the street, the sun in the sky. Impossibly, unfathomably, they all kept going the way they always had. Every day at the same time, the shadow on her office floor would begin its slow, steady crawl from one side of the room to the other until it swallowed everything.

When Alma could no longer bear to go to work, she stayed in bed and stared into space for hours. The same moving shadow that had driven her out of her office followed her home, where she watched it pass over her bedroom floor again and again.

Alone, thoughts came, thoughts of things she had seen and things she could not stop imagining. Images of Mia right before the wave hit, walking through the foreign streets full of strange sights and sounds, holding a stranger's hand. When that cold dark wall hit them, how long had she managed to hold on to Hashani's hand? Which one of them had let go first?

The vodka bottle that used to wait for her on top of the refrigerator until five o'clock now came down to her desk and stayed. There was no more five o'clock. No more daytime or nighttime.

Alma tried to make the minutes and the seconds slow down to nothing, but somehow she could not make the clock stop. Like everything else, it kept going without her.

An angry buzzing reached her through the depth of sleep. She reached out with one hand and found the source; her phone, cool and smooth and hard against her cheek. The voice on the other end, distant but familiar.

"Mrs. Randall…Mrs. Randall, can you hear me?"

"Yes…" she muttered, not really understanding.

The man's voice spoke again but broke apart into a shower of static noise.

"I…I'm sorry," she said, "I can't hear you. You're breaking up…"

Like fractured glimmers of light, the pieces of the voice came back together for a moment. *I am sorry…it is…it is very difficult. It is very difficult here…"*

"Where are you?" She didn't ask *who are you* – she'd known from the moment she heard the melodious accent and polite voice, shredded and strained thin like it was about to unravel into nothingness.

"There are…there are many of us…many of us here…"

She could hear the static sound that kept rushing up, threatening to swallow him, and realized what she was hearing – the sound of voices, thousands and thousands of voices all calling out at once, blurring together into a rush of wind or water.

The call from her friend Helen came the next morning. "Darling, there's a job opening in Westchester, at Vanderberg Manor. One of those old historic sites. They're looking for a Program Director. You know, public events, overseeing staff…" Alma had listened, only half-comprehending as Helen's voice droned on. "It's not healthcare or human services, but it is non-profit. With your experience, believe me, you could walk right into it."

Alma could hear Helen breathing on the other end, waiting for her answer. On the floor in front of her, the shadow of the afternoon had already started it's slow, steady crawl toward her. She could see motes of dust drowning in the last trapped beams of sunlight.

The train ride from the city was almost two hours long and ran alongside the Hudson the whole way. The sun was low over the Palisades and set the wide river on fire, blinding Alma so she had to turn her face away.

The board of directors had sent a car to the train station. When the great house rose out of the trees in front of her, Alma had to choke back a harsh laugh. The stone towers, the great leaded glass windows that seemed to trap the fire of the setting sun, the Greco-Roman statues posing on the lawn. It all seemed so foolish. So self-important and trivial. She knew that rich people like to build monuments to themselves. What was this one thinking, she wondered, building so close to the water? He must have thought he would never die.

The woman who conducted the interview was young and

obviously impressed by Alma's resume, especially by the many places she'd traveled and lived. "I really envy you," she'd said. "You must have seen so many wonderful things." There was an ornate-looking letter opener on the desk between them, possibly made of bronze. Alma thought of picking it up and plunging it into the young woman's face, into her eyes.

"Yes," Alma said, straightening her skirt and remembering to smile. "So many wonderful things."

The first few weeks Alma told the staff not to disturb her and immersed herself in reading files, old proposals, final reports and correspondence. She started to enjoy the feeling of learning things again, even boring things. But not the people around her. She didn't want to learn about them, or have them learn about her. What was the point?

A realtor had found an apartment less than two miles away. An old three-story brick house, it sat back from the road at the edge of the woods. The apartment was not large, but the high-ceilinged old rooms made it feel larger. She'd brought very little with her from the city, and her footsteps echoed on the bare white walls and wood floors.

It was late October and Alma's staff had begun to decorate the grounds for Halloween. Children from the local school came in long yellow buses for their annual scarecrow-building contest, and soon the south lawn was occupied by an army of awkward-looking figures in mismatched clothes standing in uneven rows against the horizon.

Late one afternoon as Alma was leaving for home, a movement from above caught her eye. She looked up and saw something waving at her from high above in the tree branches – tattered strips of cloth fluttering in the breeze from the river, twisted rags with empty eyes and silent howling mouths. Alma felt a great crack in the earth open up beneath her, a thousand screaming voices threatening to drag her down.

When she could move again, Alma walked back to the office and threw the door open. Her staff looked up with startled faces.

"Those things," she said, struggling to keep her voice even. "Those things up there. In the trees. I want them taken down."

One of the women who handled ticket sales looked up at her and spoke slowly and carefully. "But…it's Halloween. We decorate like that every year…"

"Well, they're ugly. Take them down." Alma saw the looks on her staff's faces and tried to soften her tone. "Please. I want them all taken down by tomorrow morning." She couldn't stand the way they were looking at her, so she left quickly, got into her car and drove away, careful not to look up.

Later that night, Alma awoke suddenly, a sound she must have heard in her sleep still ringing in her ears. She lay there in the darkness, wondering if she'd dreamed it. Then a terrible shriek split the air, pushing her heart into her throat. It was a cry like she'd never heard before, a raw distillation of rage and terror, coming from right outside her window. The shriek came again, freezing the breath in her lungs.

Alma got out of bed and walked across the cold floor to the window. She hesitated, then stepped closer and tried to peer through the glass. Even with the lights turned off in her bedroom, the woods outside were a wall of solid blackness, the shapes of the trees not even visible. The shriek came again, further away this time, it seemed, but she still took a few steps away from the glass and the unseen thing on the other side.

Alma looked over at the green numbers glowing on her alarm clock. 3:47 AM. She climbed back into bed and closed her eyes, waiting for the terrible shriek to come again. When she finally fell asleep, it followed her into her dreams.

The next morning Alma arrived at work exhausted and irritable. The scarecrows that the children had built stood in silent rows along the driveway. With their mismatched ragged clothes and sightless eyes, they reminded her of blind beggars standing in rows along the street.

When she got out of her car, Alma risked a glance upward. She was relieved to see that the branches were bare again, except for the few burnt-looking leaves that were already beginning to fall.

Then she saw it, high above in the farthest branches. One tattered white shape still fluttering in the river-breeze. Even from this distance she could see the mouth frozen open in a silent howl and the hollow black eyes staring down at her accusingly.

"I thought I said I wanted those things taken down," Alma said when she entered the office. Her aide looked up at her, surprised and distracted.

"We did," the woman said. "Yesterday, after you left."

"Well, you missed one," Alma said. She held the door open and glared at her aide until she could see the woman realize what she wanted. With a sigh of barely concealed annoyance, the woman stood up from her desk and followed Alma outside.

"There," Alma said, pointing upward. The woman lifted her hand to her eyes and peered up into the branches above.

"Oh, *that*," the woman said. "That's been up there for years. It's too high for anybody to reach."

"How did it get up there, then?"

The woman shrugged. "Nobody knows. It was there when I got here…it'll probably be there long after we're gone."

After we're gone. Alma knew what the woman had really meant. *After* you're *gone. Why don't you just leave now, you fucking bitch?*

That night the screaming in the trees came back again. Insistent, unrelenting. This time an angry heat filled Alma's veins and she was on her feet, digging through the kitchen drawer for a flashlight. She tried to shine it out the window but the glass threw the light back into her eyes, so she put it down, took hold of the window sill with both hands and dragged it open.

The cold night air washed over her body, along with the thousand night-scents of the woods. The scream came again, clearer and closer without the glass in-between. Alma shone the flashlight out into the trees, watching the wavering cone of pale light illuminate the dead branches like arteries and veins.

The shriek came again, and the light caught two blazing orbs of blind hatred, and below them a gaping red mouth like an open wound.

A wild cry caught in Alma's throat, her hand spasmed and the light veered away from the thing in the trees. When she brought it back, there was only the naked branches and the blackness in-between.

The man with the cherry-picker arrived at noon the next day. Alma stood in the shadow of the great house while the crane slowly stretched itself all the way up to the highest branches. She watched as the man riding in the basket at the tip of the crane reached out, took hold of the white, fluttering thing in his hand and pulled it free. Alma felt a sharp pain like something tearing inside her chest as the thing came loose from the branches.

"What do you want to do with this?" the man asked, holding the ragged white thing out to her. Alma had not thought of that. She had not expected to be asked this question.

She looked closely at the thing in the man's hands without touching it. It was just a rag, a piece of white cloth, probably cut from a sheet long ago, stuffed and tied at one end to give the appearance of a small head. The face drawn on the head was not as fearsome as it appeared from far away. The wide, howling mouth, the staring eyes were still there, but they were not angry. In fact, the expression that the thing wore was more of a look of terror and surprise.

Alma woke in the middle of the night, a sound she couldn't recognize reverberating in the empty room. When her phone rang again, she clawed at it clumsily, managed to push the answer button, and brought it to her ear. A rushing sound filled her head, something coming from far away but getting closer every second. The sound grew closer and louder. In the moment before she cried out and dropped the phone, she realized it wasn't static. It was water. The sound of water rushing toward her at terrible speed.

When Alma woke late the next morning and looked in the mirror, the black circles under her eyes frightened her. Sunlight stunned her when she stepped out of her house. At work, the voices and sounds of her co-workers were too loud and grated on her nerves. She locked the door of her office and sat behind the large antique desk, staring at the piles of unread papers without seeing them.

When she saw the shadow of the afternoon creeping closer across the room, she stood up and left through the back door where her co-workers would not see her.

There was a walking-trail behind the manor that lead down to the river and a footbridge over the train tracks that shook whenever the express commuter train passed beneath it. Alma stopped on the bridge, and instead of looking out over the river, she turned and looked down the train tracks that she knew stretched all the way to the city. She heard the train before she saw it, first two short howls in the distance, then the faint rumbling that grew louder until it seemed to come from all around. Alma closed her eyes and waited.

She knew that a young woman had been killed here last year. When the train passed beneath her, the roaring sound enveloped her and a huge clap of air struck the whole front of her body like a blow. She tried to imagine what it would be like, whether there would be a moment of pain, or if it was possible that there might be no pain at all.

When Alma first heard the sound of knocking outside her apartment door, she tried to ignore it. The walls were thin, and more than once she'd gone to answer her door to find no one there. But this knocking didn't stop. The knock was gentle but insistent, even polite. Alma rose wearily from her chair and opened the door.

At first she didn't understand what she was seeing. The bearded man standing in the hallway looked familiar. His heavy coat was too large for him, and he looked lost in it, like a child. It was the wire-rimmed glasses that made her realize what she was seeing, and the bright smile that broke through the straggly beard. Then, the voice.

"Mrs. Randall…It is good to see you."

Alma clapped a hand over her mouth to stop the sob or scream that rose into her throat. The bright smile dimmed and the dark eyes behind the glasses looked sad. "I am sorry," he said. "I have frightened you. I have tried to reach you by telephone several times, but the connection has been very bad."

"No…please," Alma said, finding her voice, "Please. Come in."

Alma stepped aside to let Dr. Kumar enter. As he passed close by, the urge to touch him or throw her arms around him almost overwhelmed her, and she forced herself to stand still while he carefully removed his winter coat and then glanced around, still looking a little lost.

"Here," she said, stepping toward him to take his coat. "Let me take that."

"Thank you," he said again, the familiar smile back in place. "I realize this must be a shock to you. I apologize. You see, I have been in the hospital at Ampara. For many weeks."

"Ampara? But…they told me…they told me you were not there."

Kumar shrugged. "So many people, unidentified. I'm afraid they did not know who I was. To be truthful, for a while, I did not know who I was myself." Alma noticed for the first time how gaunt his face looked under the patchy beard.

"You are wondering why I am here." His bright smile faltered. "The truth is, there is no place for me there now. The District General Hospital was destroyed. Beruwala, Dharga Town. They are all gone. There are many doctors, like me, but no hospitals. I tried to work in the clinics, in the streets. But I could not live." He paused and took a deep breath before continuing. "My family there…they are all gone now. I have a cousin in New York who offered to help me. So…I have come here. To start over." He looked up at her. "You have come here to start over too."

Alma could only nod. She was grateful he had not mentioned Mia. If he did, she knew that she would break into a million pieces. She felt somehow that this would be unkind to him.

"Please," she said, gesturing toward the kitchen. "Let me make you some tea."

"Yes," his smile returned. "That would be very nice."

After she'd made two cups of tea, Alma brought a carton of milk and set it down in front of Dr. Kumar. He looked up and smiled. "I see. You remember. Thank you." Gazing down into his tea as he stirred it, he said quietly, "I was very sorry to hear about your daughter. She was a beautiful girl."

Alma closed her eyes and waited for the lightning bolt that would strike and erase her. When it didn't, she opened her eyes and felt surprised to see the table still in front of her, the walls still standing around her.

"Can I ask you…" she said, carefully, "why did you come here?"

"I have been thinking about something," he said. "It is something I believed you might understand…" He paused. Alma could see him gathering his words, trying to think of the right way to say whatever he'd come to tell her. "My sister. She was killed in the tsunami."

"Oh no…I'm so sorry…"

"Yes…We were very close, she and I. When I was in the hospital, those first few weeks…I thought I saw her. At night, she would come to my window. I believed I could hear her crying and screaming. Every night, this happened. When I left the hospital, I thought it would be better, but it was not. I could still hear her. Every night. It was terrible. I could not sleep, I could not work. One day I decided that I would walk into the ocean and drown, like she did. I believed that this was what she wanted me to do."

Dr. Kumar paused. "The night before I was going to drown myself, my sister came to me in a dream. She looked as beautiful as she had always been. She said that she had come to tell me something, something very important. *The thing that you hear at night,* she told me, *that thing in the trees. It is not me. Whatever it tells you, whatever you may think. It is not me.*"

Alma was afraid to speak, but she had to know. "Do you still hear it?"

Dr. Kumar glanced away, out the kitchen window where the light was fading in the trees. When he looked back, his jaw was set and his eyes fixed firmly on hers. "Yes. Sometimes. But I do not listen, because I know it is not her." He kept looking into her eyes like he was searching for something. Then he relaxed and sat back in his chair. "That is the thing I have come to tell you," he said. Then he smiled. "Thank you very much for the tea."

Later that day, Alma went to the closet where she'd hidden the ragged thing the man had taken down from the trees. She'd started to throw it away that day, but a sudden feeling of panic had stopped her, and here it had stayed ever since, alone and in the dark. Today when she reached up and took it down, the faded expression drawn on its face looked like one of astonishment. It seemed smaller now, fragile and delicate, like a doll that a child had made.

Carrying the thing in her hands, Alma stepped outside where the wind was making a rushing sound in the trees. She closed her eyes and took deep breaths until her mind felt clear. When she opened her eyes, she saw the branches moving above her, and one oak tree, older and larger than the others. Walking to the edge of the woods, she knelt down at the foot of the tree, laid the poor ragged thing down between the roots, then started covering it up with fallen leaves. She stayed there for a long while, gathering more leaves and letting them fall on the small mound below the tree, smoothing them over with her hands again and again, making it perfect.

That night the screams followed Alma into her dreams and found her naked and alone, curled on the forest floor at the foot of a great tree in a bed of dry leaves. The screams called to her from somewhere deep in the woods, terrible and wrenching in their grief and rage.

This time, Alma did not lay still and listen. She did not hide from the terrible screaming. She rose up to meet it. She ran toward that sound, feeling the change take hold of her. She ran and ran until she found herself rising into the night air in a new body, one with wings to fly and talons to rip and tear and do what must be done.

the sound that
the world makes

They were too old for this – that was the thought that kept coming back to her as she watched the bare trees fly past the car window, the hum of the engine blending with Jerry and Gordon's voices and the ancient-sounding croaking of Peter Gabriel coming from the speakers.

"Daddy, are we there yet?" Gordon said in a whiney kid-voice and then chuckled, cracking himself up. Gordon had always been a lightweight since they'd started these midnight rides back in college. One-toke Gordon. At least some things stayed the same.

"Patience, sonny boy," Jerry boomed in his best fatherly baritone. "Patience…"

Maddy liked how Jerry still retained some of his actor's skill and presence, even though he now used them not on stage but in the lecture hall. Jerry had not planned on being an adjunct professor in the psychology department, nor had Molly planned on being married to one. *Plans change* – that was how Jerry put it. The important thing, he said, was not to be so attached to your plans for the future that you can't handle it when a whole different future arrives.

Jerry's profile against the dim blue light from the driver's-side window could have been the same one captured in the old Polaroid she'd found last week when they were cleaning house. The same proud Roman nose, the same flowing, tousled mane of hair, although occasionally a square of illumination from a streetlight outside would pass across his head and show for a moment the balding forehead, the creases and sagging skin around the eyes, before the light moved on and darkness covered him again.

"Hey, doc…" She turned and saw Gordon handing the joint toward her. She'd already declined twice, but Gordon, like a goldfish swimming around the bowl, kept coming back to the same spot with no memory of having been there before. Good old Gordon.

Maddy shook her head, "No thanks." They didn't smoke that often anymore, so she knew her refusal would not attract attention. Drinking was a different matter. Jerry had already remarked once about her not sharing their nightly bottle of wine. *You making me drink alone again?* She'd pleaded fatigue and a weak stomach – that much was true. Also, she needed a clear head to finish working on her doctorate. Almost two months since her last drink and her head was anything but clear.

"Jerry," she said, "can you roll down the window, please?"

"It's pretty cold out there, sweetheart," he said.

"I don't care," she said, the harshness in her own voice startling her. Then a little softer, "Please."

Jerry pushed the button, the window next to her moved down a few inches and in a second the cold winter air was all around her, numbing her cheeks and filling her lungs. With every breath, she felt the first traces of nausea subside.

"So how long before we get to this place?" Gordon asked.

"Few more miles," Jerry said, with the kind of bold assurance that Maddy knew meant he wasn't exactly sure. "In the meantime, enjoy the pretty lights."

At those words, Maddy suddenly thought of the song that her mother used to sing years ago when her parents drove her around to look at the Christmas lights. She hadn't thought of it…for how many years? It should have been a good memory, even a comforting one. But the searing pain it caused made her want to tear the sound of her mother's voice out of her head.

"Holy shit," Gordon laughed. "Look at *that* one!"

A blaze of light and color appeared on the right and moved toward them. Maddy saw a two story house strung with blinking lights and a dozen or more illuminated plastic figures planted on the lawn; a nativity scene complete with all three wise men, plus a row of open-mouthed Dickensian Christmas carolers, Santa in his sleigh with all eight reindeer, and even Snoopy smiling blissfully in a Santa hat.

"Jesus, where's the Easter Bunny?" Gordon said.

"He's on his government-mandated fifteen-minute break." Maddy could hear the smirk in Jerry's voice. *Here we are again,* Maddy thought. *Enjoying the things we have contempt for – what would we do without them?*

Maddy felt a surge of nausea returning. *Not now,* she thought, *not here.* Why did she agree to come along on this ride? She was too old for this. Too old and too pregnant.

She'd almost told Jerry about it tonight. She'd planned to, like she'd planned to tell him the night before, and the night before that. But then he'd asked her to come along on this stupid midnight ride out to the country and he'd seemed so excited that she didn't want to spoil it. She was angry at herself now for that. For thinking of him first. That was going to have to stop. That was going to have to stop soon.

Another garishly decorated house rose out of the night and moved toward them on the right. Maddy flinched at the chaos of plastic holiday figures clustered together in the snow.

"Are the giant candy canes actually supposed to be *touching* the Nativity scene?" Gordon asked. "Christ, my parents never spent that much money on Christmas decorations in their whole life. What about your family, Maddy. Did they…" Gordon stopped himself even before Jerry's hand reached across the driver's seat to touch his arm. "Shit, sorry…" Gordon mumbled.

"It's okay, man," Jerry said, patting Gordon on the knee. "Betty and Henry were into all this Yuletide stuff big-time. They would have loved all this, right sweetheart?"

Maddy didn't answer. This was Jerry's way of dealing with it, of helping her deal with it. No use tiptoeing around or keeping it hidden. Bring it all out, bring *them* out into the open. It was a way of keeping them alive, Jerry said. And it might have worked. If it hadn't been for that news item in the paper.

It was a single line, a quote from a nameless source, a truck driver who'd seen her parents' car go off the road and over the cliff, who'd *followed the sound of screams to the crash site.* That one line was the worst thing she could imagine, worse, even, than their deaths. It was all she could think about, day and night. She told Jerry and he'd tried to play the therapist with her. That one moment, terrible as it may have been, was not her parents' whole lives. Their lives, he tried to assure her, were more than that, and that one moment could not wipe all that they were. She listened in silence and thought, *but it already has.*

She drank wine and vodka every night to shut off that terrible sound in her brain until the news came from the doctor and she had to stop. No more drinking. No more looking back. Only looking forward to the new life inside her that would be the start of a new life for her too. That was how it was supposed to work, wasn't it? One generation dying to make way for the next? It was natural. But that thought couldn't keep out the feeling that there was still something horrible and unfair about it all.

She glanced up at her own reflection in the passenger window and was instantly sorry. The haggard face, the flesh starting to sag under the eyes and at the jawline. She was going to be forty-one years old in four months. What business did she have giving birth to a child? Who did she think she was? No one ever believes they're as old as they really are. Not even her mother. On one of their last visits, over their third glass of white wine, her mother had admitted that she couldn't believe she was seventy. *I look in the mirror sometimes and I wonder, who is that old lady?* Old age had taken her by surprise. A reasonable, intelligent woman, she had still somehow thought, against all reason, that it would somehow not happen to *her*. Just as she had probably not thought that she would die in a dark ditch by the side of the road, screaming in the crushed wreck of a car…

Maddy squeezed her eyes tight shut and pressed her fists against them, trying to push the thought out of her brain. When she opened her eyes again, things had changed. It was darker outside the car now. All the lights of town far behind them. They were in what Jerry liked to call *the old, real country*. It was a phrase he'd gotten from a book by one of his favorite writers. Agee, she thought it was. Yes, it was Agee. She'd given Jerry a picture of Agee once for his birthday and he'd never put it up; when she asked him why, he said it was a picture of the older, dissipated Agree, his movie star looks destroyed by alcohol, and it made him sad. She wondered if that was why Jerry didn't like to see pictures of himself.

Maddy saw a small, ramshackle wood house with several oblong blobs of ghostly white light standing between the trees. The shapes were vaguely human, with the contour or suggestion of a face, an arm, or a leg, a few smudges of cracked and faded color still hiding in the creases. Maddy could tell which ones were animals and which ones were supposed to be human, but which figure was supposed to be Joseph, which one Mary, which one a wise man or shepherd, she couldn't tell at this distance.

"Wow. How old do you think those are?" Maddy said. The cold

air had made her feel almost normal again. "Guess that's what happens when you can't afford new decorations."

"It's not about that," Jerry said in that all-knowing tone that always annoyed her; tonight it set her nerves on edge. "If those people had a million dollars they still wouldn't throw those things away."

"If they had a million dollars, they would live like fucking trailer trash," Gordon said. Maddy grit her teeth.

"No, no," Jerry said. "That's the *good* stuff. The *real* stuff…"

"You mean it's because they're poor," Maddy said, sounding a little harsher than she meant to. "You think it's cool because they're poor."

No one spoke for a moment. Then Gordon chuckled, "Wow. Someone's grumpy."

"There's nothing *cool* about poverty," Jerry said in his measured teacher's voice. As if she had suggested that there was. "What I love is what they do with what they have. Remember that graveyard in Mexico? Those wooden crosses with the names and dates spelled-out in roofing nails and thumbtacks?"

Maddy remembered stumbling through the desert graveyard with Jerry – was it twenty…twenty-five years ago? Jesus. She'd agreed to split a hit of acid with him, the first and last time she'd ever done that. The little wooden crosses with their thumbtack names made her think of a child's art project, and before long she became convinced that it was a cemetery for dolls. They'd sat on a stone bench and watched the sun turn the Western sky blood-red, and she'd felt like the sunset, or something *in* or *behind* it, was coming to take her. It had been waiting for her – now she was here and it was going to take her with it. She sat there holding her breath longer than she thought was possible, waiting for it to happen, not understanding why it was taking so long.

Jerry was good at seeking out places like that. The strange, out-of-the-way corners of the world. Like the place he was looking for tonight. God only knows where he'd heard about it. Gordon had asked him what kind of search he'd done for it, what the "link" was. Jerry had smirked happily. "No link. No URL. It's completely off the grid." This was typical Jerry. *Off the grid* was where the good stuff was, the *real* stuff, and that was where he was taking them tonight.

"Seriously, Jerry," Gordon asked. "How'd you hear about this place? A hundred and fifty year-old monastery is kind of hard to hide, don't ya think?"

"Not if no one's looking for it. They're a separatist group. They left the Church, or the Church kicked them out. Not sure which. It was a long time ago. So they're really off the map."

"So what's up with this service we're going to see?" Gordon said. "And what makes you think they'll even let us in?"

"Dr. Cosgrove saw it," Jerry said. "About fifteen years ago. He told me about it last year before he retired. He said he went there one Christmas Eve when he was younger, back when he was an adjunct. I asked him how he got them to let him in, and he said he didn't have to do anything. He said they didn't seem to care if he was there or not."

"Yeah? What else did he say? What do they do? Sacrifice chickens?"

"No. He just said it was something he'd never forget for the rest of his life. Probably some kind of archaic form of the Christmas vigil." Jerry took a deep breath and started chanting in his best spooky baritone, *"Kyrie…Domine…Dominus…"*

The hills and trees that had crowded around the sides of the road had begun to fall away. Maddy could sense more than see the barren fields stretching out around them. Occasionally the lights from a far away farmhouse would float by in the distance like the lights of a ship far out at sea.

A Christmas Eve mass. The last time she had been to one was with her parents – how many years ago? She closed her eyes and saw again the glow of candlelight, smelled the scent of pine and hot candle wax. The memory of an old song was stirring inside her chest, almost rising to her throat. What was it? More than once she had awoken with tears on her face from a dream of music so intensely beautiful and moving that she'd thought her heart would burst. Jerry had explained that it was just another trick that her brain was playing on her, that there really was no music, just the sensation of beautiful music that our brains manufacture for us. That didn't seem right to her. Just because she couldn't remember the music, the exact melody or the words, that didn't mean it had never been there.

Looking out at the few stars glittering over the barren snowy fields, it came to her – the child she was carrying inside, this would be its first time in church. She decided it would not be the last. It didn't matter what Jerry said about it. It was what her parents would have wanted. She would give that gift to her child. And to them.

A light appeared far away in the darkness, a pale glow that looked like a single lamp moving slowly across the frozen fields. "There it is," Jerry said.

As they got closer Maddy could make out the shape of a rectangular building far off the road, and that the light was coming from a single window. Jerry slowed down and turned onto a long, narrow road that took them down into the fields and closer to the building. The road had not been plowed and there were no tire tracks in the snow. The tires rumbled and crunched and occasionally banged over deep holes hidden by the snow.

"Shit," Gordon said. "Are we even on the fucking road?"

"Don't worry," Jerry said through gritted teeth as the car banged its way over the rough surface. "We can't get lost. It's right there. All we gotta do is follow the light."

"Follow the light, Jerry… follow the light!" Gordon said in a spooky falsetto.

As they drew closer Maddy could see that the building was made of bricks that had once been covered with white paint, now grown thin and worn away. The roof was flat except for a kind of square tower at one end. The windows were all small and dark, except for one that threw a narrow trail of pale, weak light on the snow.

"Looks more like a prison," Gordon said.

Maddy looked around and saw there were no other cars or trucks in sight. "Are we the only ones here?" she asked.

"Looks like it," Jerry said. "I guess they don't get a lot of visitors out here…"

They all sat in the car for a minute, looking up at the tall, weathered brick walls and the single lighted window above. Maddy noticed that Jerry hadn't turned off the ignition.

"Are those *bars* on the windows?" Gordon said. Maddy looked up at what Gordon was seeing, but the small windows were so dark and grimy it was hard to tell.

"Jerry," she asked, "are you sure this is the right place?"

"Absolutely," he said, finally shutting off the ignition. He sat there for a another few seconds looking at the building. Then he opened the car door. "Come on."

Maddy's legs sank up to the knees in the snow as they plodded toward the building. "Don't these guys believe in shoveling?" Gordon groaned. "How do they get in and out of this place?"

"Maybe they don't." Jerry said what Maddy had been thinking. No cars, no trucks, no vehicles of any kind. No tracks in the snow, which was four days old by now. Under any other circumstances, Maddy would have concluded that the building was abandoned – if it wasn't for the pale yellow light burning in the little window above. As she looked up, Maddy saw a thin shadow pass behind the window, blotting out the light for a second.

"Jerry," she said, taking his arm. "Look – somebody's home."

"Yeah?" he said with a forced-sounding cheerfulness. "See? I told you this was the right place. Come on…"

They approached a double wooden door set deep into the wall, the old wood painted an ugly institutional brown. "Shouldn't there be a bell or a buzzer or something?" Gordon said.

"Do you think this is the right door?" Maddy asked.

"Hey, do you *see* any other door?" Jerry said, sounding strained for the first time. He reached out, took the doorknob in his hand and pushed, and the door swung open a few inches.

"See?" Jerry said. "If they weren't expecting anybody, why would they leave the door open?"

"Maybe because they *weren't* expecting anybody," Maddy said, angry at the stirrings of fear deep inside her. She had wanted this to be beautiful. She had needed that. She still did. And she didn't want anything or anyone to ruin that. "Come on," she said, stepping in front of Jerry. "We don't want to be late."

The first thing Maddy noticed was how cold and empty it was inside. Bare, whitewashed stucco walls. Worn wood floors. No furniture. No decorations of any kind. Not even any sign that this was a church. "Which way is it?" she whispered. She could see ghost-traces of her breath from the corner of her eye as she spoke.

"Shit, these guys don't believe in turning up the heat, do they?" Gordon said.

"Cosgrove said something about a balcony…" Jerry said. A flight of steep, boxy stairs led up the wall on their left to a closed door. Jerry led the way, followed by Maddy, then Gordon. At the top of the stairs, Jerry opened the door and Maddy followed him inside.

She could feel the space below them before she could see it, a drop-off hidden in the dark. She hung back, not wanting to step over the edge until her eyes adjusted. Soon, she saw a faint, throbbing light coming from below. A balcony. They were on a balcony like Jerry had said. Jerry was already standing at the railing looking down and he beckoned her over silently. Maddy walked over to Jerry's side and looked down.

The space below them was filled with row after row of burning candles, casting enormous wavering shadows on the walls. Some of the candles were moving in a line and Maddy saw that they were being carried by men walking slowly toward a plain altar with only with a rough wooden cross nailed or bolted to the wall. The monks all wore plain brown robes and the tops of their heads were shaved in the traditional tonsured style. One of them – Maddy couldn't see which one – was chanting words she couldn't understand but recognized as Latin, the sound of his voice made larger like his shadow in this cavernous space.

Maddy felt Jerry's hand on top of hers where it rested on the railing. "Isn't it beautiful?" he whispered in her ear. She turned and saw his tender smile and felt surprised to realize that he'd done this for her, that she was the reason he'd brought them here tonight. He'd known what she needed. For the first time she felt a surge of warmth and certainty, knowing he would be a good father.

A bell rang somewhere and all the monks joined together in the chant, which was not a song but *like* a song in the way that the tone of their words seemed to reach inside her and move things, touch things. She swallowed the lump that had risen in her throat and took a deep breath, letting the sound of the monks' voices and the glow of a hundred candles take her back to a time before the terrible thing had happened, before she'd read the words that wiped out the happy memory of her mother's and father's lives, far worse than that car wreck had done. She closed her eyes and breathed in the scent of burning candles and could see her mother's face again, young and smiling and looking down at her. *Yes. Beautiful. Isn't it all so beautiful?*

The bell rang again. Maddy opened her eyes and saw four monks appear below from under the balcony, pushing wheelchairs, then two more. Elderly monks slumped in the chairs, small as children, their thin bodies appearing to melt into their brown robes. The monks brought the wheelchairs down the aisle and arranged them in a line directly in front of the altar.

"They must have come from the infirmary," Jerry whispered. Maddy could see one of the elderly monks nodding his head endlessly, another with arthritic hands drawn up under his chin, trembling violently. How kind, Maddy thought. To bring these aged, sick men into this circle of light one night every year. This was how it should be.

Another bell rang. Maddy looked down and saw five more monks appear from below the balcony carrying wheelless chairs by long wooden handles. In each chair sat an ancient-looking monk, more decrepit and emaciated than the last group.

"Jeez, how old are *those* guys?" Gordon whispered.

The monks brought the chairs to the front and sat them down close to the altar. Their backs were turned but Maddy could see the profile of one seated monk illuminated against the candlelight. His sunken eyes were hidden in shadow, his mouth wide open in a kind of frozen, silent howl. A string of spittle hung suspended in his open mouth.

"Wait…wait a minute," Gordon said. "What…"

Maddy looked closer and saw that what was hanging in the monk's open mouth was not spittle. It was a spider web.

"Oh Jesus," Maddy heard Gordon start to whine. "Oh God…"

"No, no…" Jerry was speaking fast in a brittle-sounding monotone. "This…this is…There are churches in Italy…This is what they do."

Maddy couldn't see the faces of the other monks seated in the front but she caught a glimpse of their hands clutching the arms of their chairs, the bones thin and fragile-looking as sticks, the skin bled dry of color and worn paper-thin.

The bell rang again. Two monks appeared carrying a wooden chest about three feet long The chest was decorated with some kind of tarnished gold metal and studded with crude-looking gems that glowed dully in the candle light. As the two monks passed slowly with the chest, Maddy saw the other monks bow their heads, except for the ones seated in the front. The two monks set the chest down on a wooden stand in front of the altar and the chanting stopped.

"Jerry, please, let's go," she said, digging her fingers into his arm. "I want to go."

"Wait…" Jerry whispered, his eyes fixed on the scene below. "Wait…"

The two monks moved to either side of the wooden chest, undid the metal latches and lifted the lid. It took Maddy a moment to understand what she was seeing. Inside the chest on a bed of white cloth was a small child, no more than a baby, dressed in a worn-looking white and gold brocade gown. The child's mouth was open wide and the blackened gums were peeled back from the tiny yellowed teeth. In the hollow eye sockets were two large red gems that reflected the candle light and seemed to wink and move.

The bell rang one more time. Then the monks began to scream. They all stood where they were with their mouths open wide and screamed as though the skin was being flayed from their bodies. The terrible sound rose up and filled the space around her until she could not hear or speak or breathe. She saw Jerry pressing his arms over his ears, his mouth moving like he was screaming too but she could not hear it. She saw Gordon huddled on the floor in a corner, clutching his head and rocking back and forth.

Without looking back, Maddy turned and ran from the balcony into the stairwell where the screaming was somehow even louder. Clutching her hands over her ears, she stumbled down the stairs and almost made it to the door before the terrible sound drove her to her knees. The screaming was coming from the walls around her and from the cold stones beneath her knees where she found herself kneeling and rocking. She knew that even if she opened the door and ran across the frozen field, the screaming would follow her; it would rise up from the ice and snow below her feet and pour down from the stars above, no matter how far she tried to run or how long she lived. The screaming was the sound that the world made, and always would be.

last ride of the night

Cedar Grove Park had been there since before we were born; now it looked like we were going to outlive it. Just another old-school roadside attraction bound for the bulldozer. But for everyone of my generation and at least two generations before us, the name *Cedar Grove Park* conjured up a parade of decrepit, indelible images. Firetrap arcades and ancient rides that smelled of rust and vomit, the racetrack that roared like war and raised a cloud of gasoline and oil-smoke thick enough to blot out the sun. Then there was the zoo. Everyone said they remembered it but no one could call up a clear picture of what they'd actually seen. Instead, we were left with partial impressions, like sifting through the pieces of a jigsaw puzzle and finding only a patch of striped fur, a piece of dusty wrinkled skin like old leather, a single huge eye filled with pain and hatred and no understanding.

It was Sharon's idea to make one last trip before they shut the whole thing down. What I wanted wasn't a return to my childhood, not a ride back into the past. I wanted the shock of contradiction, to have the flaws and falsehoods in my memory confirmed and held up to my face. I knew what I remembered and I wanted to be wrong.

At the foot of the roller coaster was a measuring-stick with a sign, *You must be this tall to ride.* Some kids who weren't tall enough took it hard and had to be dragged away red-faced and screaming. Not me. I loved that stick, just as long as it ruled me out and kept me safe. I remember the day I realized that it wouldn't last, that one day my body would betray me, and there was no way to stop it. I always knew it would happen. Just like I always knew that Ron would come back one day.

Nothing lasts forever. Those were the first words in the only email Ron sent me from Iraq. He'd been gone for twelve months and none of us had heard from him. I'd read the stories in the news, seen photos of the war on the internet, so I'd started to prepare myself for the worst. I think part of me had gotten so used to thinking of Ron as gone, as *really* gone, that when I opened that email it was a shock, almost like he was writing to me from the other side – which, in a way, he was.

Nothing lasts forever. What does that mean? Most people say it means that everything dies, that everything is doomed to disappear. But what if that's not what it means?

Ron never talked much in class when we were in school together. He didn't know how to put his thoughts out there in a way that other people would understand. It hurt him to try. But with me, somehow, it was different. Maybe it was because I never treated him like he was crazy. Or because his kind of craziness was easier for me to understand.

What if there's something that does last forever, and that thing that lasts forever is called "Nothing"? If nothing lasts forever, maybe the only way to last forever is to become Nothing.

Ron didn't say much in his email about what was going on around him over there. Daryl said it was because Ron was probably under orders not to reveal the places he'd been or the things he'd seen. *If he told you, he'd have to kill you.* But I knew it was because whatever was going on inside Ron's head was more interesting to him than what was going on outside it.

How do you become nothing? Some people spend their lives chasing after the wrong kind of nothing. They take drugs, jump off bridges, and never become nothing. They just die. So…what's the right kind of nothing? Maybe it's all around us. Maybe we just need to close our eyes and step into it.

I didn't understand everything Ron was taking about, but I did feel like I knew about *the wrong kind of nothing.* The wrong kind of nothing was all around me. The signs and storefronts of our little town, the streets I'd learned to drive on, the faces of the people I'd known all my life seemed one moment to be full of some kind of important mystery so deep and powerful that I could feel my heart breaking; then the next moment it would all feel empty, flat and meaningless.

More than anything, I felt like I was waiting, like I'd always been waiting – to get out of school, to get away from home, to get out of the job I hated and find the right one. But even though the things I was waiting for didn't seem so important once I finally had them, I still couldn't stop myself from wanting things.

I felt that same *wanting-but-not-having* every time I heard Daryl's voice on the phone. At first I thought that being with Daryl was what I wanted. Lately, it was just getting rid of that feeling of wanting that mattered.

When you're born in a trap, you look for the people who can get you out. It's like you're on one side of the wall and they're on the other, and maybe, if you're lucky, they might reach over and pull you through. That's what Daryl looked like to me at first, especially after Ron was gone. Daryl was a little loud, a little crazy, but at least he was *real* in a way that I was beginning to think Ron had never been.

"You know why you think so much about Ron?" Daryl had said to me one night when we were lying in bed. "It's because you don't know anything about him. He's like a blank piece of paper. Like some kind of fucking coloring book you can fill-in with anything you want."

I'm real, was what Daryl was saying. *This is reality.* The fact that Daryl was married made things even more real, and made that wall he was going to pull me over just a little higher. I wanted to see how he was going to do it. Two years later, I was still waiting.

When I looked down and saw Daryl's name light up my cell phone, I felt the usual rush of excitement, guilt, and worry. But the feeling was weaker now, like a radio signal that's getting too far away to hear.

"Hey, baby." Daryl's usual greeting.

"Hey," I said, the sound of my voice coming back to me over the phone, faint and thin as I felt inside.

"So," Daryl said, "you coming out to the bar tomorrow, right? Seven o'clock? There's gonna be a party…"

"Is Sharon coming?"

There was the pause that I knew meant *yes*.

"I'm sorry," he whispered, like she was standing right over his shoulder. For all I knew, she was. "She's all excited about this party and everything. What am I supposed to do?"

"Yeah? Why don't you just go with *her* then?"

"Jesus, Laurie, why do you have to make it sound like we're in fucking high school or something?"

Because, that's how this makes me feel, I wanted to say. *I'll be thirty years old next month and I feel like I'm in fucking high school.*

"Look, baby," Daryl whispered. "You know it's not gonna stay this way much longer."

"Yeah? How am I supposed to know that?"

"*Because*," he hissed. "Because it *can't*, that's why." Daryl was always bringing me these little passionate assurances every time I backed him into a corner like this. They used to make me angry, sometimes they even made me cry. Now all they did was make me want to lie down somewhere and go to sleep.

"Guess who's coming?" Daryl said. Changing the subject to distract me, I thought.

"I don't know," I said. "Surprise me."

"Ron. Ron's coming."

At the sound of that name, all the words I had inside me went away. I closed my eyes and waited. I was glad we were on the phone and Daryl couldn't see my face.

"Ron's in Iraq," I finally said.

"Not any more. He got back Tuesday."

My mind raced. I was flailing, reaching for something to say, something to feel. I swallowed hard and took a deep breath. "So…the party…it's for him?"

"Yeah. It's Sharon's idea. She wants to throw some kind of big homecoming thing for him. She already bought decorations and everything…" He paused and waited, like he thought the decorations would be the thing that would convince me. "So…you're coming, right?"

"Yeah. I'm coming."

Reading Ron's email was one thing. Seeing him face to face was another, and I spent the rest of the night and all the next day trying to figure out how to get out of it. I thought of getting in my car and driving all night to Cincinnati where my sister had a house with an empty bedroom where I could disappear for a few days. But I knew there'd be questions, and even more questions when I came back – unless I never came back. Unless I just kept driving all the way through Ohio till the sun rose over some town I'd never seen before where I could disappear for as long as I needed to. I shut my eyes and tried to make myself believe in that possibility, but I couldn't. It was like that measuring stick with the sign I remembered: *You must be this tall to ride.* I could avoid what I was afraid of for just so long – but not forever.

Sharon called it a *welcome home* party. I couldn't help but wonder if Ron still considered this his home. The house he'd grown up in was still here, although his mother, who had just died in it, was not. That was the only thing that was bringing him back here. Not the *welcome home* party. Not to see his old friends. Not to see me. Although I couldn't help but worry about that too.

When I walked into the bar and saw the shiny cardboard *WELCOME HOME* banner strung across the wall along with dozens of paper American flags, my heart sank.

"Jesus, Daryl," I whispered, "Ron's gonna hate this. He's gonna take one look and turn around and walk out."

Daryl rolled his eyes at the decorations, like *what can I do about it,* and pushed a bottle of cold beer toward me. Sharon was at Daryl's side, talking a million miles a minute as usual.

"Isn't this *great*?" Sharon said, waving one hand at the cardboard flags and banner. "He's gonna *love* it! Laurie, don't you think he'll love it?"

I took a long drink from the bottle Daryl had just handed me and put on the same fake smile I always wear around Sharon. "It's nice," I said.

"Well, *I* think he's gonna love it," Sharon said, then went rattling on about where she'd bought the decorations, how much they cost, and a hundred other things. It was like listening to a record playing on fast forward. I kept smiling and tried to remember when Sharon's manic phases had started. Or had she always been this way and the rest of us were just too young and crazy ourselves to notice?

"Where *is* he?" Sharon whined, casting a glance at the clock. "He should be here by now."

"I don't know, Sharon," I said cautiously, "Maybe you shouldn't have put all this stuff up. Ron's kind of shy…"

"*Shy?*" Sharon laughed. "Doing all that stuff he's done over there? Seeing everything he's seen? You're telling me he's too shy to come to a little party?"

"Yeah, Sharon," Daryl muttered into his whiskey glass, "That's what she's telling you."

"Well," Sharon said, straightening her back and lifting her chin in an attempt to look serious, "*I* think Ron is the bravest person I know."

And just like that, a picture rose up in my mind so fast that I couldn't stop it – a hot, cluttered room filled with shadows and red light, the silhouette of a small boy standing alone in a doorway… I kept my eyes shut tight until that image left my mind. Then Daryl's voice cut through.

"What do you know about how *brave* Ron is? For all you know, he could be doing his soldiering behind a desk somewhere…"

"No," Sharon shook her head, "not Ron. Ron never hid from anything his whole life."

Daryl chuckled and took another drink of whiskey. He was just being an asshole, but in a way, he was right. What did Sharon know about how brave Ron was? Everything she knew came from movies and things she'd seen on TV. What I knew came from a real place, and a different time.

Ron and I had come to Cedar Grove Park on one of those school trips at the end of the year when the teachers have run out of things to teach. We were about nine or ten. I don't remember how we got separated from the group, if they'd lost us or if we'd just slipped away somehow. The two of us were wandering around the midway, all out of tickets, when a man called out to us from between two vendors' booths. He was wearing a dirty white tank-top stretched tight over his swollen belly, but the rest of him looked thin and scrawny. There were white whiskers on his jaw and his greased-back hair looked a few shades darker than it should have been. "You kids wanna ride?" he said. I noticed he wasn't shouting like the other vendors and barkers; he was keeping his voice low. His long arms had wrinkled like leather in the sun and were crawling with tattoos.

I'd been told not to speak to strangers but what was both obvious and strange to me was how often I was expected to speak with adults who I didn't know; teachers, store clerks, doctors, nurses, policemen. An amusement park vendor, it seemed to me, was no different than any other adult professional who I was expected to treat respectfully; he just wore a different type of uniform.

I explained to the man that I didn't have any more tickets. I could feel him looking down at me. "Don't need no tickets," he finally said. "Last ride of the night, always free."

The man unhooked a chain that blocked our way and gestured for us to enter. I looked at Ron and saw him scowling at the man in a way that struck me as rude. "You comin'?" the man said to him. Ron kept glaring at the man and shook his head. "Suit yourself," the man said and held the chain back for me. I didn't hesitate. I left Ron standing there and slipped right under the chain without looking back. In the years that followed, I wondered how I could have been so reckless. There's no good answer for that, except maybe that I sensed something extraordinary was being offered to me and I didn't want to miss out.

I followed the man down the dark space between the vendors' booths. I was surprised when we passed behind the bumper cars and the tilt-a-whirl, through the loud grinding racket of gears and throttles and the stink of gasoline and oil-smoke.

The man lifted up a flap of canvas and gestured for me to enter. I could see red-colored light gleaming inside and figured it was some kind of fun-house. I hoped it wasn't a haunted ride; I didn't like scary things.

I found myself inside a tent where a couple of red lightbulbs hung from a wire and threw a hellish light over stacks of boxes, old clothes hanging from a pole, and a sagging cot. A terrible animal smell hung in the air and I had to stifle a gag. The man walked over to a table and picked up a bottle that was half-full of something clear that I knew wasn't water. When I asked him where the ride was, he took a long drink from the bottle and looked at me. His eyes looked red and, it seemed to me, a little sad. "Best ride," he finally muttered in a low voice, like he was talking to himself. "Best ride there is."

Then the look on the man's face changed and I realized there was someone behind me. I turned and saw a small body silhouetted in the doorway of the tent. It was Ron. Ron had come back for me.

"Here he is! Here he is!" Sharon's shrill voice brought me back to the present. She'd leapt out of her seat and was practically jumping up and down, looking over my shoulder toward the door.

I was afraid to look. I don't know what I expected to see. Ron hadn't sent me any pictures from Iraq, so for all I knew he might be missing an arm or a leg or an eye, and for a terrible moment I caught myself wondering which would be worse.

The man moving toward our table looked like the Ron I remembered, but changed. His hair was shaved close to his head, making me think of a puppy or a baby bird. I saw with a rush of relief that both arms and legs were still there. Both eyes too, although it did seem to me like something else was missing.

I thought I saw him pause for a split-second, although he never actually stopped moving. It was like I could see him pause *inside*, draw back inside himself. Then he came toward us and we were all standing up and taking turns hugging him. I hung back and took my turn last. Ron took his hugs like a tree, quiet and unbending. The hard muscles I could feel under his green T-shirt were new, the downcast brown eyes that looked up cautiously now and then were not.

"Damn, Ron, you look good," Sharon said when we'd all settled back down into our seats. "Doesn't he look good, Laurie?" I didn't answer, but just managed to smile.

"Jesus Christ, Sharon, stop hitting on him and get him a drink," Daryl said. "What are you drinking, Ron?"

"Beer's good." He spoke in the same quiet, tight-lipped way I remembered.

"Get the man a goddamn beer," Daryl shouted, red-faced and louder than he needed to be.

"So how long are you here for, baby?" Sharon asked.

"Little while." Ron said in a voice so low it was hard to hear.

"You still with the Marine Corps?" Ron didn't answer and took a long sip from his beer, his eyes cast down again.

"If he told you, he'd have to kill you," Daryl chuckled. "Isn't that right, Ron?"

I saw a pained expression pass across Ron's face and felt a flash of the old protectiveness.

"Leave him alone, Daryl."

"Shit, are you kidding me? Old Ron here could snap me like a twig with one finger with all that kung fu tai chi shit they teach him over there…"

"I don't believe it," Sharon said. "I was talking to Cora Jean…you remember Cora Jean, don't you, Ron? I told her you were coming back and she said you must've killed people, that nobody stays in the service that long without killing someone. But I told her no, our Ron's not a killer. He never killed anybody."

There was a moment of the deadliest silence you can imagine. I couldn't bear to look at Ron's face. "*Sharon…*" Daryl spoke her name in a hard, warning tone. Sharon stopped and looked around the table like she didn't recognize us for a moment. Then she seemed to gather herself together, leaned closer to Ron and put one hand on his arm.

"Ron," she spoke in a calmer voice, "I'm so sorry 'bout your momma. She was a real nice lady…"

I felt Daryl's foot nudge mine under the table. He got up, muttered, "'Scuse me a minute…" and went down the hall toward the restroom. This was Daryl's signal to follow him. I couldn't believe it. Why now? I waited for a couple of minutes, then excused myself, stood up and slipped down the hall where Daryl had gone. I turned the corner and saw him waiting for me by the red exit sign, one hand on the door. He pushed the door open and I followed him outside.

At the corner of the parking lot was a high wooden fence around a dumpster. As soon as Daryl and I were behind it, he pushed me against the fence and put his mouth over mine. I could taste the whiskey on his tongue and the smell of the thousands of cigarettes he'd smoked since he was thirteen rising up from his lungs. For a moment I resisted, then I settled in and let the old feeling wash through me and push out all the other thoughts crowding my head.

I ran my hand up under Daryl's shirt and felt something strange, some kind of rough interruption in the smoothness of his skin. I drew back for a moment; he must have read the question in my mind, because before I knew it he was unbuttoning his shirt and pulling it off. In the faint glow of the street light I could see angry-looking red scars criss-crossing his chest, a few more on his arms.

"Jesus, Daryl…what the hell?"

"It's Sharon," he said. For a few seconds I didn't understand what he was telling me. "She finally did it," Daryl said. "Came at me with the kitchen knife."

"Oh my God, Daryl…And you brought her *here?*"

"She doesn't even remember it," Daryl said. "Went upstairs and took a nap, came out an hour later and asked me what I wanted for supper."

I tore my eyes away from the fresh scars on Daryl's chest and tried to see the look on his face in the dim light. For a horrible moment I thought he might be smiling.

"Sweetheart," he said. "This is what we've been waiting for. All I gotta do now is file a police report. Sign an order of committal, whatever they call it…" He paused, waiting for me to fill in the rest. He spread his arms open, showing me his scars like he was giving me a gift.

"Fuck, Daryl, why didn't you do it already?" I asked. "What the hell are you waiting for?"

"Sweetheart, it just happened. I just want to get my head clear first, you know? Figure out the details, make sure I do it right. Besides," he said, starting to button his shirt back up, "she went to all this trouble putting on this party for Ron. Kinda seemed like a shame to ruin it."

I stood staring at him, trying to figure out who was crazier, Sharon or Daryl – or me, for letting myself become part of their craziness.

Daryl slipped back inside, leaving me standing in the dark behind the dumpster. I couldn't wrap my mind around it. How was I supposed to go back in there now and face Sharon? Smile and laugh and act normal like nothing had happened? Then I realized – I'd already been doing that for a long time.

When I got back to our table Sharon was leaning close to Ron, talking and waving her hands around. I thought about those hands holding a kitchen knife, and the scars Daryl had just shown me. It was hard to believe – the worst things always are. I wondered how long it would take once Daryl filed the police report. I thought of movies and TV shows I'd seen, men in white coats, padded vans and strait jackets. I looked at Sharon talking away on the other side of the table and I didn't feel afraid, or angry – I just felt sorry for her. This was like her last night on earth; she just didn't know it yet.

"Let's go to Cedar Grove!" Sharon shouted suddenly. "Come on, it'll be great!"

"That old piece of shit?" Daryl said. "You need a fucking tetanus shot just to walk in the place. No wonder they're tearing it down…"

"I know!" Sharon said. "That's why we've gotta go!"

The old feeling of dread rose up in my throat. I was afraid to look at Ron, but I made myself do it. He was looking at the wall or at something beyond it.

"Come on, Ron," Sharon said. "It'll be fun. You want to go, right?"

No, I thought. *Please…*

Ron didn't look at me or change his expression. He just shrugged and said, "Sure."

The road to Cedar Grove was exactly as I remembered – long and narrow with wild, steep hills that rose and fell like waves in a typhoon and left my stomach somewhere behind us. It was the closest thing to a roller coaster I'd ever been on, and as we got closer I could feel that same old childhood dread start to clamp down on my guts. Of course, none of us were kids anymore. We were grown-ups playing at being kids. And while we used to come together for pleasure, tonight we were celebrating the memory of that pleasure. In a way, it felt like a funeral.

When the trees parted and we pulled into the barren field that served as a parking lot, I could see the roller coaster tracks rising above us, but no cars were plunging up and down, no wild screams rising and falling on the wind. Orange plastic barricade netting sealed-off the entrance like some kind of brightly colored spider web.

"God damn it!" Sharon said. "I don't fucking believe it!"

While the others cursed and grumbled, I felt a familiar wave of shameful relief wash through my body.

I saw a few other people wandering around the near-deserted midway, some couples our age and older. No children. Talking in hushed voices, like we were walking through a museum or a graveyard, we passed by the boarded-up vendors' booths, the tilt-a-whirl that looked frozen in mid-spin.

"I can't believe we came all the way out here and they shut down all the rides," Sharon moaned.

"Not all of 'em," Daryl said. "There's the merry-go-round. Maybe the train's still running..."

"Oh, the train!" Sharon practically squealed, "Remember the train? I used to *love* that train!"

I did remember that train. It was one of the only rides I wasn't afraid to ride when I was younger. A perfect little replica of an old-fashioned steam-engine with its smokestack puffing clouds of faint white vapor. I liked how it took me away from the clamor and stench of the midway and out across the open fields, where you could imagine you were going on a real journey to a place you'd never seen, not just circling back around to the place where you started.

Daryl led the way around a corner to the far end of the midway. And there it was, four little carts hitched to a rusted red engine, a little smaller and a lot less grand than I remembered.

I watched Daryl walk over to a skinny young man with long, greasy hair who looked like he was manning the switch, then walked back toward us, a big grin on his face.

"How much?" Sharon asked.

"Nothing. It's free. He says it's the last ride of the night. "

I felt a chill go right through me. *Last ride of the night. Always free.*

"Daryl," I said, "let's do something else, okay?"

"Like what?" Daryl said. "There's nothing else running. Besides, you gonna turn down a free ride? Hell, we might be the last people ever to ride this thing."

I looked over at Ron to see how he was taking all of this. As usual, his face was a solemn blank, unreadable.

"What's the matter, Laurie?" Sharon laughed, "You not big enough for this one either?"

Sharon climbed into the first cart with Daryl. There was room for two more people, but I got into the second cart. I felt Ron climb in next to me and the train starting to roll forward.

We rumbled and rattled down the midway, four grown-ups squeezed into a children's ride. I saw Daryl turn his head to sneak a look at the two of us, at Ron and me. I knew Daryl was jealous, but he was jealous for the wrong reasons. The things that had happened between Ron and me weren't the kind of things that Daryl could understand.

Like the time right after my dad died when I was fourteen, when Ron showed up at our front door, standing quietly on my doorstep in his green army jacket. I don't remember what we talked about, or if he said anything at all. What I remember is walking together to the end of our street where the asphalt turned to weeds and dirt, and then out into the old fields where we all used to play together when we were little.

We walked in silence across the winter stubble, past fallen-down fence posts and dry cow-ponds. As we walked, I could hear the sound of the interstate like the hushing of ocean waves somewhere behind the trees. Then we stepped through the trees and there were all four lanes of I-65 rolling out in front of us like a river in the sun.

Ron led me down the slope and right up to the gravel shoulder where I could smell the stink of exhaust and feel the wind from passing cars plucking at my clothes. Then he explained what we were going to do. I can't remember exactly what he said, and I doubt if I even heard all of it, because my mind was filling up with a kind of fear that felt like excitement. *Close your eyes*, Ron said. Then we stepped out into it.

What happened next is hard to remember, and harder to describe. I remember the roaring sound all around us and the feeling of huge, powerful things flying past. It even felt like they were flying *through* us. I knew that was impossible, but somehow I knew that if I opened my eyes, the spell would be broken and we'd both be killed. Then I felt Ron pulling me back to the side of the highway. When I finally dared to open my eyes, we were both standing on the gravel shoulder again, untouched and unhurt. I remember feeling stunned and a little changed, like I wasn't the same person anymore.

The little train clanked and shuddered under us. I looked over at Ron's face, older now, with the carnival lights passing over it, and wondered if he still knew how to make things like that happen.

A string of naked light bulbs hung across the track overhead. I closed my eyes as we passed under them. When I opened my eyes, the park was gone and we were in the open fields, the weak light at the head of the train making a faint trail in the darkness ahead of us.

The little train started it's long, slow curve to the left, rattling and clacking as it went. A thick fog had started to rise from the ground and cover everything in a dim grayish haze. "Oooo, *spooky!*" Daryl said in a corny monster-movie voice.

I turned around and looked behind us. The lights of the park had blurred into a ghostly haze. The black shapes of trees kept materializing ahead of us and dissolving again into the fog. It was colder out here in the fields, a raw, wet cold that crept up from the ground and into your skin. I glanced over at Ron and had a momentary vision of snuggling into his side, his strong left arm curled protectively around me…

A sudden jolt threw me forward against the back of the cart in front of us. Sharon gave a startled cry and I heard Daryl curse. I reached up and touched my forehead, feeling a bump already rising. The train had stopped.

"What the fuck…?" Daryl said, twisting around in his seat. I felt Ron touch my right shoulder. I turned and saw him looking intently into my face.

"You okay?"

"Yeah…" I nodded. "What happened?"

"Stupid piece of shit broke down, that's what happened," Daryl said, glaring around in all directions like he was looking for someone to blame. I looked behind and could no longer see the blur of light from the midway. All around us, the fog had risen so high that only the tops of the trees were visible like islands in the distance.

"You think it's gonna start again?" Sharon asked, her voice already turning high and whiny.

"I don't know," Daryl said. The four of us sat there, waiting.

"Fuck it, let's walk," Sharon said and started to climb out of the cart. Daryl reached out and put a hand on her arm to stop her and a flash of rage flared up inside me.

"Just wait a minute," Daryl said. "Maybe it'll start up again."

Sharon climbed out and stumbled a little on the track. I watched her turn and face the direction we'd come from, cup her hands to her mouth and yell, *"Hey…Hey…we're stuck out here."*

"No one's gonna hear you," Daryl said. Ignoring him, Sharon yelled even louder, *"Help…help…"* My skin crawled. Yelling *help* made things seem so much worse than they really were.

"So are we really just going to sit here and wait?" I asked. Daryl cursed and stood up, climbing down out of the cart. I got out too, then Ron followed. The four of us stood by the little train, looking around in the thick fog.

"Okay," I said. "I guess we can just follow the track back…"

"What are you going *that* way for?" Daryl asked. "The track loops around. Let's keep going this way. It's probably closer."

"How do *you* know?" I asked, annoyance rising up inside me. And it hit me – here we were, arguing like an old married couple in front of everyone. "Okay, whatever…" I said, and the four of us started walking, following Daryl through the fog.

The grass out here was high and in a few minutes the legs of my pants were soaking wet. We stayed close to the track and walked in single-file. The bump on my head was throbbing.

Someone touched my arm and I jumped. I looked to my left and saw Ron walking next to me, a concerned look on his face. "Laurie," he said, "you're bleeding." I reached up and touched my forehead, then looked at my fingers that came away dark red and wet.

Sharon turned to see what was happening. "What's the matter?" she said. When she saw the blood, I saw a look of horror come over her face. "Oh my God!" she whined. "Oh my God…" She clamped one hand over her mouth, her eyes huge above it, turned and vomited into the grass. "I'm sorry…" she moaned, still doubled-over and not looking at me, "I'm sorry…I just can't…I can't look at that…" She retched again. Ron stepped closer and rested a hand on her back while Daryl stood at a distance, a look of embarrassment and disgust on his face.

Before I knew it, Ron was taking off his shirt and handing it to me. I wasn't sure what it was supposed to mean until he pressed a corner of it gently to the side of my forehead. I took it and pressed it to the place on my head that was still throbbing. Then we kept walking.

The cold came up from the ground through the soles of my feet and into my bones. I felt like I was moving more and more slowly, like in a dream. I looked ahead and saw Ron walking next to Sharon, making sure she was okay. She was walking with her head hung down, arms wrapped around herself. Whether it was because of the cold or sickness, I couldn't tell. It was strange to think of her that way; Sharon, afraid of blood. Of all the things Daryl had told me about her, he'd never told me that.

Then it hit me. It hit me so fast and so hard I felt the strength drain out of my body and I almost had to sit down right there in the cold wet grass. I reached out and took hold of Daryl's arm and stopped him while Sharon and Ron kept walking ahead of us. Daryl glared at me, startled and annoyed. "What?" he whispered.

"She never cut you," I said.

"What are you talking about?"

"Sharon. She never cut you like that. She couldn't." Daryl said nothing. I thought of those red, angry-looking wounds I'd seen and touched on his arms and chest. And then the picture came to me. "Oh my God," I said. "Oh my God. It was you."

It was too dark to see the look on his face. "What does it matter?" I heard him whisper. "She would have done it herself sooner or later. This way, it's just sooner."

I knew the next words out of his mouth would be, *I did it for us,* or, even worse, *I did it for you,* and I walked faster to get away from him so I wouldn't have to hear that. What I couldn't get away from was the picture that had just come into my mind – Daryl standing alone and shirtless in front of his bathroom mirror, a bottle of bourbon in one hand, a kitchen knife in the other.

I saw a dark shape materializing out of the fog ahead of us. Not like the tangled branches of trees, but straight lines and hard angles. More shapes rose out of the fog, dark vertical lines rising up with the heavy mist passing through them. Suddenly, we walked into a wall of odor so strong it stopped us in our tracks. It was like the smell of a kennel or dog-pound magnified a hundred times, a solid cloud of wet fur, diseased skin, and excrement.

"Jesus!" Daryl groaned from behind the hand clamped over his mouth. "What *is* that?"

I knew then what these things were. They were cages. And they were not empty.

I stood about ten feet away from the bars. I didn't want to get any closer. From that distance I could feel more than see something moving inside, something large and old that didn't want to be seen.

"Oh my God…" Sharon whispered, stepping closer to the bars. "What *is* that?"

"Don't get too close…" Daryl said. Sharon ignored him and drew closer, pressing her face between the bars. That was when I heard it. A low, dry, rattling sound; a harsh, labored breath from a throat was wasn't human. It was coming from the cage in front of us, and from the others all around us. Large, huddled shapes shifted and stirred in the dark.

I could hear another harsh sound closer to us; Sharon was crying. At first I couldn't understand what she was saying. "Bastards," she was sobbing. "Fucking bastards…"

"But…they shut down that zoo years ago…" Daryl said, unbelieving.

"Don't you get it? They brought them out here and left them," Sharon said, "They brought them out here and left them to die."

I moved slowly along the cages, both wanting to see and not wanting to. The smell of filth and disease radiated from the dark corners, along with something else – a feeling of awareness, and a slow-running current of hatred and pain.

A loud metallic banging started a few feet away from me. I turned and saw Sharon clutching a big rock in her hands, raising it over her head and smashing it down again and again on the lock on one of the cage doors. "Fucking…bastards…" she kept saying and pounding away at the lock. In a moment Ron and Daryl were on her, trying to pull her away, but she kept swinging, wildly. I heard Daryl curse and saw him stagger away from the struggle.

While Ron wrapped his arms around Sharon from behind and carried her away, Daryl walked up to me, his hand over his mouth. He looked down at his hand and then raised it toward my face so I could see the blood smeared on his palm from where Sharon had cut his lip with the rock.

"See?" he said, "What did I tell you – just a matter of time."

Sharon broke away from Ron and ran off into the field. The fog was so heavy now that she almost vanished into it and I could just barely make her out, standing alone with her back to us, arms wrapped around herself against the cold. "Leave the stupid bitch out there," I heard Daryl mutter.

Ron walked out to where Sharon was. They looked like a couple of ghosts, and for a moment I thought I could see through them. A minute later the two of them came trudging back through the high grass, then we all started following the track again, away from those cages and what was in them.

It was hard to see more than ten or twelve feet ahead, and the track came out of the fog in front of us a piece at a time. None of us spoke. A couple of times, I thought I heard something that might be music in the distance, very faint and strange-sounding, and I thought we must be getting closer to the park. But there were still no lights ahead of us, only fog and darkness. And something else was wrong. I'd felt it for a while but wasn't sure what it was until Daryl said it.

"This isn't right. This track is supposed to circle back around…"

He turned and looked at me for confirmation, and I could see what looked like the beginning of panic in his eyes.

"Maybe you just don't remember it right," I offered. "Maybe it goes on like this for a while at first..." But even as I said it, I knew he was right. The track should have started curving back long before now. Instead, it was leading us further and further out.

"Maybe they changed it," Daryl said. I could hear the strain in his voice. "Yeah, they must've just changed the track or something..."

"Yeah," I said. Then I looked down at the track and saw that the metal wasn't new or shiny; they were the same dark, rusted rails as before, leading in a straight line that stretched out and vanished ahead of us.

It felt colder than before as we walked on in silence. I heard a faint sound of wind in the trees, and other sounds I didn't recognize.

Suddenly I realized Ron wasn't walking next to me. I turned to look for him and saw him standing several yards away, looking back at where the track disappeared into the fog behind us. Then I smelled it. That same sickening wave of diseased fur and skin.

Ron turned and quickly walked back toward us, a grim look on his face. "Don't run," he spoke in a low, even voice. "Keep walking."

I tried to do what Ron said but my legs wouldn't move. All I could do was stand and stare at the spot behind us where Ron had been looking. I thought I could see something moving in the fog, then Ron took me by the arm and spoke in a low, firm voice, "Come on, Laurie." Daryl turned around to look at us, then I saw all the expression drain from his face. "Oh Jesus," he said in a hollow voice. "Jesus, no…"

"Don't run," Ron said again, a little louder this time. "Keep walking." This time I did what Ron told me. The tall grass grabbed at my legs and slowed me down until I wanted to scream but I choked it back and kept going. I could hear Sharon crying in quiet broken sobs, and Daryl still praying between ragged breaths. "Jesus. This isn't happening…" I heard him say. "This is *not* happening…"

My mind felt frozen. For a while the noises behind us would stop and I almost thought we'd imagined it. Then I heard them again, the sound of large bodies moving through the high grass, a low rattling from deep inside strange chests and throats. And that horrible smell overtaking us.

"Don't run," Ron kept saying. "Don't run. Keep walking." He stopped again and waved us on, looking back into the dark and fog where the noises were coming closer.

"Big fucking hero," I heard Daryl mutter.

"What are you talking about?" I asked.

Daryl's face was pale and wet and I realized with a shock that he'd been crying. "Don't you know? They kicked him out of the Marines, three months ago. *Psychiatric disability.* He's crazy."

"You're crazy," I said. "You're a fucking liar."

"Yeah? Ask him. Ask him yourself. You know where he's been? Living in his mother's basement."

Suddenly it all made sense. The silence. The secrecy. For a moment it felt like the earth had tilted under me, and I had to close my eyes to keep from falling down. I couldn't speak or move. It felt like I was never going to be able to move again.

Then I heard Ron's voice. It was a small voice, but it was strong and sure and it cut through the fog of my confusion and paralysis and it made me feel like I could move again, and that maybe this wasn't really the end of everything after all.

Come on, Laurie.

I opened my eyes and I was back in that tent again years ago with the heat and the red light all around me and the old man who I'd let lead me here looking down at me with those hungry red eyes.

"Come on, Laurie," Ron had said in his flat voice, not taking his eyes off the man.

"Hold on," the man said. "Where you think you're goin'?"

"Come on," Ron said it a little louder this time.

"No sir," the man said, "That ain't how it works. Ain't both of y'all leavin'. Maybe one of you. Not both. You said you wanted a ride. Now one of you gotta stay. That's the rules."

The man stood where he was, looming over the both of us. He could have closed the space between us in one step and blocked our way, or worse, but he didn't have to. We were the children, he was the adult, and he had just told us what the rules were.

"Go on, Laurie," Ron finally said. He spoke so low for a moment I wasn't sure what he'd said. He stepped a little closer to the big man and stood partway between us. When he did that, I thought I could see the man start to smile.

"That's right, little girl," the big man said. "You go on now."

For a moment I couldn't move or speak. I think I shook my head. The next thing I knew I could feel Ron's hand on my chest pushing me backward toward the tent door, and I heard his voice, louder and firmer, *"Go."*

Then I did the thing that would not leave me for twenty years, the thing that cut me off from Ron and tied us together forever. I left. I walked out of that little tent and between the vendors' carts and games and out onto the midway again where men and women, boys and girls were walking and talking and laughing like nothing had changed. I remember feeling shocked that there was still so much sunlight outside, that the sky hadn't turned black already. It felt to me like the whole world should be black by now.

I looked back down the tracks and saw Ron standing between us and whatever was coming, saw the eagle and death's head tattoos on his back. I thought about what I'd done and what Daryl had just told me, and what I felt wasn't shock, or pity. Because I knew it didn't matter anymore, none of it. None of it mattered now.

I walked back toward Ron and stood at his side. The noises were getting closer and I thought I could see forms taking shape in the fog – slouching, hulking shapes moving slowly but deliberately. The bad thing that I'd always felt was coming, the thing that I'd always known was going to happen to me. It was going to happen now.

"Ron," I said. "I'm sorry. I'm sorry about everything."

"Go on, Laurie," he said, not taking his eyes off of the fog where the noises were coming from. I felt him put his hand on my chest and push me back toward Daryl and Sharon. "I said *go on*."

"*No!*" I shouted as loud as I could. My eyes were shut but I saw waves of my voice rushing out of me in all directions like tremors in the earth, the sound of it ringing in my skull. I was saying *no* to what was going to happen to us and what had happened to us long ago, *no* to the dark tent and the red light, to everything I'd done and hadn't done. I shouted until I was empty inside and there was nothing left to hurt.

What happened next was something I wasn't born with the words to describe. They came through him. That's the only way I can say it. They came right through him. They came through both of us, Ron and me. It didn't hurt, but it should have. All the pain and hate in the world was right there in that place. It had come looking for us with its teeth and claws and red, red eyes. Now there was nothing left for it to hold on to. Because that's what we'd become, Ron and me. We'd become *nothing* together, and this thing that had been coming toward us for so long couldn't hurt us. It thrashed and howled like the storm that's coming at the end of the world. But the world didn't end.

When I opened my eyes again, the fog had started to lift and a few stars had come out. Ron and I were alone. I saw him step off the track into the high, wet grass, hold out his hand and say, "Come on Laurie." Then it was just Ron and me walking together a long way into the field.

We've been walking like this for a long time now. I can see lights ahead of us shining through the mist like the lights of an ocean liner, a whole city adrift in the gray. They're not the same lights we saw when we started, like the music drifting toward us through the dark isn't the same music as before, although it feels like I've heard it all my life. I know what we'll find when we get there. The tent at the end of the midway, and inside the tent, the red light and the man who's still there waiting for us. This time he can't touch us. Nothing can.

The music sounds closer than ever now. We're almost there.

David Surface lives in the Hudson River Valley of New York. His stories have appeared in a wide variety of genre journals including *Shadows & Tall Trees, Supernatural Tales, Nightscript, Morpheus Tales,* and *The Tenth Black Book of Horror,* as well as in literary journals including *North American Review, Crazyhorse, Fiction, and Doubletake.* His stories have been anthologized in *Darkest Minds* from Dark Minds Press, *Ghost Highways* from Midnight Street Press, and *Twisted Book of Shadows* from Twisted Publishing/Haverhill House Publications. A story co-authored with Julia Rust, 'TallDarkAnd', appears in the Swan River Press anthology, *Uncertainties III.*

David is also a regular contributor to *Black Static Magazine* where his column 'One Good Story' appears in the Case Notes section. To learn more about David and his writing, visit his website at *davidsurfacewriter.wordpress.com*